# The
# Opposite
## of Love

www.rbooks.co.uk

For more information on Julie Buxbaum and her books, visit her website at: www.juliebuxbaum.com

# The
# Opposite
# of Love

JULIE BUXBAUM

**BANTAM BOOKS**
LONDON • TORONTO • SYDNEY • AUCKLAND • JOHANNESBURG

TRANSWORLD PUBLISHERS
61–63 Uxbridge Road, London W5 5SA
A Random House Group Company
www.rbooks.co.uk

**THE OPPOSITE OF LOVE
A BANTAM BOOK: 9780553818833**

First published in Great Britain
in 2008 by Bantam Press
a division of Transworld Publishers
Bantam edition published 2009

Addresses for Random House Group Ltd companies outside the UK
can be found at: www.randomhouse.co.uk
The Random House Group Ltd Reg. No. 954009

The Random House Group Limited supports The Forest Stewardship Council
(FSC), the leading international forest certification organisation. All our titles
that are printed on Greenpeace approved FSC certified paper carry the FSC
logo. Our paper procurement policy can be found at
www.rbooks.co.uk/environment

Typeset in 11/15pt Janson by
Falcon Oast Graphic Art Ltd.
Printed in the UK by CPI Cox & Wyman, Reading, RG1 8EX.

2 4 6 8 10 9 7 5 3 1

*For my dad, with love and gratitude
And for my mom, who is loved and
remembered, every day*

# The
# Opposite
# of Love

# Prologue

*Your picture is already hanging on the fridge. Black and white, 3 x 5— unposed, unselfconscious—you, curled up and in profile. You, wholly contained inside of me.*

*Here's what I know: I eat mass quantities of red meat, curse religiously, sing out of tune but with conviction. I cry when it suits me, laugh when it's inopportune, read* The New York Times *obituaries and wedding announcements, out loud and in that order.*

*You: You weigh less than a pint of milk. You are no longer theoretical. You are a girl.*

*When the doctor told us today, he clapped, as if taking credit for the whole shebang. As if he were the one to transform you into an exclamatory event, from the intangible to the concrete, an* it *into a baby girl. I didn't want to disappoint him, but we knew I was having a daughter all along, from the first second we found out I was pregnant, just as we knew we would name you Charlotte. (Your dad keeps correcting me—*we *are pregnant, he* *says, not just* you—*but are his ankles so swollen that it looks like he's under house arrest? Are his breasts hanging like water balloons? He may be expecting, but I am pregnant.)*

*"A million women have peed on these sticks. You can do it, Emily." That's what your dad said to get me into the bathroom to make what we suspected official. I was nervous, though, and it took a good hour and a half until I went anywhere near the toilet, and then another one after that, because he came in with me and I got stage fright. But I did it, like the millions of women before me, and then there was a plus sign, which, after triple-checking the box and confirming with a 1–800 number and peeing on a few more sticks, told us all we needed to know.*

*I understood then, in a way that went beyond want, in a way that may have bordered on need, that you were going to be a girl. I understood, too, that nights like tonight were coming, almost looked forward to them, when I would sit up while your dad slept, when my emotions would waver between excitement and fear.*

*Your dad, who is made of sunnier material, who sings in the shower and doesn't knock on wood, whose body is curved toward mine now, eyes twitching in time to dreams filled with super-heroes and award-acceptance speeches, thinks my need to document my life for you, by words and by photographs, is a morbid indulgence. He wonders why I flirt with life's shallow paradoxes—the line between love and its opposite, the line between holding on and letting go.*

*But it's not that simple, really. This chronic chronicling, this eulogizing of sorts, falls outside my conscious choice. Sometimes I try to rewind twenty weeks, to before, to remember when you were an idea, something we dreamt up in darkness when sleep wouldn't come. But even then— even in that pre-you world—I felt this compulsion to preserve us all into a pile of memory and render us indelible. One way to guarantee the crossing of any future temporal divide: You will always find me here, in these pages, even long after I am gone.*

*And let's be honest, who knows how long I'll be around? We Haxby women aren't known for our lengthy life spans.*

*But that is somewhat beside the point, because no matter when I go, be it when I am forty-two or eighty-two, you will forget whole parts of me. That's the blessing and the curse of loss: You don't get to choose what falls within the inevitable dissolution of recollection or what lingers and haunts you late at night, your head heavy with memories, while your husband dreams of scaling walls in spandex tights.*

*My own mother, for whom you are named, has been mostly lost to recycled anecdotes and left behind to the angles of a few arbitrary photographs. Not so much lost and left behind, then; more distorted and distilled. And though I often find comfort in this airbrushed facsimile of who she once was, I long for the real thing on nights like these.*

*The real thing. The flesh and the bones.*

*Maybe the aftermath of loss—the crumbs of memory—has, in some ways, scarred me more than the loss itself. The truth is I've never learned to ride a bicycle, because, among other reasons, it is something you can never forget. This is who I am: someone who simultaneously longs for and fears the commitment of remembering. There is the forgetting, the disintegration of memory, morsel by morsel; and there is the impossibility of forgetting, the scar tissue, with its insulated layers of padding. Both haunt me in their own way.*

*You will never get to meet the person who I once was, the one pre-you, before in some ways I was even me. But it is your legacy as much as mine, this story of how you came to be, this story of us.*

*And now that your portrait is on the fridge, now that I got to play my part as a Russian nested doll, now that there will be no living for me in a world without you, I pass along all that I can preserve: this story of how we became a family—of your dad and me, of Ruth and Grandpa Jack, of my own father, who is awake right now too, busy assembling a crib with pink trim. This story of the dividing line I love and live and bequeath, the one that lies between remembering and forgetting, commitment and liberation, getting left and leaving behind.*

*The line, always the line, the same line that separates me from my mother. The same line that separates me from you.*

# One

Last night, I dreamt that I chopped Andrew up into a hundred little pieces, like a Benihana chef, and ate them, one by one. He tasted like chicken. Afterward, I felt full but slightly disappointed. I had been craving steak.

I plan to forget this dream. I will block out the grainy texture of moo shu Andrew. The itch of swallowing him dry. I will erase it completely, without lingering echoes or annoying déjà vu, despite the possibility that my dream led me inexorably to this moment.

Because I already know that, unlike the dream—this dead end—this one is going to stick. I am living an inevitable memory.

Today, I break up with Andrew in a restaurant that has crayons on the table and peanut shells on the floor. A drunken young woman in the midst of her bachelorette party, wearing little more than a cowboy hat and tassels, attempts to organize a line dance. I realize now that I should have waited for a better backdrop. It looks as if I think our relationship adds up to nothing more than a couple of beers and some satisfying, but fiery, Buffalo wings. This is not the effect I was going for.

I had imagined that disentangling would be straight-forward and civilized, maybe even a tiny bit romantic. The fantasy breakup in my head played out in pantomime; no explanations, only rueful smiles, a kiss good-bye on the cheek, a farewell wave thrown over a shoulder. The sting of nostalgia and the high of release, a combustible package, maybe, but one we would both understand and appreciate.

Instead, Andrew looks at me strangely, as if I am a foreigner he has just met and he can't place my accent. I refuse to meet his eyes. I quell the overwhelming desire to run outside into the swill of Third Avenue, to drown in the overflow of people spilling out from the bars and onto the street. Surely that would be better than feeling Andrew's confusion reverberate off his skin like a bad odor. I lock my legs around the bottom of my bar stool and stare at the bit of barbecue sauce that clings to his upper lip. This helps assuage my guilt. How could I be serious about a man who walks around with food on his face? In all fairness, Andrew is not walking around anywhere. He perches there, stunned.

And I, too, am adorned in condiments. The ketchup on my white tank top makes it look like my heart is leaking.

"This was never going to be a forever, happily-ever-after

sort of thing. You knew that," I say, though it is clear from his silence and from the last few days that he did not. I wonder if he wants to hit me. I almost wish he would.

Seems strange now that I didn't realize this moment was coming, that I hadn't started practicing in my head before yesterday. I'm usually good at endings—pride myself on them, in fact—and I always find people disingenuous when they claim that a breakup came out of nowhere. Nothing comes out of nowhere, except for, perhaps, freak accidents. Or cancer. And even those things you should be prepared for.

I guess I could have just let the weekend unfold, followed the original plan with military precision, and woken up tomorrow with Andrew in my bed and his arm thrown across my shoulder. Later, at work, I would have been able to tell some funny Labor Day anecdote around the proverbial water cooler, the weekend always better in rose-colored instant replay. But though I firmly believe that a tree does not fall in the forest until someone later tells an amusing story about it, I realize now that there will be no tidbits to share tomorrow. At least not funny ones. I have made sure of that.

Today, during the last moments of the Labor Day weekend, I find myself sitting across from Andrew, the man with whom I have spent the past two years, attempting to explain why it is we need to stop seeing each other naked. I want to tell him it is merely our ages—I am twenty-nine, Andrew is thirty-one—that are at fault here. We are acting under a collective cultural delusion, the one that demands random connection after the quarter-life mark, a handcuffing to whoever lands by your side during a particular game of musical chairs. This is the only way I can explain how Andrew went so out of bounds yesterday, with his intimations of a ring and permission, with his hints of an impending proposal. But I don't say any of this out loud, of course. The words seem too vague, too much like an excuse, maybe, too much like the truth.

We had never been one of those fantasy-prone couples who presumed a happy ending or named their unborn children on their first date. Actually, our first date was at a restaurant remarkably similar to this one, and rather than talking about the future, or even ourselves, we had a fierce competition over who could eat more hot wings. We left the restaurant with lips so swollen that when he kissed me good night I could barely feel it. Four months later, he admitted rushing the date because the wings gave him diarrhea. It took me two more months to confess that I had let him win. He didn't take that so well.

Whenever the future did come up, though, we always included convenient "ifs" in our language, deflating whatever followed into something less loaded.

"If we ever have kids, I hope they have your eyes and my toes," I would say, while tracing circles on Andrew's stomach with my fingertips.

"If we ever have kids, I hope they have your intestines. That way, we could enter them in competitive eating contests and retire to Mexico on their winnings," he would say, and gather my hair into a ponytail and then let it slip back through his hands, like the strands were only on loan.

Perhaps the lesson here is to pay attention. There is always a lesson, isn't there? There has to be, because without one, what would be the point? So maybe this time it is to be vigilant, to watch out. Because somehow, sometime yesterday, without my noticing, without my *perceiving*, our fault line shifted.

The plan was to walk up to Central Park with our friends Daniel and Kate, to jointly celebrate our limited free time by wantonly wasting it. The curtain of Manhattan humidity had been replaced with a whistling breeze, and after a choking August, we were relieved to be balancing between seasons. Since the rest of the city had better places to be over the holiday weekend, we took advantage of having the sidewalks to ourselves. Andrew and I weaved back and forth, elbowing each other in the ribs, sticking out our feet to trip the other, pinching sides in a game of gotcha-last. I was feeling pure pleasure, not dithering happiness. No buzz of anxiety or free fall in my stomach to warn of what was to come.

Daniel and Kate walked in front of us. Her engagement ring, whose presence loomed out of proportion to its size, would occasionally catch the sun and paint shadow shows on the sidewalk. Our closest friends—we could still say "our" yesterday, we were still a "we" then—and somehow, more than that, they were also symbols of how things can be for some people, how effortless commitment can look. Daniel and Kate were the adults leading this brigade, though at a languid pace, since it was clear that we should savor this last bit of summer before the trees shed their leaves to make room for the snow.

After I caught Andrew in a sneaky gotcha-last move—the never-fail distract-and-mislead maneuver—he ended the game by lacing his fingers in mine. We walked that way for a while, hand in hand, until I felt him start to toy with my empty ring finger, wrapping it with the whole of his palm in an infant grip. And though he kept quiet, it was as if he said the words out loud. He was going to ask me to marry him.

His thoughts, I could tell, were wholly methodical—the hows of proposing, not the ifs or the whys. Finding a free day to take the train out to Connecticut to get my father's permission or to Riverdale to ask my Grandpa Jack. Conjuring up the name of my favorite restaurant and his family jeweler. No meditation on whether he knows me well enough to zip together our futures, no concern that he can't decipher the infinite thoughts that run through my inaccessible brain at any given moment. But that's who Andrew is, ultimately; someone not overly bothered by the ifs and the whys.

Before I could wonder if my rising panic was merely the result of an illusion, he pulled me toward a jewelry-shop window, his arm cupped around my back. I imagined the rings winking at me, laughing at my discomfort.

"Do you like anything?" he asked.

"That bracelet is pretty," I said. "Oh, and those earrings are gorgeous. I like how dangly they are. I never wear dangly. And, look, they have a one hundred percent money-back guarantee. I like when you can get your money back."

"How about those rings?"

"Too sparkly. I prefer the dangly earrings."

"Come on, what kinds of cuts do you like? Princess, oval, marquise?" The man had clearly done his homework. This is not the first time he has thought about this, I realized.

*Fuck.*

"I don't know the difference. It's not my sort of thing," I said, which was true. I thought Marquise was an island in the Caribbean. And then, because I didn't know what else to do, I pointed far into the distance.

"Look!" I said, like a child who has just learned a new word. "A puppy."

The rest of the afternoon unraveled like a well-scripted sit-com, with the four of us playing a silly game of monkey-in-the-middle in the park, jokingly competitive, and tackling one another unnecessarily. I was perhaps the silliest of all, overcompensating for the dread I was feeling, somehow believing that goofiness would stave off the inevitable.

But there was no way out, really. I had made a promise not to work this weekend, even "accidentally" left my BlackBerry behind in the office, something I had never done before in my almost five years as a litigator at Altman, Pryor and Tisch, LLP. I was off my leash, which had seemed like a good idea before the weekend, when I thought I needed a break from the billable hour, not from my life. I hadn't known I would want to dive right back into the pile of papers on my desk, run away to a place that has no room for words like "our" and "we."

But work would have been mere procrastination. I had come to my decision in front of the jewelry store. I was going to break up with Andrew before he knelt down and asked an impossible question. I would shatter our naïve and comfortable world like the kid who plays with a gun in an after-school special.

Self-awareness is a slippery thing, though, when you find yourself at odds with a "supposed to" in life. I understand that I am supposed to want to marry Andrew. That some women wait their whole lives to stand before a bended knee or fantasize about a sparkly stone that silently announces to the world, *See, someone loves me. Someone picked me.* That some women dream of that choreographed first dance with their new husband before the crowd erupts into a vigorous "YMCA."

Or, better yet, that almost all of us want someone to be our very own partner in crime, to drive us home from the airport, to cheer when we succeed, and to hold our hair when we vomit. And if I am honest with you, I do want that, in one form or another.

But getting married? To Andrew? 'Til death do us part? I can't do it. I would be nothing more than a fraud, a pretend grown-up, a con artist playing the role of bride. I don't even want to spend the rest of my life with me. How can Andrew? And how do you explain to someone you love that you can't give yourself to them, because if you did, you're not sure who you'd be giving? That you aren't even sure what your own words are worth? You can't tell someone that, especially someone you love. And so I don't.

Instead, I do the right thing. I lie.

"Well, I guess that's it, then," Andrew says to me now, his voice barely audible over the jukebox. His tone is hard and resigned, without even a hint of pleading. He handles this like a professional. Clinical acceptance.

"I'm sorry."

Andrew just nods, as if he is suddenly sleepy and his head is too heavy a burden to carry.

"I want you to know I care about you a lot," I say, like I am reading from a book on how to break up with someone. I even have the nerve to add "It's not you. It's me."

Andrew lets a strangled laugh escape. I have finally

provoked him. He has moved from confusion to sadness and now, finally, to what I am most comfortable with, anger.

"You're fucking right. It is you, Em. Don't you worry. I know that this is all about you." He grabs his jacket and is about to leave. I want to stop him, to prolong this terrible moment before finality. But there is nothing left to say.

"I'm sorry," I whisper, as he throws some bills onto the table. "I really am." This takes the air out of the moment, and the tightness in his shoulders softens at the sound of my words.

"I know," he says, and his eyes bore into mine. Surprisingly, they are not filled with anger or sadness or love, but with something that looks a hell of a lot like pity. Andrew clears his throat, kisses me on the cheek, and walks calmly out of the restaurant.

Within seconds, he gets absorbed into the swell of Third Avenue. And it is me who is left sitting alone, watching the door and chewing on the bones of his leftover hot wings.

I walk the twenty blocks to my apartment, and it helps to clear my head. The air tingles in my nose, another hint that autumn will soon relieve summer. I take Madison Avenue and watch the crowds savoring the last few moments of the long weekend and the season, sitting with shiny cocktails on makeshift street-level patios. I envy them their last taste of freedom before the workweek. For a moment, I consider stopping for a cosmopolitan at a swanky bar; maybe I can pretend to be one of them, in camouflage, and postpone feeling anything for another hour or two.

Instead, I keep going. I focus on the street numbers as I walk; the counting slows my pulsing thoughts. *Fourteenth, you did what you had to do. Thirteenth, we were never meant to be. Twelfth, this is my fault. Eleventh, I did this.* I find comfort in the rhythm and that I'm solely responsible for how things turned out. I know I let the relationship go too far. I should have said my good-bye months ago, when it would have hurt both of us less, long before I was steered in front of a jewelry-store window. At least, I reason, at the very least, I took back control. *Tenth, things are under control. Ninth, you will be fine. Eighth, he would have left anyway, sooner or later. He would have left you anyway.*

When I get to my building, Robert, my doorman, ushers me inside. He is in his early seventies, with a comically white head of hair and matching beard. He looks like a benevolent God or Santa Claus and has the same tendency to meddle. Robert's constant presence, even his rapid-fire questions, soothes the tenants of the building, which is filled with mostly studios; we know that someone will be there when we get home, that someone will ask how our day was, that someone will notice if we don't come back at all.

"Where's your other half tonight?" he asks.

"Staying at his place." He smiles at me and steps out of

the way so I can get into the empty elevator. "Have a good night."

"Good night, Emily."

From now on, my day will end right here. Right at the front door. Robert's is the last voice I will hear most evenings. His is the last face I will see.

# Two

The first time Andrew laughed in his sleep, I should have woken him and broken up with him right then and there. No one deserves to be that happy.

Instead, though, I curled my body around his, pushed my belly tight against his back, and absorbed the vibrations. I had hoped that whatever made him that *free*, that *pure*, was contagious. It wasn't.

When I sleep through the night, I dream in black and white. I see images of men chasing me through circular mazes, of getting sucked into an envelope shaped gutter, of disappearing into a crowd at Times Square. Some days, my anxiety dreams are prosaic, the kind that have all been dreamt before: teeth falling out, showing up at work naked, screaming until my throat dries up. Even the steamy ones can turn on me, switching genres from romance to noir. In those dreams, I stand up after passionate sex with a stranger, let cigarette smoke billow out a darkened window, and contemplate the person I have forgotten and wronged.

I don't always have nightmares. Sometimes the night brings only sweet relief. But I can tell you this: I may have laughed at my dreams, the next morning mocking their high-school-level special effects or grade B porn, but I have never laughed in my sleep. I am just not that happy.

Last night, I lay in the middle of my queen-size bed in an effort to reclaim the space, to eliminate any evidence that it was once split into sides. I erase the crease Andrew left behind just twelve hours earlier by making vigorous snow angels on the ivory sheets. Sleep never had a chance.

The alarm goes off at eight a.m., and I drag myself out of bed. A quick glance in the mirror confirms what I already know—I look like crap. I have shiny dark circles under my eyes, as if someone attacked me with a purple Crayola marker. My stomach feels raw and empty. *You did this*, I tell myself. *You are not going to start feeling sorry for yourself now. Get over it.*

I dress in my favorite black suit, which always feels like a costume, its thin pinstripes elongating my body, the cut managing to be both professional and sexy. When I put it on, I transform suddenly into the comic-book character that Andrew and I used to call, in unison falsetto, "SuuuperLawyer." I wear it today for that extra boost.

My commute seems strangely solitary. The number 6 train, normally packed by the time I get on at Bleecker Street, holds only two other people: a homeless guy, with ink-stained fingers and a pile of newspapers on his lap, and a young woman in a skirt and sneakers, reading *Harry Potter*. Neither looks up when I take my seat.

The train lets me out at Grand Central, and I walk two more blocks to my building, a skyscraper that looks much like its neighbors and has thousands of small windows that do not open. They seal them to keep people from jumping.

I flash my security badge at Marge, the guard at the turnstile. She is about six foot one, both in height and width, her biceps and thighs indistinguishable. A human palindrome. Her face, too, has an eerie symmetry, with features that form parallel lines; her eyes, set too close to the nose, mirror her lips—thin, wide, and cinched in the middle. Every day, Marge wears a navy-blue polyester suit that pulls around her back, steel-toed boots, and hot-pink lipstick, the latter probably purchased to fight a rapidly approaching or recently arrived middle age. I wish I had Marge's presence. When she walks into a room, I imagine people notice. *This is a woman*, they think, *who can kick my ass in ten seconds or less. This is a woman*, they think, *whose makeup wouldn't even smear.*

I have walked past Marge at least twice a day, five days a week, for the last five years, more than 2,600 times in all—I once did the math—and she has not once wished me a good morning. When I first started at Altman, Pryor and Tisch, it was dehumanizing, somehow, that our daily encounter would go unacknowledged, and it became my mission to get Marge to notice me. It was one way to make my work life more interesting, since the rest of my hours were spent locked in a conference room reviewing millions of accounting documents for a fraud case. Some of my male colleagues, I found out from my friend Mason, would numb their own pain by masturbating in the bathroom. I now, of course, avoid shaking hands in the office.

Marge seemed like a more appropriate project. I was trying to carve out my own, friendlier New York. My tactics were harmless. I tried smiling and using her name, complimenting her hair. I even tried poking her once. I admit that was a mistake.

Despite my valiant effort, though, Marge has never said a single word to me. Never even smiled at me. I like to believe this is because she was trained at Buckingham Palace and that, should she speak, she would have a posh British accent, and not the rough Brooklynese of the other guards.

I like to believe it is her civic duty to stare straight ahead.

After about a year, I finally gave up my crusade. I just ran out of energy. New York seems to do that to people; it finally wears you down until you do things its way. I now simply nod at Marge when I walk by and imagine that she feels something resembling maternal affection for me.

When I get to my office, Karen, my secretary, has already left twelve messages on my chair, with a Post-it note that says *Good Luck!!!!* Four exclamation points, one for each message from a notoriously difficult partner, Carl MacKinnon, demanding to know why I did not respond to his six e-mails over the weekend. I write him a quick passive-aggressive message that is far less deferential than usual.

I just don't have it in me today to bend over.

To: Carl R. MacKinnon, APT
From: Emily M. Haxby, APT
Subject: HOLIDAY weekend
   Accidentally left BlackBerry in office over the weekend, so I did not get all of your e-mails until this morning. In answer to your urgent questions, our hearing date on the Quinn matter is August 29, 2010, approximately two years from now. And, no, I have not yet started preparing.

From: Carl R. MacKinnon, APT
To: Emily M. Haxby, APT
Subject: Re: HOLIDAY weekend
   Emily, you have been with the firm long enough to know that "accidentally" forgetting your BlackBerry is an unacceptable excuse. See me in my office at noon. We have issues to discuss.

A few years ago, Carl's e-mail would have reduced me to tears; today, I laugh it off. If he wants to fire me at noon, it will be a blessing.

Julie Buxbaum

From: Emily M. Haxby, APT
To: Mason C. Shaw, APT
Subject: FW: Re: HOLIDAY weekend
   Oops. Mason, can you please get Marge to go
kick Carl's ass? I bet she would let you watch.


To: Emily M. Haxby, APT
From: Mason C. Shaw, APT
Subject: Re: FW: Re: HOLIDAY weekend
   Will do. But from what I hear about Carl, I think he
might enjoy it. He's the kind of guy who likes a good
spanking.
   Lunch Thursday?


Thank God for Mason. At four o'clock in the morning—
when I am drowning in a pool of deposition transcripts and
haven't gotten more than a couple of hours of sleep over
the course of the week—Mason is the one who trots out
well-worn imitations of the senior partners to keep me
laughing. He manages to make the absurdity of our daily
existence at APT an endless source of entertainment,
magically manipulating tedium into a form of sport.
Mason's the type of guy who exploited the small victories of
high school—simultaneously captain of the football team,
student-body president, and deflowerer of the entire cheer-
leading squad—but instead of peaking like so many
homecoming kings of yesteryear, he continued to pillage all

the way to graduating first in his class at Stanford Law School. He's a serial monogamist with a short attention span, which means he always has a girlfriend but never for long enough that I need to remember her name. They are usually interchangeable, anyway: blond and silicone and placated by shiny objects. They demand little and get less. I am not sure Mason and I would have crossed paths and become friends outside the bizarre snow globe of law-firm life, but now that we have, he's a keeper.

To: Mason C. Shaw, APT
From: Emily M. Haxby, APT
Subject: Re: Re: FW: Re: HOLIDAY weekend
    If I still have my job on Thursday, we're on. If not, you're buying.

Before I have time to respond to my other work messages and dig out of the big hole I created for myself by not checking e-mail this weekend, Kate swings by my office and pokes her head in the door frame. Her hair is pulled back into a tight chignon with a thin headband, and her tailored shirt is tucked in and belted. Everything kept in its place. Her look is softened, though, by the crow's feet at the corners of her eyes; somehow, the lines manage to make her look younger, playful even.

"Em," she whispers. "What have you done?"

At first I think she is talking about my lie to Carl, and I

Julie Buxbaum

feel a shot of fear that I actually may be fired. How did she know so quickly? How will I pay rent? But then I remember last night and see the hurt look on her face, like I broke up with her and not Andrew.

"I guess good news travels fast." My flat voice belies my smile.

"Andrew called Daniel last night."

"Ah."

Kate sits down across from me and kicks the door closed with her spike heel. "I'm worried about you, Em. I don't get it."

"I know. I'm not so sure I get it either."

"But you guys were happy."

"I guess. Sometimes. Us getting married though? Not a good idea." Kate's eyebrows crunch together, and she looks at me, really looks at me, like she is not sure who I am all of a sudden.

*I'm still here. I'm still me*, I want to say, but I don't, because I am not surprised by her reaction. I knew she would be upset, mad at me even, for breaking up with Andrew, since she was the one who brought us together in the first place. Kate had arranged our blind date under the theory that it made sense to seal the friendship gap, that it was only logical that one of your best friends and one of your fiancé's best friends would be a perfect fit. She wasn't half wrong.

When Kate first came up with the idea to set us up, she

described Andrew as a "great catch," which instantly made me reluctant to meet him. Though everyone I knew seemed to be either settling down or looking to settle down, I was never on a deep-sea fishing expedition to find a boyfriend. And a "great catch," well, that seemed to be begging for heartache.

Though Kate didn't believe me, I liked being alone. As an only child of easily distracted parents, I have never had trouble entertaining myself. Preferred things that way. When I was kid, even before my mother died and I retreated into my bedroom and Sharpied the words GO AWAY onto the door, I spent much of my time tucked away in tight corners reading Nancy Drew mysteries, a place where kids seemed smarter and more capable than grown-ups. I barely noticed when my parents blew kisses on the way out the door to cocktail parties, unfazed by their desire to enter a world where I didn't meet the height require-ment. As an adult, I haven't changed all that much.

But to be fair, Kate was absolutely right; Andrew was a catch. Irresistible, if I had been inclined to resist him, which I wasn't. He checks off all of the boxes: He is smart, successful, and funny. He is good-looking, but not scarily so. His left eye dips just a tad lower than the right, and he has this endearing way of cocking his head to the side to even them out. He always takes out the garbage, changes the toilet-paper roll, cleans the hair from the shower drain. Sure, he leaves his toenails behind on the coffee table, consistently runs twenty minutes late, and secretly enjoys Internet porn, but I have no doubt that he will make a wonderful husband to some lucky *wife*. The truth is, he would have been wasted on me.

"Andrew really liked you. He told Daniel. You did well," Kate reported to me after our first date. As if the date was a performance and I had gotten good reviews. And later, when Andrew and I had officially become a couple, Kate would gloat about her matchmaking abilities. I now feel guilty for tarnishing her reputation. She had wanted to put a marriage on her résumé, and she would have been excited about being one of my bridesmaids. She actually likes that kind of stuff; her smile is eerily unaffected by the prospect of head-to-toe taffeta. In fact, I wouldn't be surprised if she had already ordered me a T-shirt that says *Mrs. Warner* on the back.

"Em, please just tell me why," she says, and suddenly, with all of the strength I have left in my body, I want to make my friend understand. I am just not sure how. I am not sure I even understand.

"I don't know why. I just couldn't see myself as Mrs. Warner. Or Mrs. Haxby-Warner. Or whatever I would be called. I can't marry him, Kate. I can't. I'm not sure I would still be me if I did." I concentrate on doodling empty hearts on my legal pad. "Whoever the hell that is."

"You don't have to change your name."

"I know that. It's not about my name." I start drawing large bouquets of flowers, making circling loops for the petals.

"But I don't get it. He hasn't even asked you yet. You guys don't have to get married right now, if you're not ready." She glances at her ring and covers one of her hands with the other.

"I'm never going to be ready, though. Andrew is great. We both know that. But it's just not enough. I can't become his other half. You know what I mean?" I ask, though I know she does not. She has never had to question things between her and Daniel. She has always just known. Kate's charm lies in her placid consistency.

"Maybe you are holding out for something that doesn't exist," she says.

"It's not that I am looking for someone better, or anything like that. He's the best. But he doesn't understand me." I know I sound full of lame excuses, but I can't bring myself to say what I really want to. *I ate him, Kate, and he tasted just like chicken. I ate him, Kate, and I barely felt a thing.* I keep these thoughts to myself, because I know I don't make any sense.

"I guess the truth of the matter is this isn't about Andrew at all," I say instead.

"No. No, I don't think it is," she says, and the look she gives me now is identical to the one Andrew gave me last night; it looks something like pity. She crosses the room and kisses me on my forehead, a gesture only she can get away with. No condescension or judgment, just a move to bring the mood back to level. Kate never leaves a wake; instead, she makes sure to smooth things out.

"All right, we'll talk more about this later. I've got to get back to work," she says. Kate is three years senior to me and is aiming to make partner next year. If she does—and she will if there is any justice in this world—Kate will become the second woman litigation partner in the two-hundred-year history of APT. I, on the other hand, was told at my last review that I need to work on my *dedication* to the firm.

"By the way, be careful, Em. Avoid Carl today at all costs. He is looking for someone to work on the new Synergon water case."

"Please, please tell me you're making that up. I already have a meeting scheduled with him this afternoon."

There is no doubt about it, the look in her eyes now is definitely pity. I am screwed. Day one at APT, we were taught by the senior associates that there were only three things you needed to avoid at the firm in order to survive: Synergon, Carl MacKinnon, and the Chinese take-out place on the corner.

"It gets worse. Carisse has already been assigned to it, so she'll be the most senior person under Carl."

Now, I like to think that I don't hate anyone in this world, but that would be a big, fat lie. I hate Carisse. Even Kate, who does not hate anyone, makes an exception for her. Carisse is one of those women who should be kicked out of the Sisterhood. Her transgressions, beyond sleeping with various married partners, include playing games with her underlings, such as Passing the Blame and Do My Work for Me and I'll Take the Credit, Thank You. She's famous for saying things like *Wow, you look terrible/ tired/bloated*, or congratulating you on your nonexistent pregnancy. Although she is only two years ahead of me at the firm, just another cog in the associate ranks, she commands as if she is managing partner. I sometimes think that if I could murder her and get away with it, it would not be hard to pull the trigger. The world would be a much better place without her.

"Sorry, Em," Kate says, and walks out the door. I look down at my notepad and notice a new set of doodles. I have been drawing little daggers.

At noon, I walk into Carl's office in what I hope is a defiant way. Maybe my unfriendly demeanor will change his mind about assigning me to the case. I channel Marge. She brings me strength in times like these.

Carl sits behind an enormous mahogany desk that is empty except for a sleek flat-screen monitor. Although not a tall man, his chair is pumped up to what seems like ten feet off the ground. I notice that his guest chairs rest about two inches from the floor. He is on the phone, and he signals me to enter with a flick of his wrist.

I sit on the minuscule seat. The chair thing actually works. I feel like a five-year-old getting scolded in the principal's office. Impressively framed degrees line the wall, and the names jump out. Princeton. Wharton Business School. Harvard Law School. Could he possibly have gone to all three? An award from Save the Children hangs beside them; apparently, Carl was Donor of the Year in 1994, 1999, and 2005. A picture of him hugging a skinny African kid shares the frame.

Carl stares at me, evaluates me, while he sweet-talks a client on the phone. I cradle a legal pad against my chest to avoid him taking a peek at my cleavage. He's the type who somehow thinks it's perfectly acceptable at one moment to scream at an associate and in the next, if the associate happens to be wearing a skirt, to put his hand on her thigh. Rumor has it that though his partnership shares have been cut more than a few times for sexual harassment, he'll never be fired, because he could take too many big clients, like Synergon, with him. There is also firm lore that he once threw the annotated *New York Civil Procedure and Laws Rule Book* at an associate's head.

*That had to hurt.*

Oh, and did I mention his pregnant wife? She's expecting twins.

Usually, if I know I will be meeting with Carl, I wear my dowdiest clothing, leave my makeup at home, and pull my hair back in an old-lady bun. I like to believe this is why he has never hit on me. Of course, I am firmly anti-sexual harassment, but I have to admit that I worry about the fact that my costume works so well; I'm the only woman in the office he has never made a pass at.

"So, I am assigning you to the new Synergon water case. It will be you, me, and Carisse, though as the most junior person, I expect you to do most of the legwork on this one," Carl says, after he hangs up the phone. There it is. My stomach drops. The fact I already knew it was coming does not cushion the blow.

"I expect you to devote one hundred and ten percent of your time to this. It requires all the manpower we have and is a great opportunity to show your *dedication* to the firm. I expect that there will be no incidents like this weekend?" I nod, and Carl sniffs the air as if he smells something bad.

"Of course, Carl. I'm sorry about that." The apology slips out before I can stop it, and I am ashamed of myself for giving in so easily. I might as well just give him a blow job and get it over with.

"All right, now here are the details. Synergon is being sued by about fifty different families in Arkansas state court. Basically, we are defending against a bunch of Erin Brockovich-type cases, though fortunately that bitch isn't involved this time. You know, she looks nothing like Julia Roberts."

"Oh," I say.

"All these poor people in the middle of nowhere

Arkansas have gotten cancer and are growing third eyes and the like, and they are claiming it's because we have been dumping chemicals in the water."

"Is there evidence of dumping?"

"Yeah, Synergon has been dumping petrochemicals in the Caddo River for over fifty years. They just assumed none of the WT who live nearby would be smart enough to sue."

"WT?" I ask.

"White trash. But, honestly, dumping does not necessarily equal cancer. Yeah, they have been spilling chemicals, but no one has proven this is why these people are getting sick."

I look up at Carl and see a small smile playing at the corners of his lips. He enjoys this, I realize, this squashing of the little guy. Carl must have been pantsed daily in high school, been beaten up in the cafeteria, perhaps even swirlied. There is just no other way to explain his level of evil. His aimless revenge.

"Really, this case is simply the plaintiffs' bar trying to squeeze some more money out of corporate America," he says.

"But if there was dumping—"

"Do I really need to repeat this? Write this down, Emily. Dumping does not necessarily equal cancer. Dumping equals dumping. Not cancer. Got it?"

"I guess . . ."

"So here is our plan of attack, though I will leave the details and the heavy lifting to you. We are going to go *A Civil Action* on their asses. Did you read that book?"

"Yup, it was required my first year of law school." I don't add that it was for an ethics class and that the point was to teach us how not to practice law.

"Good, good. Here is the big picture. First, we get some expert reports from a few scientists who will say that there is no causal connection between the chemicals and cancer. Which, really, I don't think there is." Carl looks down at his notes. "There is a list of experts Synergon always uses. We'll also serve the plaintiffs with tons of discovery requests and file as many motions as we can get away with to ratchet up their legal costs. Synergon has piles of money to throw at this, but the other side clearly doesn't.

"After we win on summary judgment, which we will because they can't prove a damn thing, then comes act three. We sue them for our attorneys' fees. We probably won't get 'em, but it's still a win-win for us. Synergon is impressed by our aggressive stance, we get to bill more hours, and best of all it teaches people not to mess with Synergon."

He smiles again, and I swear I see his chest puff out.

"Get started drafting the first set of discovery requests immediately. I expect them on my desk tomorrow morning. Also, plan on traveling to Arkansas a lot over the coming

months. Get some decent luggage. And one more thing."
He pauses and waits for me to catch his eye.

"Nice suit, Emily." And with a wink, I am dismissed from
his office. Somehow he leaves me no doubt that he just
pictured me naked.

When you take a job as a litigator at a large law firm, you
know that you are selling your soul. Anyone who tries to
tell you otherwise is either lying or fooling themselves. But,
until this moment, I had always thought about it as selling
my life, and not really my soul. I knew going in that the job
would require all of my time, leaving little for anything
resembling a social life. As an associate, canceling plans,
doctors' appointments, and vacations all comes with the
territory. Most of us spend Friday afternoons keeping our
fingers crossed, praying that this week will be the
exception, that a partner will not drop work on our desks
that invariably "needs" to be done by Monday morning.

But soul-selling aside, being an associate is still a pretty
good deal. Though most days I feel overworked and under-
stimulated, the salary leaves me enough room to pay off my
gigantic law-school loans and to rent my own studio in the
Village. Though the space is only four hundred square feet,
in Manhattan, where people sell their organs for an apartment, having my own little corner carved out feels
luxurious.

I start looking over the complaints that have been filed

against Synergon. I read about some of the plaintiffs, impoverished people from a tiny little town that no one has ever heard of: Caddo Valley, Arkansas. Population: 565. The first complaint is from the Jones family, and they are suing because their mother, Jo-Ann, died from acute lymphoblastic leukemia. Mr. Jones has five kids to raise alone now, all between the ages of two and nine. They live .25 miles from the Caddo River, and Jo-Ann is the seventh person in Caddo Valley to get the diagnosis. This gives the town a cancer rate five hundred times the national average.

While I consider the details of the complaint, I sit on the forty-fifth floor of a high-rise building smack in the middle of New York City. My office is a large box constructed from gleaming steel and glass, a lofty perch, with a view of the city's grid of organized chaos. The only thing I have in common with the Joneses is that my mother, too, died of cancer. That suddenly doesn't seem like all that much.

A wave of shame passes over me when I realize that this is my job. This is what I am paid to do. I get a check every two weeks, a 401k, and health-care benefits (which cover me should *I* ever get cancer), and in exchange, I will spend this evening, and the next six months, manufacturing ways to prevent Synergon from redistributing a tiny portion of its wealth to fifty families that need, and deserve, the help. I wonder what Andrew, who paddles people back to life every day in the E.R., who *makes the world a better place*, would think about the case, but I push him out of my head.

I then wonder briefly, like a flicker, what my mother, whose own hair fell out strand by strand and whose breasts were carved out of her chest, would say if she knew who I have grown up to be. I don't want to know. Instead, I click over to the American Cancer Society Web site and make a hundred-dollar donation, a small penance, nothing in comparison to the fifty million at stake in the litigation.

And then I begin drafting the countless discovery requests for Carl and block everything else out. I don't look up until my window has gone dark and night has fallen on Manhattan. The only sound, the periodic bleating of distant sirens, is soothing, a New York lullaby.

It does not once occur to me to quit.

# Three

I go home to a pile of laundry in the center of my apartment. Its staggering height pushes the alert level from yellow (elevated) to orange (high) that I will not have clean underwear tomorrow. I decide it doesn't matter if I rebel against the panty police; no one will be checking under my skirt at work. If they do, they get what they deserve.

The light of my answering machine double-blinks: *Blink. Blink blink. Blink. Blink blink.* This is answering-machine code for two messages.

"Hey, Emily, it's your father. Just checking in." *Click.*

"Hey, Em." Jess's voice bounces against the walls of my apartment and reminds me that I live in a perfect square. "Hope you're holding up okay about the whole Andrew thing. Friday night. You. Me. Merc Bar. We're going out on the town. I will not take no for an answer." Although I met Jess as a consequence of a random room assignment my freshman year at Brown, she has morphed from college friend into my Siamese twin/Magic 8 Ball/Jewish mother/codependent/Tony Robbins. I want to call her back, but I know it's past her bedtime. Jess goes to sleep every weekday night at 10:43, the only remnant of her childhood struggle with OCD.

I pick up the phone to call my father back instead, since he—unlike Jess or the rest of us, for that matter—does not believe in sleep.

"This is Lieutenant Governor Haxby," my dad answers the phone, apparently under the assumption that whoever would be calling him on his personal cell at one a.m. does not already know that he is the lieutenant governor of Connecticut. Or that anyone cares. I wonder if it was such a good idea to call after all, wonder if I should have continued our endless game of phone tag. Talking to my dad has the unfortunate side effect of making me feel very much alone in the world.

"Hi, Dad. It's Emily. How are you?"

"Good, sweetheart. Good. Keeping fit. Went for a six-mile run this morning. Five a.m."

"Wow, Dad," I say, as if he doesn't tell me this every single time I call. I think this may be a passive-aggressive way of criticizing me, since he knows I have not—have never—done the same.

"Yeah, well, it's important to stay fit. You should try it sometime. Maybe in Central Park."

"Dad, I live downtown."

"Oh. Maybe you could run up to the park then. That reminds me, I need to come see your new apartment one of these days."

"Not so new. I've lived here for over a year now."

"Right. Right. So what is the superstar litigator working on?"

I tell my father about the Synergon case, mostly because we find it easy to talk about my job. As I describe what is going on in Caddo Valley, though, I worry, for perhaps the first time in my life, that I am giving my dad good reason to be ashamed of me. He is, after all, a civil servant.

"Wow, kiddo. It's great to make connections at Synergon," he says. "You better put your time in on this one. This is the kind of thing that can make your career."

"But, Dad, I'm defending Synergon. I mean, I know they can't prove anything, but still."

"Business is business, Em. You know that. And it never hurts to make friends in high places." I realize now that I had wanted a different reaction from my father; I wanted him to scream at me, to tell me that what I am doing is wrong, that my work makes the world a worse place. I wanted us to have a fight about it, which is ridiculous, really. My dad and I have never had a fight. It is just not something my father does. Fighting is petty and distasteful to him, something better left to children.

My father has that shellac that coats all politicians: the shine, the charm, the boyish good looks and graying temples. When he shakes hands, he uses both of them, to show how interested he is in meeting you. He'll look you right in the eye too, as if to say I *care*. I don't know what is underneath all the polish, though. He has never shown me.

The truth is, I love my father, but I don't particularly like him. I guess I don't particularly like him because I am not sure if he likes me.

After my mother died and it was just the two of us in the house, there was a small window of opportunity when we could have at least tried to communicate. We could have screamed and cried and said all the things that would normally have been unforgivable. We could have wept together until we recognized that we had both lost one of the few things that connected us. Or we could have laughed maniacally, as I did with my friends in the corner after the wake, as if to say *This doesn't hurt, this doesn't hurt, this doesn't hurt.*

But that never happened. My mother died on a Thursday afternoon, and I was back in school on Monday morning. I wasn't given the choice to stay home. We both figured out a way to feed ourselves, separately, and we went about our usual routines. As if we had always lived this way, as if nothing had changed, as if we didn't suddenly feel like a three-legged dog.

Though I know my father cried late at night while I lay in the bedroom next door, though I heard his heartbreak in the form of quick, strangled intakes of breath, the muffled sobs into pillows that echoed my own, I didn't knock on his door, and he didn't knock on mine. I thought about it, of course. Would stand outside his room sometimes, motionless, unable to lift my arms, unable to brush knuckle against wood. I am not sure why our doors felt so impenetrable. Maybe we felt some ownership over our grief, worried that by sharing it, we would be giving our only pieces of her away. Or maybe, neither of us had the strength left to console the other in the scary depths of night, since we exhausted all of our energy by day, busy, busy, busy pretending that we were just fine.

"Dad, you know what? I've got to go. I still have more work to do tonight," I say. White lie number one.

"Okay. Please send my regards to Andrew," he says.

"Will do." White lie number two. I am not ready to tell him that Andrew and I broke up. Like my job, my relationship is a source of contentment for my father; it means that my happiness is no longer his responsibility. I am complicitous in this. Over the years, I've religiously followed our single unspoken rule that, whenever possible, I would take care of myself. Being a widower is hard enough without the added burden of having to parent.

"By the way, I'm going to visit Grandpa Jack on Saturday. You want to come?"

"Can't, Em. You know how it is," he says. "Tell my father that I'm too busy. Things are going crazy at the office."

"Will do." White lie number three. I would never

insult my grandfather with my father's favorite excuse.

"Keep up the good work, kiddo," my dad says, and then replaces his voice with a dial tone.

I crawl under the covers, exhausted, and glance over at my windowsill, empty except for a few photographs. Andrew and I at my last birthday dinner, candles glowing eerily under my chin, as if my face is lit up from within. Jess and I at her sister's wedding, both of us in purple taffeta and smeared eye makeup. And one small photograph of my family, all three of us together on the front steps of our house in Connecticut. I am wearing OshKosh overalls and holding up my new Wonder Woman lunch box proudly for the camera. It is my first day of kindergarten, and I look fearless. The only thing holding me in place is the second I have to wait for the camera to click.

Tonight, I leave the bathroom light on and double-check the lock on the front door. I rest in the middle of the bed again and make a few more snow angels. It is a fruitless exercise though, because when I am done moving my arms upward and downward, I end up in exactly the same place I started.

# Four

"How *are* you?" Jess asks, when I call her back the next morning. Her emphasis on the "are" makes it sound like someone just died.

"I'm fine."

"I'm worried about you." I picture Jess on the other end of the call, sitting in her hot-pink half-walled cubicle. I bet she's curling the phone cord around her fingers into elaborate animal shapes, like she used to in college. Though her business cards say she is a graphic designer, Jess gets paid to doodle on a computer.

"No need to be worried. I'm fine. I broke up with him, remember. This was my decision."

"That's why I'm worried."

"Jess—"

"No, seriously, that's why. I've been thinking a lot about this. You're probably the best person I know, and you'd never hurt Andrew unless you absolutely felt you had to. I just wish I could make some sense of it all. You seemed so good together."

"Jess, I'm not trying to punt here, but can we talk about this later? I'm in the office." When I first called Jess to tell her that Andrew and I had broken up, I had naïvely hoped she would follow the universal breakup rules and indulge me in some ex-boyfriend bashing. I wanted her to say *I never liked that guy*, or *I always thought he smelled kind of funny but didn't want to say anything*. Instead, Jess's reactions have ranged from: (a) "But I thought he was the best thing that had ever happened to you," to (b) "Fine, if you don't want to marry him, I will," and (c), my personal favorite, "Are you out of your fucking mind?"

"Okay, I'll drop it only because it's before noon and I can tell you haven't had your coffee yet. But Friday night we're going out," she says now, her voice, unlike mine, not deadened by work. Jess's office has that infectious Internet start-up energy. The potent effect of combining modern furniture, a high-tech latte maker, a pinball machine, and a staff made up solely of people wearing funky glasses.

"Absolutely." I wish I could be at Jess's office right now, wearing jeans and sipping Red Bull. I would be trading one kind of conformity for another, maybe, but her type is still better. In her world, flip-flops are encouraged.

"Absolutely?" she asks, unable or unwilling to hide her surprise.

"Yeah, of course. Can't wait."

"Seriously? I was gearing up to convince you. I had a whole speech prepared. Do you want to hear it?"

"Not really."

"You sure? It's very inspirational."

"I'm already inspired, but if you want me to play along, I will."

"No, the speech won't be as good now. I don't need you to pretend for me."

"Seriously, I am happy to play along. Which way did you expect me to go? Too heartbroken to go out? Or too busy with work?"

"Of course too busy with work. You would never go the heartbroken route. Not your style."

"Yeah, you're probably right."

"Em, maybe you're not ready for an Andrew."

"Please, let's drop it. I don't even know what that means."

"Can I just ask you one more question? Just one?"

"Sure," I say. "Okay."

"Are you really fine?"

"I think so. I think I did the right thing here. For everyone. I really do."

"If you say so." Her tone makes it clear she doesn't believe me but she doesn't have the time right now to deal with it. Instead, she talks to one of her colleagues in the background. "You have to make the cartoon's boobs bigger, and Mark said he wants to see a hint of nipple. It makes them look healthier."

"What are you working on?" I ask, grateful for the opportunity to change the subject.

"A kids' vitamin label."

# Five

Over the next few days, work pulls me under. Carl keeps giving me Synergon assignments, endless, numbing tasks, and I conquer them, one after the other. The monotony and its low, rhythmic hum leave little room for thoughts of any kind. I spend twenty hours each day in my office and do not get out of my chair until my eyes glaze over and pins and needles prickle my feet. I eat all of my meals in this square cell, food that falls from a vending machine, and I litter important documents with their crumbs and smudges. In a law firm, these marks are a badge of honor.

I do not think about Andrew. Instead, I feel an empty space, a white noise, where the thoughts of him, the memories of him, used to live. My apartment feels like that too, since there is now an overwhelming stillness to the place. The Cheerios are tucked away in the cabinet, my toilet seat is down, Andrew's pillow is not indented. But I haven't been home much.

I leave early in the morning, when the streets are still quiet except for the sounds of garbage trucks taking away the trash. The few other people who share the city blocks with me at this hour walk with their heads down and their collars up. We all look guilty. Just before dawn, when I leave the office, I take a car with tinted windows home. I look out and blindly watch as the city passes in a dark blur. I climb into bed, my head too numb to notice Andrew's absence, and sleep for just a couple of hours before I start all over again.

There is a part of me that relishes the bags under my eyes, the fact that my body is sore from lack of exercise. I find myself saying things like "I might bill close to three hundred hours this month," or "It looks like it's going to be another all-nighter," to my fellow colleagues when I pass them in the hallways to and from the bathroom, as if this is something to be proud of, this self-flagellation. I like to think they are a little in awe of my *dedication*, but I know better.

I convince myself that I am having fun playing big lawyer in the big city—working all hours, surrounded by a ringing phone and day-old pizza crust. That I am reveling in this life of a caricature.

But that would be a lie, because the truth is that I don't really feel much of anything at all. Just a dull ache around my edges.

\* \* \*

"Ready?" Mason says, as he knocks on my door and takes a shocked glance around. My office, which is usually reasonably tidy, looks like the scene of a hit, as if the perps trashed the place to make the homicide look random. I can also tell he notices the stale smell in the air, from last night's dinner and probably because I haven't showered in a few days, but he is too polite to comment. Mason looks out of place here, his hair still wet and neatly combed.

"Ready for what?"

"Lunch." Mason fixes the cuff of his shirt, as if my messiness is contagious.

"Oh, can't. Sorry. Forgot. Too much to do. I may bill close to three hundred hours this month," I say, because those seem to be the only words I know how to put together into a sentence.

"Shut up. You sound like Carisse. Now get that adorable ass of yours out of that chair. We're going out. And by the way, you look and smell like the gift Rambo left for me last night." Rambo is Mason's basset hound; all jowls and drool. Guess Mason is not so polite after all.

"Thanks."

"Come on. We're going to Charlie's. And you're getting that steak you're always talking about."

He leads me out the door with his hand on the small of my back, and his movements follow his speech, both commanding and lazy. He's from Texas, and despite spending the last decade above the Mason-Dixon Line, he hasn't let go of that slow, sensual Southern pace. I melted the first time he called me "darlin'," but now I don't notice so much anymore. I sometimes look at Mason, though, and his over-size hands, and think, *The only cowboy left in New York.*

I follow him out of the office, and he leads me into the sunlight, which burns my eyes, and then, mercifully, back into the darkness again. Charlie's has chocolate-brown leather booths, wood-paneled walls, and waiters in green felt jackets. It screams, *Men eat steak here.* I love everything about it: the small groups of businessmen with their shirt-sleeves rolled up, digging into plates of ribs; the generous amount of olives that come with a martini; Charlie himself, who stands behind the bar and greets some of the customers by name.

Mason sits down across from me, falling heavily into the booth. He likes to take up a lot of space, and he spreads himself out along the bench. I think it is his way of express-ing his masculinity, this elaborate unfolding of his arms and legs, long and muscular.

"Heard you're working on the Synergon thing. My condolences," he says.

"It's not that bad."

"Right. No, really, what's up with you lately? Normally I have to kick you out of my office so I can get some work done, and now suddenly you're billing like a maniac."

"Yeah, well, you know what it's like working for Carl," I say. "I've been very busy." I wonder if I have to tell Mason that Andrew and I broke up. I feel as if saying it out loud, especially to him, will make it more real, more official. I have always gotten the feeling that he never liked Andrew, and telling him now feels something like a betrayal.

I practice in my head a few times. *Andrew and I broke up. I broke up with Andrew.* These descriptions seem imprecise. Not exactly right. *The truth is I broke Andrew and me. I broke us.*

"I broke up with Andrew," I say, out loud.

"I see," he says, as if he needs a moment to figure out what to say next. Unlike my other friends, he doesn't jump into apologies or bombard me with expressions of sympathy.

"What happened?"

"He was getting ready to propose."

Mason nods, as if there is nothing more to be said. As if he knows me, and this makes perfect sense. As if I am not crazy. On the other hand, it may just be his male impulse not to talk about these kinds of things.

"Let's order." He signals one of the waiters over, and it seems, at least for now, like the conversation is over.

"For me, the bacon double cheeseburger and a basket of onion rings. And for the lady, the twelve-ounce tenderloin. And please give her extra fries, 'cause she needs 'em," he drawls, and then smiles up at the waiter. "She just gone and broke some poor man's heart."

Andrew does not come up again for the rest of lunch. We

chat about everything else, though. We talk about work, about Carl, about Rambo. We talk about Laurel, Mason's current girlfriend, who recently made a copy of his keys without asking. By the end of the meal, I am nourished by the conversation as much as the food. When we leave Charlie's and walk back out into the light, the sun feels good too, warm against my eyelids.

I almost feel normal.

The funk of my office hits me as soon as I walk in. I vow to go home early tonight, get a good night's sleep, perhaps take a long bath to soak away the residue. I am refreshed just thinking about it, until I see Carisse standing in front of my desk. She looks like a bobble-head doll, the cranium of Cro-Magnon man balancing on toothpick legs. She dives right in. Teeth first.

"Heard Andrew broke up with you. That sucks. He was a hottie." Who uses words like "hottie" after the ninth grade? I consider correcting her, that I, in fact, broke up with Andrew, but realize with a flush of pleasure that I don't care what she thinks.

"You should probably put that away, then." Carisse goes right for my jugular, pointing to the framed photo I keep on my desk of Andrew and me. In the picture, we stand shoulder to shoulder and hold hands, muddy after a camping trip in New Hampshire last summer. I had not yet decided what I was going to do with the picture. It felt wrong, somehow, to hide it in the drawer. Like throwing away exculpatory evidence.

"I guess." I must look sad, because Carisse actually smirks at me, as if we are playing tennis and she has just scored a point. Her thin lips slightly curl under, like a comic book villain, and I wonder if I smack her upside the back of the head if her face will stick that way.

She waits a beat, as if we are friends and she expects me to confide in her. When it becomes clear that I am not going to, she drops a huge file on my desk. Did she think we were going to have a heart-to-heart and that I was going to cry on her shoulder? If I did, would she take the file back?

"Carl wants you to write a motion to compel and to send me the first draft. All of the information is in there." She starts to walk out of my office, tugging on the hem of her gray pencil skirt, which, like her heels, is at least four inches higher than what is office appropriate. She stops and looks back, as if she has an afterthought.

"I need it by nine a.m. tomorrow morning."

Game, set, match.

After Carisse leaves, the stink of her perfume remains. I look at the file and realize she has left me with about fourteen hours of work.

I do a shoddy job. The only reason we are filing the motion is to force the other side to waste legal fees, which does not seem like a good enough reason for me to lose another night's sleep. Even though I write as quickly as possible, I don't finish until well after midnight.

Before leaving the office, I set the e-mail attaching the document for a late delivery to Carisse. Four-thirty a.m. Serves her right for bragging that she sleeps with her BlackBerry under her pillow. I imagine Carisse twitching awake when my e-mail arrives. The loud beep making her drool like a Pavlovian dog.

At least we're playing a new game now. Fifteen-love.

# Six

"I am wearing white after Labor Day. I don't care. Just arrest me and get it over with," Jess says on Friday night, and by way of greeting, puts her hands out to be cuffed. She prances through my apartment door in a white halter top with a yellow ribbon that ties around her neck and tight white pants. An outfit only about three people in America can get away with. Jess happens to be one of them. "Anyhow, *Vogue* says that it's totally allowed nowadays."

"Since when do you read *Vogue*?"

"I don't. I just made it up," she says. "Did you believe me?"

"No," I say, and smile. Jess would never pick up *Vogue*. It would never occur to her to look at pictures so she could dress like other people. I, on the other hand, dress to blend.

"All right, missy. Let me get a look at you." Jess manhandles me toward the full-length mirror. She grabs my makeup bag and starts to paint my face, adding a lot to the little I have put on. Since we have been doing this routine for years, Jess knows my limits by now—just how much color I will allow, just how much makeup pushes me from feeling attractive to pathetic—and stays within bounds.

We have developed a division of labor. She is my personal stylist and interior decorator. I am her tax accountant.

Jess takes a wand from her bag and dots glitter above my eyes. I immediately look more awake. Just before we leave, we stand side by side in the mirror and take pleasure in the fact that we are physical opposites. She is tall and angular, with sharp corners for elbows and knees. My edges are rounder, curvier; my bones comfortably padded. She has blond, almost white hair, kept close to her scalp, uneven enough to make it obvious she cut it herself. My hair is so dark it bleeds in photographs, and hangs long and wavy. When we walk into a bar, men immediately turn to get a better look at her. I tend not to be picked out from a crowd. I'm occasionally noticed, *recognized* over time. I don't mind, really. Men who are interested in a woman like Jess won't be interested in me, and vice versa. For all intents and purposes, we are different species.

We have a couple of glasses of Two Buck Chuck while we get ready, so by the time we are outside I am feeling lighter. Jess tucks her arm under my elbow, and we teeter on our heels as we head farther downtown. For a moment, it feels like we are back in college, giggly and full of optimism. A spectacle, regardless of whether anyone bothers to look.

"Have you spoken to Andrew?" she asks, and my lightness deflates.

"Nope. He is definitely not going to call me." I shrug, like it is out of my control. Like she didn't just kick her heel right through my bubble.

"Maybe you should call him."

"Nah. To say what?"

"I don't know. You miss him, don't you?"

"I don't know. I've been way too busy at work this past week to even think about it."

"Why do you keep doing this to yourself?" She stops walking to turn to look at me on the sidewalk.

"Doing what?"

"You're your own worst enemy. It's like you get pleasure out of breaking your own heart." She shakes her head at me, as if I'm amusingly incorrigible, like I'm an old man telling a dirty joke.

"That's not true," I say. "It just wasn't right, Jess. I can't marry him. I just can't." My lower lip starts to tremble. I take my fingers and dig them into my palms, and the threat of tears pulls away.

"Oh, Emily," she says, and draws me into a hug. The full use of my name hits a false note, and when I come up to her collarbone, her height is an insult.

"How is it that you are the most fun person I know and

also the most unhappy? Doesn't it get exhausting?" she asks.

I don't know what to say to this, so I don't say anything at all. I want to smooth it over with a joke, maybe make a reference to the Energizer Bunny, but that would only prove her point. Instead, we walk the rest of the way in silence. I spend the whole time thinking that I should have stayed home and rented a DVD. Maybe masturbated to the miniseries version of *Pride and Prejudice*. It's over six hours long.

That would have been less tiring than this.

The bar is filled with college students and a few, very recent, graduates. The women wear baby Ts embellished with juvenile images—Mickey Mouse, the Superman symbol, Smurfs—above exposed, pierced midriffs. On the bottom, they wear short cutoff denim skirts with the seams dangling. The men wear fitted black shirts, the two top buttons opened. The air is thick with the smell of hair gel.

"Is it just me or is everyone in here about twelve?" Jess asks, and I am surprised she notices.

"I'm tempted to order a Shirley Temple just to fit in."

She sidles up to the bar and orders us each a vodka tonic, which we down in about thirty seconds.

"Tequila?" she asks.

Three shots later, the bar looks very different. *I miss this*, I think. *You never know when you're going to meet someone who's going to change your life.* New York, its consistent throb of potential, can be a dangerous place for the overly imaginative; everyone you see is a possible route toward a different future. That guy in the grocery store with the green Pumas asking for cruelty-free eggs, the man in the suit and tie brushing your back when the subway lurches forward, the one in the Strand with sideburns and stubble reading *The Believer*. All lifestyle prototypes, maybe, but possible rebirths as well, like the freshman year of college all over again.

Just as quickly, though, the tide turns when I glance at the men gathered in small groups around the bar. They all look like little boys, with their spiky hair and clear eyes. I feel overdressed and out of place. *What am I doing here?*

This happens to me often, the moment never quite living up to the anticipation. At least I can hope that later, much later, my memory, like a revisionist historian, will retouch tonight's event by deleting my existential angst. I will remember laughing and getting drunk with Jess; I won't remember wanting to go home.

Years ago, when we went to Paris for the first time, Jess and I spent the months before reveling in blind excitement, memorizing travel guides and practicing our nonexistent French. I remember two days into the vacation, picnicking with a baguette and *fromage* on the lawn of yet another church and feeling like we looked very grown-up, even though we were not yet twenty.

While we sat there talking up the bitter cheese, I felt a familiar pang of disappointment. *This is what I spent ages looking forward to? Wasn't I supposed to feel different here?* And later, while dancing with a handsome French boy in a club, knowing I looked carefree, my youth something to be relished, I still needed to repeat in my head, like a mantra: *This is fun, this is fun, this is fun.* Of course, placing my tongue in his mouth did help mute the voices somewhat. Months later, though, I began to remember the vacation as idyllic, and would joke about my French conquest who was, appropriately enough, named Jacques. The trip paid for itself in afterglow.

I look over at Jess now, and she is chatting with a guy who has one eyebrow. He looks like Frida Kahlo. I tap her on the shoulder and tell her that I am going to step outside to make a quick phone call. She grabs my wrist. Hard.

"Calling Andrew?"

"No."

"Don't do it. If you're going to call him, wait until you've sobered up. Trust me. You'll thank me for it tomorrow," she says, like she is an authority on the perils of drunk dialing.

"I was just going to call and say hi."

"Give me the phone." I hand it over. Jess, despite her scrawniness, is stronger than I am and could beat me up. She turns my cell off and hands it back. Clearly, I'm very drunk, because it appears to me that the matter is now closed.

Four hours and countless shots later, Jess and I are sitting on stools talking to Frida and Frida's friend. Ironically, it turns out that Frida is a painter. Frida's friend, whose name I don't know or can't remember, says he's an entrepreneur, but when I ask him in what field, he looks at me blankly. I spend much of the conversation staring at his eyebrows, which in contrast to Frida's mustache-on-the-forehead look, have been recently overarched and waxed by a professional. They are perfect right triangles.

When the room starts to spin and I have grown bored of internally debating the relative disadvantages of over- and undergrooming, it's time to go home. Jess, who has the biggest libido of anyone I know—she calls herself a "sex-positive feminist," though I suspect this is grounded less in philosophy, more in pleasure—stays behind, presumably to pursue Frida. I admire the fact that her approach to sex is so simple. I could use a healthy dose of her nonchalance.

I go home alone and greet Robert at the door. As I stumble onto the elevator, he calls out to me to drink a couple of glasses of water before bed. It takes a few attempts to get the keys in the lock, but eventually I get inside and weave toward the bathroom.

And I stay there, crouched on the floor, with my head resting on the toilet seat, content to feel the coolness against my cheek, until the sun shines through my window and announces that it is morning.

This is the best sleep I have gotten all week.

# Seven

I hurt everywhere. I can't cross the room without succumbing to the spins. I glance at the clock, but move my head too quickly and cause a fresh rush of nausea. I am supposed to meet my grandfather at ten in Riverdale. It is 8:55 and I need to make a 9:15 train. Which means I should have left for Grand Central about ten minutes ago. Shit. I consider canceling, but I just can't do that to my Grandpa Jack. Anyone else, maybe, but not my Grandpa Jack. He has always shown up for me.

I drag myself up off the floor, brush my teeth, and swish around some mouthwash. Better to not show up at his retirement home smelling like tequila. Since there is no time to shower, I swat a Clearasil face wipe under my arms. It stings. I grab a T-shirt and a ratty pair of jeans from the tower of dirty laundry, throw my purse over my shoulder, and run out the door, down the six flights of stairs—there is no time to wait for the elevator—and out onto the street.

There will be no winning contests for good hygiene today. A quick look at my watch dashes any dreams of coffee. I sprint unevenly toward the subway and weigh the possibility that I may still be drunk. I reach the platform just as the car is pulling away. Damn.

It takes at least six minutes until the next train arrives. *I cannot miss the train to Riverdale*, I mutter to myself, possibly out loud. Definitely out loud. I'm still drunk. Fuck. The other people on the train move away from me, as if my kind of mental illness is contagious. I want to tell them not to worry, that I've just been drinking, but I realize that this will probably not help matters, seeing that it's only nine a.m. Instead, I drop my head in my hands and moan softly to myself. The car rocks back and forth, provoking my hangover.

"Emily?" asks a disembodied voice from above. I see freshly shined black shoes in front of me, but I don't lift my head. *This cannot be happening. I have to be imagining this. Please God, tell me that this is not happening.* I wonder if I keep my head down and pretend like I don't hear Andrew, he will walk away. I squeeze my eyes closed, hoping this will make him disappear. It doesn't. When I open them, he is still there. Freshly shined black shoes.

This is really happening.

"Hey," I say. He looks at me curiously, and I can tell by the hunch in his shoulders that he is trying not to laugh. I look down and realize I am wearing his old T-shirt from the

MIT swim team, the one he had promised me he would throw out. The words WET SHAVED BEAVERS are written in black letters across my chest. Although the first time I heard the story of the shirt I found it mildly humorous—apparently the school's mascot is the beaver, and the team used to shave their legs so they could swim faster; you get the picture—it's not amusing right now. The only benefit to being drunk is that I don't quite feel the full depth of my humiliation.

"Do you need help?" I can tell he is enjoying this, and I don't blame him.

"Fuck," I say out loud, though I mean to just think it.

"Fuck," I say again out loud, this time for saying it before when I meant to just think it. *Get yourself together, Emily.*

"Hey there," I say. "Sorry. Still drunk from last night."

"I can see that."

"Tequila. Going to Grandpa Jack's. Am late." I keep my head down to avoid the spins.

"You went out with Jess, didn't you?" Jess is notorious for taking me out and getting me obliterated. She seems to think it's healthy to lose control of your bodily functions every once in a while. To her, vomit signifies the end of a good night out.

"Yup. Shots. And T-shirt because I was late." My lips keep failing me. I have clear sentences in my head, but they won't translate into words. Andrew sits down next to me and starts to look concerned.

"You sure you're okay?"

"Fine, just late. And a little queasy." The electronic voice announces Grand Central Station.

"This is my stop," I say, proud of forming a full sentence and relieved that I have an escape. To my surprise, though, Andrew gets up to follow me off the train. He walks up the two flights of stairs, taking my elbow as I wobble. We make it into the main area of the terminal, which feels oddly empty and almost intimate in its vastness; the constellations on the ceiling seem to be hovering lower than usual. The place is empty enough for us to hear the ticking of the big clock, which I imagine must be symbolic of something, though, in my current state, I couldn't tell you what.

I feel Andrew next to me, and my arm gets warm and tingly. *Stop it. This is not the time for this*, I tell myself. The tingles make me anxious suddenly, remind me of the rocking train, and I consider the possibility that I might throw up on Andrew's shoes. I time my breaths to the ticktocks— inhale on the tick, exhale on the tock— and, thankfully, the nausea passes.

"You are in no condition to go anywhere," he says. And though I feel like saying something juvenile and smart-ass, like *You are not the boss of me* or *Who died and made you captain*, I hold back. Andrew is absolutely right. I let him steer me toward a Starbucks, and I sit down. He asks for my cell phone, and I hand it over. It is still turned off from last night. He flips it open and scrolls through for my grandfather's number.

"Grandpa Jack," he says. "It's Andrew." I can't hear what my grandfather is saying on the other line, but I'm sure it's something cheerful, because Andrew smiles into the phone.

"Unfortunately, Emily is going to be a bit late." He glances back at me and frowns. "No, no, nothing to worry about. There was a problem with the subway and she missed the train. She'll probably be on the ten–fifteen.

"Will do, Grandpa Jack. I hope to come by sometime soon as well. Give my love to Ruth." Andrew hangs up and hands the phone back. He gives me a look, as if to say *I can't believe I just had to lie to Grandpa Jack*. He heads to the counter and comes back with two cups of coffee and two chocolate croissants.

"Thanks," I say.

Andrew doesn't respond. He sits down across from me and his shoulders start to tremble slightly and then shake. He looks like he is sobbing, and my heart blinks with guilt. I never meant to hurt him. But it turns out Andrew is not crying at all; he is cracking up. He starts with small giggles, but within seconds he is doubled over with laughter, his head between his legs. I start laughing too. I can't help myself—his laugh has always been contagious—and fat tears roll down my cheeks.

We collect ourselves, and it seems the fit is over. But then I hiccup, and it starts again. Andrew slaps his knees, I grip my stomach. We are laughing so hard it hurts; it is too much to expect out of our tiny mouths.

I look up, our eyes meet, and just like that, we stop laughing, and the moment devolves into awkward silence. I wish we could keep on forgetting to remember ourselves.

"So how have you been?" I ask, to break the tension.

"Good," he says. "Great, actually. Really great."

"Good, I'm glad."

"And you?" he asks, like we are just neighbors, like it wasn't just a couple of weeks ago that we had sex on my kitchen floor. And in my bathtub. And in the dressing room at Saks.

"Okay. Busy with work. Very busy." I wrap my hands around my coffee cup to warm my fingertips. I take a sip of coffee, and it burns.

"Interesting case?" He bites into a croissant. A flake clings to his mouth—he always has sticky lips—and I want to lick it off. This wouldn't be the first time.

"Accounting fraud," I lie. "Absolutely fascinating. You? Anything interesting going on in the E.R.?"

"I delivered a baby yesterday. That was cool," he says. "Miracle of life and all."

"Wow," I say. "Wow."

"Yeah. Well, okay, then." Andrew gets up, a signal that our conversation is now over, and he dumps both of our unfinished croissants into the trash. I am not ready to leave yet—wasn't even finished with my breakfast—but I follow his departing back into the main terminal anyway, until he stops in front of the big clock.

"Take care of yourself," he says, and I glance downward, hoping he will kiss me good-bye. I know it is more than I deserve, but I want to feel his lips against mine, to feel the Andrew tingles just once more. I wouldn't even mind a peck on the cheek instead, like a brother or a distant cousin. That would hold me over.

"You too. Thanks for your help," I say, but he doesn't hear me. When I look up, head tilted, expectant, I am met only by empty air. Andrew is already on the other side of the station, jogging as fast as he can toward the exit.

The Riverdale Retirement Home reminds me of a hotel in Las Vegas. It has an ornate lobby—gold-trimmed ceilings, couches with carved arms, even a concierge desk. The main floor has a movie theater, a dining room, and a café, all circling a center lounge, the layout making it next to impossible to find the exit. Televisions in the elevators assault the senses, announce events demanding your time and attention: "*The Terminator*: Action Film Night!", "Politics in the Middle East: Any hope for peace?", "Investment 101: How to make your savings go farther." I am not sure which is more depressing of the two, the retirement home or Vegas, but they share that artifice of optimism sullied by a beaten clientele. People go to both to die a slow death.

For a retirement home, though, this is as nice as it gets. My grandfather has a one-bedroom apartment on an "active seniors" floor, a "penthouse," with top-to-bottom windows. His decor is tidy and efficient, everything serving multiple functions, just the way he likes it. The coffee table has a hidden drawer for board games, the toaster makes rotisserie chicken, the toilet-seat lid sings songs. When my grandfather moved here a few years ago, after a minor stroke, it seemed like a decent compromise. At least on the surface, independence is preserved. He may have a meal plan like a college freshman and carry around medical tags, but at the end of the day, he has his own front door; he was adamant about having his own front door.

The biggest problem with this place, putting aside the fact that once a resident moves in he almost never moves out, is the forced interaction with the old and infirm. Grandpa Jack's apartment shares an elevator bank with the "constant care" floors, rendering every trip up a reminder of what the future holds. No one wants to see those ubiquitous poles with packets of fluid hanging like plastic fruit, the big nurses taking care of small people. No one wants to hear the groans that sound an awful lot like good-byes.

I wave hello to Grandpa Jack and Ruth, his neighbor and friend, when I spot them on the other side of the lobby. As I cross the marble floor, I see Ruth lean in and brush a piece of lint off my grandfather's plaid shirt.

"Have you been drinking, love?" my grandfather asks, after I kiss his cheek. The man has a nose like a narc.

"Yeah, too many tequila shots last night. Sorry, Gramps."

"I knew it. That's why you were late, right? Got your head in the toilet?"

"Something like that."

"Thanks. You just made me thirty bucks. Ruth?" He puts out his palm.

"What are you talking about?"

"I bet Ruth that there wasn't a subway problem, and she said you wouldn't lie to me. I, of course, know you a little better." My grandfather tips his newsboy cap at me, a relic from his teenage years. I am tempted to steal it from him, like I did his Burberry coat. I know he wouldn't mind. He says it makes him happy to have his clothes gallivanting around Manhattan for a second round.

"Sorry," I say to Ruth, and give her a hug. "I learned from the best."

This is not an overstatement. The truth is everything I know about life I learned from Grandpa Jack. To tie my shoes, to always carry a book, to say please and thank you and follow up with a card, to daydream as a hobby, to tip big, to question the existence of God, to grin through pain. To show up.

Next to my mother, he was my favorite person in the world when I was a kid. A real-life superhero, who swooped in and out as needed. When I failed my driver's test, when

I had my appendix removed, when Toby Myers said I had a hairy upper lip and made me cry in front of the entire sixth grade, he was the one who made it all hurt a little less. Much the same is true now.

My mom used to say that my grandfather transformed after I was born; at just shy of sixty, he went from being a man to a father. I am not sure who he was to my dad when he was growing up—maybe he was distant, busy, a lot like my dad is to me now—but in my lifetime, especially since my mom died, he has been Grandpa Jack, the person who makes being an only child bearable, the person who makes me feel less alone.

The three of us leave the retirement home behind, my grandfather in the middle; Ruth and I link each of his arms and walk out into the fresh air. We move slowly, and, from time to time, the two of them wordlessly communicate to stop and take a break. I'm sure it is my grandfather who needs to catch his breath, not Ruth, but I don't ask. Fortunately, we don't have far to go, just to the diner on the corner. I don't have to be reminded of the limits of his endurance. As it is, I think about that daily.

Grandpa Jack and I are up against statistical impossibilities. I have studied the actuary tables—another skill I picked up from my grandfather, as he was, at one time, a real-life actuary—and the numbers don't add up. Cold math says he won't make it through the end of the decade; my pure denial says he will.

I cannot, I will not, imagine life without Grandpa Jack.

When we get to the diner, we commandeer a red vinyl booth and order pickles and coffee. We go here a lot, because it's the kind of place that makes you feel like you could be anywhere in America, anywhere at all; the ambiguity makes us feel miles away from Riverdale. My grandfather looks thin, so I force him to get a strawberry milk shake. He has to lean forward to reach the top of the tall glass and ends up with a pink mustache above his lip. I don't tell him, though, because I think he looks adorable, like a small child. It helps to hide the fact that his face looks older today. His skin hangs looser, as if it has become unhinged from his cheekbones. It creates deep hollow craters below, the kind only acceptable on supermodels. In the '80s.

"So, Em, where's Andrew?" my grandfather asks. Andrew often used to come to Riverdale with me, and the four of us would play poker all day. Nine times out of ten, Ruth beat our pants off.

"We broke up."

"What? Why?" Grandpa Jack sits up straighter, stares me down.

"You know, these things happen. What's going on with you guys?"

"Come on, Emily. No one is interested in hearing how yesterday Ruth and I learned to knit. Spill it. Are you okay?"

"Nothing to spill. I'm fine. Sometimes things just end."

"What happened?" he asks.

"Nothing," I say.

"Breaking up is more than nothing," he says.

"Leave her alone, Jack," Ruth says, and takes a sip of his milk shake.

Unlike my grandfather, Ruth looks put together, almost saucy. Not young, of course, since she's somewhere in her eighties, but youthful. She wears a bouclé Chanel suit, and her hair is sprayed into a platinum globe around her head. Although I can guess what she must have looked like years ago, prom-queen pretty, I cannot imagine that she could have been any more beautiful than she is now. Ruth has the sort of beauty—the wrinkles, the spots, the lived-in skin— that makes it impossible to look away, the kind that makes you want to explore each fold further. To point to the scar on her neck, as a new lover might, and say, *Tell me the story of that one.*

Though I am unsure of the parameters of Ruth and Grandpa Jack's relationship—whether they share more than just a friendship—either way, my grandfather scored. Ruth Wasserstein is a living legend. She sat on the Second Circuit for over forty years, and at one point there was talk of nomination to the Supreme Court. (The way she tells it, "another Jew named Ruth" happened to get there first.) My grandfather teases her that he doesn't believe she is actually the famous Ruth Wasserstein, since she's way too much fun to have been a judge. Though, in her defense, she does say "objection" a lot.

"Oh, come on, I'm not giving her a hard time. This is important. I want to know what happened. Did he break up with you? Did he panic? If he did, I'll break his legs. Better yet, I'll hire someone to kill him. I have contacts, you know," he says.

"Grandpa, no need to kill anyone. I broke up with him."

"Seriously?" Grandpa Jack and Ruth ask in unison.

"Yup. Seriously."

"But he seemed like such a nice young man," Ruth says.

"And he bought me that beer-of-the-month-club thing. Do you think he'll cancel it now?" my grandfather asks.

"Jack," Ruth says.

"Relax. I'm kidding. Though that apricot ale was pretty great, right, Ruthie?"

"It was. Emily, if you don't mind my asking, why? I mean, he just seemed so . . . well, for lack of a better word, perfect for you," she says.

"Nah, not really. We were never going to get married, you know? It just seemed like the right time to end it," I say.

"But he was going to propose," Grandpa Jack says.

"What? How the hell did you know that?"

"He told me. Well, actually, he asked me. I said that he should go right ahead."

"You did what? Grandpa, why didn't you tell me? Why didn't you *warn* me? I can't believe this."

"I thought you'd want to be surprised. Was I supposed to say no? How could I say no to the guy? I'm sorry, Emily, but he's great. Most boys aren't raised to be men nowadays, but his parents did a decent job."

"You just like him because he's a doctor," I say.

"Not true. Andrew's a really good guy. He bothered to come all the way out here to ask me in person."

"He came here? To Riverdale? When?"

"I don't remember exactly. Last week maybe."

"So all it takes is someone actually asking you to get your permission?" I say it lightly, because I realize I can't blame my grandfather for how things turned out. This is my fault. My decision.

"Yup. And don't forget the beer. The beer helped too."

"What did he say?"

"I'm not going to lie to you. It wasn't pretty. He was nervous. Could barely get the words out. But he was polite and serious, and you got to give the guy credit for trying to do things right."

"We've been on pins and needles waiting for the call to say you'd gotten engaged," Ruth says. "We were so excited."

They both look at me, still with a little bit of hope in their eyes. As if this is all a practical joke and Andrew is going to walk through the door any minute. My guilt feels heavy in my gut; I've disappointed enough people lately.

"I'm sorry. I just couldn't do it. I didn't mean to let you guys down too."

"You didn't let us down. I just liked the guy, sweetheart. I've been less worried about you these past couple of years with him. He seemed to take good care of you," Grandpa Jack says. "That's all."

"I can take care of myself. I'm a grown woman." I plead like a sixteen-year-old whining about her car privileges. "Oh, God, do you know if he asked my dad?"

"I don't think so. I spoke to Kirk a couple of days ago and he didn't say anything about it, and I didn't tell him," Grandpa Jack says.

"Good. Please don't. I'm just not ready to tell Dad yet, about any of it, you know?"

"No problem. Emily?"

"Yeah?"

"All I want is for you to be happy," he says.

"I know, Gramps."

"I worry that you are not so good at making that happen all by yourself," he says.

"I'm fine, really. I'm happy. I am," I say. "I really am."

"You're full of shit," Grandpa Jack says, but not unkindly.

"What can I do? I learned from the best." My grandfather just nods at this, suddenly solemn.

"Does this mean we can't invite him to poker anymore?" he asks.

"Probably not," I say.

"Damn," Ruth says. "He was so easy to beat."

"I know," my grandfather says. "It wasn't even fair."

\* \* \*

A couple of hours later, I walk Ruth and my grandfather to their doors, units PH1 and PH2.

"See you later, Emily," my grandfather says as he kisses me good-bye. "Say hello to—" But he stops in midsentence and lets his words just hang there a couple of beats too long.

"Grandpa?"

"Say hello to, you know, what's his name—"

"Kirk," Ruth says, quickly. "Say hello to Kirk for him."

"Yeah, let him know he should visit me once in a while," my grandfather says.

"Of course, Gramps," I say. "I'll tell him."

Grandpa Jack goes inside to lie down, but Ruth invites me to her place for some tea. She says it will warm me up for the train trip back. I am happy for the excuse to spend some time in her apartment, which I love, if only because it's fun to see the polar opposite of my grandfather's. Everything here is superfluous. Instead of displaying one or two favorite photographs, pictures cover the walls, litter every surface. Her flowered couch has two throws, a solid and a pattern, since she couldn't decide which one she wanted more. She has four clocks, all antique, which riotously celebrate each passing hour.

When I come to Ruth's, I explore her one-bedroom apartment like it's a museum. I start with the bookshelf, which is built-in, overstuffed, and full of treasures: signed first editions, writers I have forgotten but always wanted to read, treatises by Ruth herself. Then I follow the progression of photographs, her three kids first as children and then later as parents themselves. My favorites are those of Ruth alone, as a young woman dressed in the court's black robes. In one in particular, her skin is smooth, her hair longer and curled into a low bun. The smile is the same, though, her two front teeth angled toward each other, her bottom lip thinned out by the width of her grin.

"I was in my early forties when that one was taken," Ruth says, and puts down a tray full of a hundred different kinds of tea. "I don't know which is harder for me to believe: that I was ever that young, or that I am now this old."

"You still look great."

"Thanks, dear. Listen, I'm sorry about Andrew. I didn't mean to make you feel worse back there."

"You didn't. Not at all."

"If you ever need to talk, I'm here. I know you talk to your grandfather about these things, but if you ever need a woman's opinion . . ."

"Thanks, I appreciate that." I look at another picture of Ruth, a twenty-something Ruth that I never met, holding an infant; it is a picture of a mother. "Really."

"That's my Sarah. She was a beautiful baby," she says, and it becomes clear that, for Ruth, it is a picture of a daughter.

"Very cute."

"She's a lawyer now too, in D.C. Though she's getting ready to retire. She's at the end of her career, while you're just at the start of yours." She looks at the picture one more time, shakes her head, and puts it back on the mantel. "Listen, I wanted to talk to you about Jack, if you don't mind. Does he seem a little different to you lately?"

"Not really. I mean, he looks tired maybe, and he probably needs to get out more. The idea of you and Grandpa Jack knitting is depressing. Why? What's going on?"

"I don't know. He just seems to get a little confused more often. Forgetting things, losing things . . ."

"I think that's just a Haxby thing. I'm exactly the same way. When I went to the bathroom before, I realized I'm wearing my underwear on inside out. The Haxbys are flaky. I'm sure that's all it is."

"Maybe, but—"

"He would have told me if he wasn't okay. When we went to the doctor's last time they said that he might start to forget things a little more. That at his age, that sort of thing is to be expected."

"But, Emily—"

"He would have come to me if something was wrong, Ruth. Seriously, my grandfather is fine." I can tell she knows what I really mean to say: *He has to be fine. He just has to be.*

"Okay," she says, and waves a hand, a gesture that I take to mean *Ignore me.*

And so that's exactly what I do. We finish our tea in a wonderfully civilized manner, pinkies out, and discuss what it was like for Ruth to be one of only four women in her class in law school. We chat and gossip and laugh, and neither of us says another word about Grandpa Jack.

# Eight

Three weeks later, I am standing on line in the Continental Airlines terminal at Newark with Carl MacKinnon. I am carrying a laptop, a shoulder bag, fifteen deposition binders, and dragging a suitcase with a broken wheel. It is four-thirty in the morning, and though my arms ache from my excessive amount of luggage, I am worried about the real possibility of falling asleep standing up. My head keeps rolling to one side as I drift off, and I feel drool gathering at the corners of my mouth. Like the consummate professional that I am, I use my suit sleeve to wipe it away. It leaves a mark.

When it is our turn to check in, the woman behind the counter smiles brightly at us despite the cruel hour. I attempt to return her enthusiasm, but my lips don't have the energy for it. The effect is something like a snarl. I begin to tell the woman that we are headed to Little Rock, Arkansas, but Carl interrupts me.

"There has been a serious mistake," he says, loudly enunciating each syllable of each word. "My colleague here is booked in coach. I request that she be moved to first class immediately and be seated next to me." The woman registers the gravity of the matter by typing furiously. Though I don't speak up, there is no mistake here. I was responsible for reserving our flights, and Carl's secretary took care of the hotel arrangements. I purposely booked myself in coach and Carl in first class. I figured the limited seat room was a small price to pay for some time away from him.

"I'm sorry, sir. First class is all booked," she says. I realize I have been holding my breath, and I let it out slowly. The thought of having to sit next to Carl for the next three and a half hours is almost too much to bear.

"That is unacceptable," Carl says, and slaps his hand down hard against the counter. "I fly over a hundred thousand miles on Continental each year. What's your name? I demand to speak to your manager." Carl throws different kinds of plastic on the counter. A platinum frequent-flier card, a black AmEx, a shiny Admiral's Club pass. The woman taps the computer keys violently in response and a bit of sweat forms on her brow.

"Well, it looks like something just opened up, sir. Sorry about that." She starts printing up documents and shuffling them together. "Unfortunately, it will be an extra two hundred and sixty-four dollars. Is that okay?"

She types some more, just to look busy.

"Absolutely," Carl says, passes her his credit card, and winks at me. This trip is on Synergon.

"You two will be in One-A and One-B. Have a safe flight."

And there goes my morning of freedom. She hands over our boarding passes, and mine has a security stamp on it and Carl's does not. Which means that before I get on the flight, all of my luggage will be hand-searched. Ironic, really, that she thinks between the two of us, I am the more likely terrorist; perhaps it is my punishment for associating with such an asshole.

As we walk through security, Carl lectures me about assertiveness, says I will not get anywhere in this world without it. He is clearly empowered by his seating coup, and his mood is jocular. We stop for caffeine and breakfast in the terminal, and he makes small talk. His personality seems to be wholly circumstantial. At counters and behind desks, he rolls over people with his aggression. But sitting side by side in attached plastic chairs, balancing bagels on our laps and coffee on the armrests, he acts human, friendly even, as if he is looking forward to our three days in Arkansas together.

I am not. I will be spending the next twenty-four hours alone with Carl. After our flight, we will drive to Arkadelphia (a location so remote that it didn't come up on Expedia when I did a hotel search) and spend the next three days in a dusty conference room taking the deposition of Mr. Jones. The plan is to grill him about the sordid details of his wife's death. I believe Carl's exact words were "Make him weep." And tomorrow it will only get uglier. At noon, Carisse flies down to join us.

When we get ready to board, airport security pulls me aside and unzips my luggage, to the amusement of all on the line. They watch as the security guard uses a plastic wand to pick through my underwear. Carl looks on, presumably to see if he can get a cheap thrill from a lacy thong. I am happy to disappoint. By the time we take our seats in first class, though, my boss and everyone else on the plane now know that (a) I am on birth control and (b) I buy my cotton briefs at Target.

After the security humiliation, the flight goes relatively smoothly. We experience some turbulence and there is much ado made about the fasten-seat-belt sign, but Carl leaves me alone for most of it, content to let me do his work. And I am content to be left alone. Since Carisse can't make it down here until tomorrow, and I will be taking most of the depositions, I have been assigned the responsibility of drafting the summary judgment motion. This is a big deal. If we win it, and by "we" I mean Synergon, the entire case gets dismissed before trial. The company will pay nothing—zip, zilch, nada—to the people of Caddo Valley. They will, however, pay plenty in attorneys' fees to us. And by "us" I mean APT.

Though I am not a fan of the subject matter, writing this motion is my first opportunity in my almost five years at the firm to show the partnership that I have a brain, that I am capable of doing more than reviewing documents day after day in a conference room. This is real lawyer work; this is my shot. I intend to take it.

When we get off the plane, the fact that we are far from New York immediately becomes evident. Everything moves slower here; the change in pace feels something like relief. The Southern drawl has a laxative effect on Carl too, magically removing the stick from his ass. He has gone from raving mad at the Continental lady, to reasonably friendly over bagels, and now to downright chummy. You would think we were in Arkansas for a couple of rounds of golf, not to "rip Mr. Jones a new one." (Carl's words yesterday. Not mine.)

Though the car-rental guy takes twenty minutes to find our reservation, Carl refrains from making a fuss. Black AmEx stays firmly in wallet, hands stay tucked into his pockets. Instead, he chats with me, starts calling me "kid." As in "It's nice to get out of the city for a bit, isn't it, kid?" And "I hope the partners haven't been working you too hard lately, kid."

I smile and nod and ignore the condescension, because truth be known, I feel different here too. The air is less charged, inserting more space in the gaps between every-thing—between my words, my steps, my breaths.

The route to Arkadelphia is a straight shot down the highway, and we drive with the windows down. I revel in the void of orchestral white noise; there are no horns, no patter of thousands of feet, no trucks loading and unloading. The road follows an empty landscape, its definition coming only from what it is not.

In this world, there are neither skyscrapers nor mini-malls. We go miles without seeing another car, not to mention a McDonald's. Instead, there is just dirt, brown and cakey, with an occasional plant, always spiky, dotting the horizon. Just Carl and me on the empty road, arms hanging out the windows, pushing back against all that air.

We eventually pull off the highway and into a Hampton Inn parking lot. Usually when I travel for work, one of the few perks is that I get to sleep in five-star resorts, like the Ritz or the Four Seasons, places I would never go if I were footing the bill. But apparently this is the only hotel in Arkadelphia, the next-best option a Motel 6. I guess on this trip I will not add to my mini-shampoo collection, I will not sleep naked under seven-hundred-thread-count sheets, and, sadly, I will not order room service to avoid dinner with Carl.

We enter the hotel, a cement rectangle that could double as a junior high school. It smells that way too, like there is a cafeteria nearby serving hamburgers and Tater Tots. The boy behind the counter has freshly slicked-back hair, a name tag that reads *Bob*, and the tragic sort of acne that makes it difficult not to stare. Above his lip, there is a tiny bit of fur, a premustache mustache. His pants sit low enough to announce that he is wearing Calvin Klein boxer briefs, and for some reason this information—Bob's choice of undies—makes me a little embarrassed.

"Welcome to the Hampton Inn, y'all," he says.

"Reservations under MacKinnon," Carl says, his voice formal again, pretentious.

"One king room, right?" Bob says. Carl doesn't say anything. Instead, he takes a keen interest in a bit of dirt lodged under his fingernail.

"Uh, no," I say. "There should be reservations for two rooms."

"Let me take a quick peek-y here, but it looks like there is only one reservation in the system," Bob says. He taps on his keyboard slowly and ignores a ringing phone.

"Okay, but we need two rooms, regardless of the reservation," I say. "Please." I keep my voice firm, as if to say *There is no room for negotiation here.* He types some more and appears to be scrolling down a list.

"No can do, little lady. We are all booked. It's county-fair season," Bob says.

"But I have a reservation," I say.

"Nope, no can do, little lady," Bob says again.

"You don't seem to understand. We need two rooms. And I have a reservation." I try to get Carl's attention. Why isn't he helping? Where is his black AmEx? I feel the betrayal of my body—my first reaction is tears, not anger—as it plays along with Bob's vision of a "little lady," of Carl's "kid."

"This is unacceptable," I say, copying Carl's tone from earlier this morning. Bob chuckles. He is not in the slightest bit intimidated by me.

"Sorry, it says here in our computer that there is only one reservation, for one room with a king," Bob says, and turns the monitor in my direction. I have to stand on the tips of my toes to lean over the counter to see.

"Look, there is a note that you specifically asked for a king as opposed to two double beds," Bob says. "There ain't anything I can do." The tears instantly morph into anger. I look over at Carl, who still has not chimed in, and see that he is casually inspecting a brochure for the Clinton Library.

"Carl?" I still hold out hope that he will jump in and help, that he didn't do this on purpose, that his secretary must have made a mistake. Screaming at the clerk will have no effect. I will only be met with more dismissive laughter. Derision, even. Carl just ignores me, engrossed in a picture of Clinton with Fleetwood Mac.

"I need to speak with your manager," I say.

"I am the manager," Bob says, and smiles. He seems to be enjoying our small battle, putting me, the uppity Northern woman, in her place. I am almost old enough to be his mother. "Sorry, like I said, there ain't anything I can do."

"How about the Motel Six?" I ask. "Do you have their number?"

"All full. We get their overflow," Bob says, his voice full of pride to be working at the second-most-popular hotel establishment in Arkadelphia.

"Oh, come on, Em. Don't worry," Carl says, tucking the brochure into his back pocket. Since when does he call me "Em"? "Bob, we can share. No big deal, right? We are both adults." Carl winks at Bob, and Bob quickly hands over some keys. I am not sure what to say, but I know I have lost. I don't have any choice here. It would seem childish to protest further, and Carl would never be stupid enough to admit that this was anything other than an honest mistake. I try to salvage the little dignity I have left.

"We will need a cot," I say, and Bob glances at me and then loops his fingers into the edge of his Calvins, to pull them even higher.

"Sure thing," Bob says, and it is clear that as long as he is on duty, there will never be a cot.

It is four hours later, halfway through taking the deposition, that I realize that things could actually get worse. I did not pack pajamas.

*Breathe deeply. In and out. In and out.* There is a court reporter who is recording each and every word I say, so any stammering or stuttering will be typed for posterity. *Let the sleeping arrangements go for the moment. Get through the deposition. Do your job. Pretend you are a professional. You are a professional.*

We are seated along a long rectangular foldout table that barely fits inside this airless square of a room. Our chairs brush the walls, our knees brush their neighbor. I am not sure why the plaintiffs' lawyers put us in here; if our walk through their office was any indication, it looks like they have plenty of space. Maybe this is some sort of trick to psych us out?

Mr. Jones sits across from me and answers my questions dutifully, even respectfully. He wears thick plastic glasses with brown frames that dip onto his cheeks, and the sleeves of his sport coat rest about an inch above his wrists. He calls me "ma'am" and nods often, as if to look cooperative.

I glance at my notes and try to focus. I ask a series of what appear to be inane questions, but in my head I am forming the basis of my summary judgment motion. Carl wants me to go the typical blame-the-victim route. My goal is to prove that there are dozens of other variables at play here that could have caused Mrs. Jones's cancer, anything other than the water polluted by Synergon.

"How much did your wife weigh, Mr. Jones?"

"Two hundred and eighty-five pounds."

"Was she ever advised by a doctor to lose weight?"

"Objection, relevance."

"You can answer, Mr. Jones."

"Yes."

"And did she?"

"No."

"Did she belong to a gym?"

"No."

"Did she exercise?"

"No. She always said you only get to live once. No use wasting time exercising."

"Did she smoke?"

"Yes. But she quit. After little Sue Ann hid her cigarettes. That got to her."

"How long did she smoke for?"

"Fifteen years."

"What was a typical breakfast in your household while your wife was alive?"

"Bacon and eggs. Sometimes sausage."

"Is it true that Caddo Valley is famous for its fried Mars Bars?"

"Yes, ma'am. You'll have to try some while you're down here."

"Thank you, sir. I'll do that. Do you live near a FarmTech power plant?"

"Yes."

"How far would you say?"

"Not far at all. About a quarter of a mile down the road."

"And does Synergon own that power plant?"

"No, ma'am. I don't believe it does."

I am ashamed to admit it, but I enjoy the deposition. *I am pretty good at this*, I think, as I pin down Mr. Jones on favorable answer after favorable answer. I must be doing a decent job, because Carl lets me run the show. It is satisfying to reassert my own power after getting so abruptly dismissed this morning by the hotel clerk. *Little ladies don't save their clients hundreds of millions of dollars*, I tell myself.

"Mr. Jones, tell me, is there a history of cancer in your wife's family?"

"Objection, relevance."

"You can answer, Mr. Jones."

"Yes, ma'am, there is. Both of my wife's parents had it too. They died within two years of each other."

She shoots, she scores, and the crowd goes wild. I feel pure pride for a moment, until I catch Mr. Jones's eye. He just looks at me. Sad and a little confused.

"I loved the part where you made the bastard tell us about all the family cancer. Great genetic argument," Carl says later, with the energy of a twelve-year-old boy reenacting his favorite action film. "Good maneuvering, changing the subject so quickly that he couldn't say that they drank Synergon water. Brilliant, Haxby. Brilliant."

It is just the two of us again, over dinner at the Cracker Barrel, a couple of miles down the highway from our hotel. Carl still has his client game face on and oozes charm and sincerity. He plays the role of suave older gentleman, peppering the conversation with interesting war stories to show off his pedigree. He drops Princeton at least twice and refers to the time he spent in Cambridge, lawyer code for Harvard Law School. He mock-complains about the amount of work he does for the trustees of the Museum of Modern Art. I wonder if some women might find him attractive, this fluid exhibition of wealth and control.

Carl is not ugly, though I'm sure he would prefer to move each of his eyes in a bit closer to his nose. Unlike most of the men in my office, he still has a full head of silver hair, cropped thick and tidy, and his wrinkles make him look more distinguished than old. Given that he never goes on vacation and lives in New York, his consistent tan must come from either a bed or a bottle. And he dresses to hide the curse of gravity; his two pudgy man boobs and wide flat butt get tucked away into pin-striped Armani suits and shirts tailored in Asia.

But he looks ridiculous here, with his bright-blue cuff links pinned into monogrammed sleeves, eating a fussy salad among the plastic plates, the free soda refills, and the families in T-shirts and jeans enjoying their fried pork tenderloin. I order the half-pound hamburger steak and ask for a side of garlic mashed potatoes, extra garlic, just in case.

I have been told that beyond hitting on women in the office, Carl is often spotted wining and dining models around Manhattan with his wedding band hidden in his pocket. I don't get what they could possibly see in him and his casual cruelty. Although I imagine there are some women out there who equate wealth with attractiveness, other than Carisse, I am not sure I've ever met any. All of the women I know are looking for Lloyd Dobler, not Gordon Gekko.

When we finish eating, Carl asks if I would like to share the chocolate cake. I decline. Digging our spoons into the same plate is somehow too intimate and certainly too date-like. On the way out, I quickly check the Cracker Barrel Country Store for pajamas, but despite about a thousand different types of bird feeders, there is not a single T-shirt or pair of shorts for sale. I'm not sure what I am going to do when it comes time for bed. All I brought were suits and underwear.

Carl drives us back to the hotel, and as I feel the night's stillness surround us, I grow increasingly nervous. I hope Carl got the message this morning with my reaction to the shared room. Surely he can't really believe that I want to have sex with him. Could he? He is twice my age. He is married. He is my boss. Maybe Bob has brought me a cot? I do not picture Carl offering to sleep on the floor and shudder at the thought of lying on the dusty Hampton Inn carpet in my suit.

I am shaking by the time we walk into the lobby. I consider working genital warts into the conversation, but can think of no casual way to bring it up and figure it is probably not wise to start that kind of rumor. Even in self-defense. I mentioned "my boyfriend" a couple of times in the car, without any reaction from Carl. If his pregnant wife doesn't stop him, I'm sure that my imaginary boyfriend won't either.

I notice a convenience store tucked around the corner, and I tell Carl that I'll meet him upstairs in a minute. He smiles at me and nods, and I wonder if he thinks I am buying condoms. *No*, I tell myself, *you are just imagining these things. He will not hit on you, and if he does, you will turn him down politely*. This is the closest thing I have to a plan. *And please, please, God, let the store have something resembling pajamas*.

Thankfully, I see a T-shirt hanging up against the wall. I ignore the fact that it says *Someone in Arkansas Loves Me*, given that my only other option is one with a cartoon image of Clinton smoking a cigar. Definitely not the message I want to send. I buy the first shirt in XXL and a pair of boxer shorts that say *Kiss My ArkansASS* across the back. It is the best I can do.

"So," Carl says when I enter the room. He is lying on the bed, wearing only his tailored shirt and plaid boxers. I accidentally glance down and see the pink head of his penis peeking out of the slit in his shorts. *I just saw Carl MacKinnon's penis; I cannot believe I just saw Carl MacKinnon's penis*. I repeat the words in my head as if on a loop, and soon the word "penis" starts to sound ridiculous. The image sears my brain too, and I wonder if I will ever be able to forget it. Although I realize that I am in trouble here, there is still a part of me that wants to giggle. The situation has moved so out of control, I half-expect him to pull out a pair of furry handcuffs.

"Where's the cot?" I ask, as if my boss is not lying on a bed in his boxer shorts, as if the flap is buttoned closed.

"Guess Bob didn't bring it," he says, and shrugs. "You look beautiful in that suit, but isn't it uncomfortable? Perhaps you should take it off." Carl looks at me matter-of-factly, as if he just asked me to bring him a file. I wonder if he knows he is sticking out. Surely, he can't.

"Nah, I'm fine. Really. Um, I'm going to call the front desk about that cot." I keep my eyes fixed on the phone and stare at its old-fashioned rotary dial.

"You don't have to. This bed is big enough for the both of us." He pats the comforter next to him.

"No, I don't think that would be appropriate, Carl," I say, hoping my firm tone implies that I have no interest in sharing a bed with him. Ever.

"Come on, Emily. Stop being so coy. It will be fun to have a sleepover," Carl says in a boyish voice. I wonder if someone once told him that baby talk becomes cute again at sixty. I have no idea what to do or what to say. I wish I had taken a course in law school on how to react to seeing your boss's member.

"I don't think so," I say. "If you're suggesting what I think you're suggesting, I don't think that would be a very good idea." I turn my back on Carl and, with a shaking finger, spin the phone dial until I get the front desk. Luckily, Bob is off duty.

"The cot will be here in five minutes," I say.

"Well, here is the thing," he says. "I'm still hungry, and since we didn't eat dessert, I want to eat you. You would like that, wouldn't you?" Carl reaches down to touch himself. This cannot be happening. I want to cry and laugh and vomit all at the same time. How will I ever be able to look anyone in the eye at work again? I imagine their faces will all be blacked out with a picture of Carl's genitals. Worse, with a picture of Carl massaging his genitals.

His flag is now at full mast.

"No," I say. "No, I would not like that. In fact, I don't want to be having this conversation. This is not going to happen. Please stop it right now."

"I thought you would be the type to play hard-to-get. Make me work for it. Don't worry, I like hard work."

"Carl." There is an embarrassing amount of pleading in my voice.

"Emily."

"Carl."

"Emily."

"No. Absolutely not. I can't do this. Please, please, please leave me alone." I am not sure why, but somehow these are the magic words, and I notice out of the corner of my eye that his hands are now tucked behind his head.

"Fine. Suit yourself," Carl says, and shrugs, as if I just

refused an offer of an extra pillow and not cunnilingus from my boss.

"Oh, by the way, I have arranged for a six-thirty a.m. wake-up call, so we can do extra prep before the deposition," he says, his tone casual.

"Sure thing," I say, ever the dedicated associate. "Sounds good."

Carl turns away from me and switches off the light. I sit in the dark, waiting for the knock on the door. I have goose bumps, despite still wearing my wool suit.

When the cot finally arrives, I tip the bellman fifty bucks. I will find a way to bill it to Synergon. But, of course, cot or not, I can't sleep in here. I am not sure what I was thinking. I can't share this small room with Carl, even though the fact that he is snoring—the fact that he is a veritable one-man band—signals that he won't be coming on to me any more tonight. Instead, I lock myself in the bathroom with a pillow and a blanket and lie down in the bathtub. I hold the removable shower head between my hands like a gun, regretting that I didn't find a Wal-Mart to buy a real firearm. You could probably do that here in Arkadelphia.

# Nine

When I wake up the next morning, flashes of last night take over my brain. I see plaid boxer shorts. I see Little Carl coming out to say hello. I see hands reaching down to play. *Please, make it stop.*

Over breakfast, Carl does not behave any differently toward me, as if the entire incident never happened. His normalcy makes me wonder if I imagined the whole thing. Oddly, I find myself acting particularly deferential toward him. My behavior is like a defective survival instinct.

Around noon, during a break from depositions, I see Carisse rounding the corner, rushing, fists squeezed tightly into balls. For the first time in my life I am happy to see her. When she spots me, her features arrange themselves into a fake smile, her lips stretching straight along an invisible horizontal line. Her face, as usual, is doughy, as if she is a Claymation character and her creator forgot to shave off the extra bits. Her brown hair is parted in the middle, wispy and thin, and tied back in a low ponytail. The pink of her scalp shows through, and for just a second I can see how someone might find this endearing.

Before she gets the chance to say hello, I tell her that we have to share a hotel room, that there has been a mistake with the reservations. She looks at me quizzically, as if I am not quite making sense. Her eyebrows arch upward and meet in the middle, shading her eyes with the overhang. I imagine this may be helpful in the rain.

"You don't expect me to share with Carl, do you?" I ask, staring at her and willing her to get the message. Even though it is Carisse, I consider begging for her mercy. I cannot bear a repeat of last night's performance.

"Of course not," Carisse says, in a tone that says she means precisely the opposite.

That night the three of us eat dinner at the Hog Pit Barbecue, which is one of those places where the inside is decorated to look like you're dining outside. Fake palm trees lean against the walls, stars sticker the ceiling, hay covers the floor. We are surrounded by pure Americana: red-and-white-checked plastic tablecloths, messy children and sticky fingers, and the requisite HPB tie around the neck bibs. I chow down, enjoying the strained expressions on Carisse and Carl's face when the waiter brings their coleslaw, the closest thing to salad in the place. I can almost see Carisse mentally calculating the fat grams in the mayonnaise.

They both recover surprisingly quickly, though, and after a couple of beers, we are all having a decent time. Amazingly, I push the images from last night out of my mind. Carl is on his best behavior again, telling stories about how the firm has changed over the past decade. I learn that the partnership is opening a Moscow office, and I refrain from suggesting that the two of them transfer there.

The only awkward moment is when Carl steps away from the table for a moment and takes a call from his wife.

"So, you and Carl shared a room last night, then, right?" Carisse whispers, cocking just her right eyebrow so high on her forehead that it melds with her hair.

"The whole town was booked, and Carl's secretary made a mistake. We didn't share a bed, though."

"Really, why not?" Her eyebrows are even again, but now her lips are pursed, as if she is putting on lipstick in a mirror. I think she likes to show off her face's cartoonish flexibility.

"I wouldn't share a bed with my boss."

"Come on, he's sort of cute. We're friends. You can tell me."

"I wouldn't do that. Besides, he's married," I say. I don't mention that we have never been, nor will we ever be, friends.

"So."

"So? Are you kidding?"

"Come on, you really expect me to believe that you didn't sleep with Carl last night?" Before I have a chance to answer, Carl comes back to the table, and Carisse quickly changes the subject.

"So, have you heard from your ex?" she asks.

"What ex?" Carl asks me with a false innocence. Of course, less than twenty-four hours earlier I had been talking incessantly about how much I love and am committed to my boyfriend.

"Oh, this guy broke up with Emily last month. It's too bad, because he was a great catch." She puts her hand on mine, to make it look like she is comforting me. It is a smart move on her part, because it keeps me from clocking her.

"Thanks, Carisse." I suddenly feel sick from my industrious consumption of pulled pork. Carl catches my eyes and looks confused. Apparently my making up a fake boyfriend to avoid sleeping with him is beyond his power of imagination.

After we finish our meal, Carl suggests we hit the dive bar across the street from the Hampton Inn. He says he feels like getting "blotto." Who uses that word? Although I am in a terrible mood and drinking will only make me feel worse, I hear myself agreeing to come along. I am not sure why I feel the need to please Carl, particularly in light of last night's debacle. But I do. I still do. Like an abused wife who somehow believes that she deserved it.

I have not seriously considered whether I should report

Carl to the firm. I'd have to go through the whole he-said–she-said thing, and it would not be handled discreetly—I know that much. Pretty soon people would be whispering, giving me weird looks in the hallways at work, and the place would become so uncomfortable I'd have to leave. I guess I could sue, but that would mean the end of my legal career. No one would risk hiring a "trouble-maker."

It seems a foregone conclusion that I will do nothing. I don't have the fight in me.

But here's what really pisses me off: I feel silly or worse, *prudish* for being upset about the whole thing. What's the big deal, really? Yes, it was uncomfortable and unpleasant, but why get all worked up over it? Carl took no for an answer.

Still, my emotions bounce back and forth, echoing, growing; I feel childish for my outrage, then outraged for feeling childish.

The place is called Sunny's Swimming Hole, and beers are only a buck. Buoys and life preservers hang on the soiled white walls, an attempt at artistic decoration, I suppose. I have always been a fan of the dive bar and am disappointed that this place is immediately ruined for me by my company. We ignore the mostly empty tables and take the three stools that line the bar. Carl in the middle between Carisse and me. The bartender throws down cocktail napkins that say *Burger King* on them, and Carl surprises me by ordering three tequila shots.

"No thanks," I say.

"Come on, Haxby. Stop being such a spoilsport," Carl says, pushing the already poured shot toward me. I wonder if he is punishing me for the Andrew lie. I don't protest further, and we all down our shots at the count of three and squeeze our teeth into bitter lemon. I feel the burn down my throat, and my arms get tingly. In thirty seconds, I know my gut will be on fire.

We all take another shot, and the nausea sets in.

"What's the matter, Haxby? Can't hang with the big boys?" Carl says, and Carisse signals the waiter for a third round. I have had enough.

"I guess not, Carl," I say, and step off my stool in surrender, a hand on the bar to steady my spinning head. "I'm exhausted. Going to head back to the hotel. Carisse, keys?" She looks at me triumphantly. Although I am not sure why everything is a competition with her, I am okay with the fact that yet again I have not won.

"Thanks for dinner, guys," I say, and walk out of Sunny's Swimming Hole, thrilled that the desire to vomit has passed. The sense of liberation is immediate; I don't even blink as I pass Bob at the hotel counter on my way in, and feel pure pleasure when I see that Carisse's room has two double beds. I throw on my new Arkansas gear and curl up under the covers.

But just as suddenly the exhilaration fades. The bath-room night-light casts vicious shadows on the wall, and the chair in the corner has mutated into something sinister. I'm afraid and alone, and all I can think about is picking up the phone and calling Andrew. I need to share the gory details of this trip. To hear him comfort me, tell me it is all going to be all right. I dial his number, quickly, before my mind registers the consequences.

He picks up on the second ring.

"Hello," he says.

I panic. I don't say anything, anything at all, because now that he is on the line, I am not sure if I have anything to say worth hearing. Surely he doesn't care about my night spent cuddling the bathtub. My problems are no longer his job.

"Hello?" he says again. "Who is this? I can hear you breathing."

I feel the weight of the phone in my hands, and it becomes too heavy to hold anymore. I hang up.

A minor relapse. A mistake.

I tell myself that I just wanted to hear his voice. I tell myself that I just wanted to hear him breathe.

I wake up to a throbbing in my temples, payback for the tequila shots. I notice that the bed next to me is still per-fectly made up, a chocolate resting on the pillow. When I go downstairs for breakfast, Carl and Carisse are already there, sharing *The Wall Street Journal*.

113

"Good morning," I say, as I join them at the table.

"Morning," Carl says, and looks at his watch. "You're late. You realize this is not a vacation."

"It's not even eight," Carisse says, and swats him with the paper. "Leave her alone."

"Yeah, well, we've been working for hours." Carl glares at Carisse, unnerved by her playfulness, and then looks at me, a slow sweep up and down. "So, Emily, Carisse and I have been talking about the summary judgment motion. I hate to have to tell you this, but I've decided that you're not ready to write the motion. I'm sorry."

Carl does not look sorry, though, but rather quite pleased with himself. Like the cat who got the cream, or, more accurately, Carisse's cream.

"Why not?" I ask, feeling the disappointment grow in my belly.

"Because I'm going to write it," Carisse says, and puts the newspaper down. Her right hand now rests just next to Carl's, so close that their pinkies are almost touching.

She shoots a look in my direction, and her face is so clear it is as if she says it out loud: *All it took was a blow job. I didn't even need to swallow.*

# Ten

Sometimes when I can't sleep, I picture my funeral and write eulogies in my head. In the fantasy, I almost always die in some tragic but unavoidable way. A drunk driver mows me down. Or a brain aneurysm. I make sure I suffer little, but die with courage and dignity and clean underwear. I like to think more about the funeral rather than how I die. Who would come? Who would face their fears of public speaking and get their ass to the pulpit? Who would decide that they had better things to do than to show up at all? I wonder if people would cry, and if there is anyone in the world who would hold the tears back for fear of never stopping.

I picture afterward, at my dad's house in Connecticut, where my friends all gather in my childhood bedroom. They feel very much like the kids at an adult event, despite the fact that they, too, are now grown-ups. Someone takes out a flask and passes it around. As they get warmed by the alcohol, they pass the time by flipping through my high-school yearbooks, which have spent the last ten years gathering dust. One of them would stop on a photograph of me at fourteen, with a perm and acne and flabby breast buds, and laugh as they held it up for the group.

*This is what Emily would have wanted*, someone would say, and gesture vaguely around the room.

At the service, my dad would give a brilliant speech, perhaps the best of his career, in which he would talk about his role as a father and the tragedy of the loss of so much potential so young. I picture him using the word "squandered," though I am not sure why. I don't think he would talk too much about me, other than maybe to list my accomplishments. I am sure Yale Law School would get mentioned more than once.

Bragging about your kid is somehow not vulgar when your kid is dead.

I bet Kate would read a poem, maybe that one from *Four Weddings and a Funeral*, and her delivery would be pitch-perfect—poignant, sad, and maybe grateful too, for having had the time we spent together. There wouldn't be a dry eye in the house. Jess, on the other hand, would turn the crowd around, make them laugh, and for just a minute let them forget about the literal dead body in the room. She would tell all the inappropriate stories from college, the kinds of stuff my father should never know: the compromising positions, the dabbling in personas, that one horrible E.R. visit. From heaven—though other than in my funeral fantasies I don't really believe in a heaven—I will look down and be proud of Jess; she will be the one who captures who I am for the large audience.

Of course, there is a large audience.

Since Andrew and I broke up, I have not yet figured out how to fit him into the scenario. Before, I would picture him standing at the lectern, my body resting just behind him in a closed casket. He would wear his black suit, which makes him look taller and broader than he actually is, and start by saying something clichéd but touching, like *Emily would have wanted us to laugh today and not to cry. She would have wanted us to celebrate her life and not mourn her death.* And as tears slide down his face, Andrew would tell funny stories about our short time together, while the congregation would laugh sadly along with him; this time, though, it's the laughter of remembering, not the laughter of letting go.

In the new fantasy, I haven't moved past seeing him in the last pew. His face is grim but not devastated. He's not even wearing black.

At my mother's funeral, which I remember only in montage, I didn't cry or speak. It wasn't that kind of funeral. A man who had never met my mother stood up in the front of the packed church and said a few things about her. His words were vague and universally applicable, like a horoscope. My father and I sat quietly in the front row—

the only time I can remember in which my father did not take advantage of an opportunity to speak—and I felt as if the entire place was staring at me, which they probably were. Who doesn't like to take a peek at tragedy?

I remember making sure I sat with my back straight, so at the very least, people could say, on the ride home, *Well, the daughter certainly has good posture*. And though I was uncomfortable because my underwear kept riding up, I stayed perfectly still. Grandpa Jack had bought my panty hose and black suit at the mall the day before. There never seemed to be a right time to tell him before the funeral that they were a size too small.

My father moved differently that day too—robotic and stiff—and he kept going to the bathroom, an excuse we both used to avoid shaking all of those stupid hands. We were too tired to hear things like *We are so sorry* and *She was a wonderful woman*. Too early for consolation, too early for what was expected of us. Too early for the past tense.

At the funeral, it felt like the whole thing was happening to somebody else. The casket laid out in the front of the church did not hold my mother, because how could it? In my experience, mothers didn't die. Especially if you lived in suburban Connecticut, in a world of manicured lawns and nails, an entire commuter-train ride away from real life. Especially if you were fourteen. In my world, the worst thing that could possibly happen was getting stood up at the prom.

It seems odd to me now, but I remember instead of focusing on the fact that I had just lost my mother, I spent that day worrying about how I looked to everyone else. I would have liked to have shed a few tears, not because I felt sad, what I was feeling was something much deeper and emptier than sad, but because tears seemed appropriate. Since I didn't trust myself to stop—didn't trust that once I let go I would not punch the man wearing a collar and spurting platitudes behind the pulpit—I kept my face dry and sat on my fists.

My father did the same. The one-size-fits-all funeral was wrong for her—he knew it, I knew it, the entire congregation knew it— but my father was powerless. We were both breathing underwater.

After the funeral, when we were back at the house, Grandpa Jack asked me for the suit, and I gave it to him, folded neatly in its original shopping bag. I changed into jeans and a T-shirt, like a normal kid, and thought about what it must have cost him to go to Macy's to pick out my funeral outfit. I hope he pretended that I needed the suit for an honor-society event or my junior-high-school graduation; I hope he did not have to say a single word out loud.

Later, when no one was looking, my grandfather, who had shed his own jacket and tie and had put his newsboy cap back on, led me out back behind the house, where he had already set up a large metal trash can. He took the suit out of its bag and threw it on top of all the garbage—on top of other people's plastic forks and knives and paper plates, on top of their picked-at quiche. Grandpa Jack let me light the match, and we stood there for a while, far away from the hands, and the apologies, and the past tense. Together, we watched as the flames licked through the material, turning it to ash.

My mother died slowly and for a long time. But there was no relief for us at the end, as there sometimes is, I imagine. Good-bye still came too early by any measure. She spent a year getting treatment, a year in which she threw up quietly behind closed doors, and asked to be left alone, and smoked joints by herself in the backyard, behind the toolshed. That year, I learned to recognize the smell of hospitals, the rhythm of bad news. That year, I watched my father unravel and shrink, as if it were him, and not her, who was dying slowly. As if it were him, and not her, who was dying for a long time.

At our last Thanksgiving as a family, my dad made a toast to my mother's health, since she was home then and it looked like things were going to get better. We clinked our glasses, and my dad even let me have some wine, which tasted both sour and sweet and made my eyes water. I hated it. My mother wore a silk scarf over her head, and I remember thinking that she looked more beautiful bald, her features unmarred by the nuance of hair. Just hazel eyes, no eyebrows, delicate, soft, and warm; young, too, their brightness rebelling against the disintegration of her body, against the new shadows on her face.

I think now, if I have to reduce my mother to snippets of memory, to a pile of adjectives, that's who she was, that's what I should hold on to—those eyes—defiant and alert, fighting like hell to hold on to us.

My dad and I ate tons of turkey, overcompensating for the fact that my mother only pushed hers around on her plate. I wonder if she knew she was dying then, whether she put on a last Thanksgiving show for us to tuck away in our memories, since it was the last one we would all spend around the large oak table. Maybe my dad knew too, and the show was all for my benefit, too young to notice the fragility of my parents' smiles. Or just young enough to play along, to let the will to believe overpower what was so clearly written on both of their faces.

They canceled Christmas that year though, because Christmas was all my mother's doing and she was too sick to get out of bed. I guess my father could have done the shopping, and put up the tree, and hung the stockings, the painstaking way my mother had done every year, but it would have been a mockery, a sham Christmas, and we had finally moved beyond pretending.

After being told that we weren't celebrating the same way we had always done—there would be fewer presents, we would skip the tree—I slammed my door and sulked in my room, an impossible child, or a typical teenager, or a bit of both. I cursed loudly at them then, feeling power from yelling words that were ordinarily not tolerated in the house. I took advantage of the one perk of my mother's illness; I could push boundaries.

"Why does fucking everything have to fucking be about her?" I screamed at the walls, at my parents through the walls, at God, though I am sure by then I had already stopped believing.

Skipping Christmas was their way of telling me that it was over, and when she was admitted to the hospital at the turn of the year, we all knew it was for the last time. No one sat me down and explained it to me; I am not sure anyone could. Instead, I learned by inference and by the fact that my mother kept getting smaller and smaller. Like Lily Tomlin in *The Incredible Shrinking Woman*, except not nearly as funny.

On her last day, my dad woke me up and told me to get dressed. All he said was "This is it."

It was winter, so I put on a wool turtleneck sweater that tickled my jaw and made me sweat in the armpits. We drove to the hospital without speaking. My dad occasionally took in sharp breaths, as if to say something, then thinking better of it; each intake, so unlike him, was a declaration of fear. I stared out the window the whole time, not able to look at my father's face, his chin decorated with something way past a five o'clock shadow, his eyes red-rimmed and watery, exactly like my own.

When we got there, my mother was asleep, or in a coma, or knocked out from morphine. It was never made clear to me, and I didn't think to ask. We each took one side of the bed. My dad held her right hand, and I held on to her left; her fingers felt foreign— rough, and cold, and unnaturally heavy. Just to have something to do, I fixed her scarf so it wouldn't slip down her bare forehead and drew on her eyebrows with makeup from her kit on the ledge. We sat there for hours, not saying a word. Just listening to each breath. Desperate for the one that followed.

At around two in the afternoon, the doctor stopped by, patted my father on the shoulder to get his attention, and said, "It won't be long now." He simply nodded at me, like I was an adult worthy of acknowledgment.

She died at exactly five p.m., as if she had clocked out of her shift for the day. We knew because the next breath just didn't come, though we waited for it. Stupidly hopeful, but both of us thinking *This is it. This is how it is going to end*. Not like in the movies, where there is a noise to warn the viewer, a machine bleating loudly so doctors can come and start pounding forcefully on her chest. A dramatic crescendo.

No, the absence of sound told us it was over. Complete stillness and quiet. If it wasn't me and it wasn't my mother who had just stopped, it would have been beautiful really, like the end of the symphony, the tiny break before the applause. But it was me and it was my mother, and now, now, it is the quiet that I find most haunting of all.

Afterward, on the way home and before the phone calls and the chatter, my dad and I went to the Stop & Shop, filling the trunk with food for the people who would be paying their respects in the week to come. I picked out the cold-cut platter my mother had chosen for my birthday party the year before, thinking that seemed appropriate. We filled the cart without discussion of what exactly we needed. We bought cookies. And frozen lasagna. Mouthwash. Enough Q-tips for the next decade.

When we got back into the car, my dad cranked up the radio as loud as it would go, and we drove that way for the rest of the ride. The lyrics to songs from the '50s— "Wake Up Little Susie," "Breaking Up Is Hard to Do," "Love Potion No. 9"—danced just at the tips of our tongues, and our mouths moved along from habit. The sounds rang mercifully loud in our ears. We sat that way for a while, in the driveway once we reached home, the motor still running, both of us not ready for the music to stop.

# Eleven

I'm not going as a fucking cat, or a fucking nurse, or a fucking flapper, or anything rubber." I run my fingers over the grooves of a corduroy blazer at the vintage clothing store in the East Village. "But I want to look fucking hot." Jess just smiles at me and nods her head. She indulges me in my rant, the same one I deliver every year around this time.

"I don't want to be one of those women who use Halloween as an excuse to go naked, that's all," I continue, as if she hasn't heard it all before. "This will be the first time I've seen Andrew since he found me sweating tequila on the subway. I need to look good. But I want a real costume too."

"Dominatrix?" she asks, holding up a studded bikini with empty holes where the nipples should go. "That'll get his attention."

Jess smacks my ass with a long leather whip. It hurts like

hell, but I don't react. "Okay, okay, too trite," she says.

"Please help me, Jess."

"How about going as Monica Lewinsky? Or, better yet, Anita Hill?" Apparently it was a mistake to tell Jess about what happened in Arkansas. After cursing for about ten minutes straight and then trying to convince me to sue the firm, I guess Jess has now decided it is sort of funny. Which it is if it didn't happen to you.

"Be serious. I need your help."

"Have you spoken to him?"

"Who? Carl?" I take the blazer off the rack and sniff it. For some reason, I expect it to smell like Grandpa Jack, musky and warm. It doesn't. It smells like dust. It smells like death.

"No, idiot. Andrew."

"No."

"Did you call him?"

"No."

"Really?"

"I haven't." She whips me again, this time harder.

"All right, once." I slam the blazer back onto the rack. "But we didn't talk. I panicked and hung up."

"Uh-oh, Em. You are even more screwed up than I thought. You really need to get some help."

"I'm fine. Really."

"Prank-calling your ex-boyfriend? The one *you* chose to break up with? Yup, sure sounds like you're doing great."

We spend the rest of the day combing the neighborhood for costumes. Though Halloween is still a few days away, most of the people walking around look like they are already dressed for the festivities. We pass a grown man in a diaper, another in a unitard and roller skates, but Jess swears she has seen them both on First Avenue before.

Jess wants to go as a sorceress, so we buy her a big cone hat, and glitter, and a velour robe. Right now, when she puts the pieces together, she looks like a homeless pimp, but I am sure she will find a way to transform her costume into something glamorous. At our final stop, one of those Manhattan stores that sells everything from feather boas to digital cameras, I find a shiny tiara tucked into a display case filled with handblown glass bongs. I ask the saleswoman if it is for sale and where she found it.

"That's from my days as Miss Mississippi, 1983," she says, as she smoothes out a large *I Love New York* sweatshirt over her belly. Her skin has a sickly yellow pallor, and she is missing one of her front teeth. The last couple of decades have been cruel to her.

"Ah, hell, who's kidding who? I'll give it to you for twenty bucks," she says, and the tone in her voice tells me this is just one more surrender in a long series of them.

"Deal," I say, and the woman takes the tiara out of the case, careful not to touch the fake pearls and diamonds that meet in repeated arcs. It is beautiful. It is ridiculous. It is perfect.

After I hand over my money, she wraps the tiara in tissue paper, tenderly covering each of the sharp edges, again and again. She takes her time.

"Wear it in good health, wear it in good health," she says, allowing herself one last long look before sliding it into the bag and handing it over.

On Halloween night, I transform myself into a prom queen. I slip on my bridesmaid's dress from Jess's sister's wedding and enjoy the feel of the cool taffeta against my skin. I figure the plunging neckline and slit up the leg balance out the fact that I am covered in iridescent sequins.

"My little girl's all grown up," Jess says, as she places the tiara on my head and pretends to tear up.

"How do I look?" I give her a final spin, knowing full well that I look pretty damn good, all things considered. The fabric clings in all of the right places, and I feel sexy. Not dominatrix sexy, maybe, but sexy enough. There is just something about a tiara.

"Fucking hot," Jess says. "And me?"

"Fucking hotter," I say, because she does. She has resewn the robe so it hangs like a glittery cape, and she wears a tight black dress underneath. Her sorceress hat sits jauntily on the back of her head, somehow provocative and edgy. And her face is glowing with sparkles, aligned to brighten her charcoaled eyes.

"Are you nervous to see Andrew?" she asks.

"Yeah." Jess takes her wand and performs a spell over my head, as if to make everything all right. I squeeze my eyes shut while she does it, hoping that might help it to work.

"Well, then," she says matter-of-factly, now that all is settled by her magic. She links her arms with mine and creates instant momentum, like we are about to embark on an adventure.

"We're off like a prom dress."

We can hear the party before we cross the street to Kate and Daniel's apartment. I can't make out any music, but there is chatter in the air. I feel that nervous energy, that kinetic buzz, that always hits before entering a room in which everyone is all dressed up and talking at once. I try to let go of my performance anxiety—*Why should I be afraid of Andrew? Why should I be afraid of anyone?*—and remember that I love Halloween. The best things in life, for one day, become socially sanctioned. The shedding of your identity. The conscious choice to assume a new one. The gluttonous sugar high.

When I was little, Halloween was a big family holiday for us; my mom, dad, and I would wander around the neighborhood in matching costumes, usually TV-themed—the Smurfs, the Bradys, the roommates from *Three's Company*. My dad loved the strategizing part: We avoided the Hogans' on the corner, because they handed out raisins, and consistently hit the Dempseys', though they were a good ten blocks away, because they were generous with king-size candy bars. My mom loved the creative part, the turning of us into a single unit with a few well-placed stitches. I loved the walking-in-between-them part, leading the way and lapping up their attention. We did that every year until I hit twelve, when I unilaterally ended the tradition. Dressing up, I decided, was only for kids.

Kate and Daniel live in Tribeca, in a large loft and, unlike my place, a real grown-up's apartment. All cement and exposed pipes and minimalist furniture. They like to describe it as "industrial," as if this is a good thing, though I am not sure why, exactly, you would want your home to resemble a warehouse. As we walk in, the two of them run up to us. I look over their shoulders to see if I can spot Andrew in the crowded room, but I can't make him out. At first count, I see six dominatrices, two black cats, and three naughty nurses. No Andrew. For now, at least, I am proud to say that I am the only prom queen in the room.

"Okay, I know you are going to hate me for this, but I thought I should let you know first off—" Kate says by way of greeting.

"Oh, no."

"Yup, Carisse is here," Daniel says, and walks away with our coats. This is how they do things. Tag team.

"Why'd you invite her?"

"I didn't. Well, not specifically. I sent out an all-associates e-mail inviting everyone from the firm. I forgot that she might actually come," Kate says.

I look over her shoulder and see Carisse standing in the corner holding a glass of wine. She wears a Hooters costume, her breasts spilling out of the official tight white tank top and her butt kept in place with the short, short orange shorts. I start laughing but stop when I see that she is talking to Andrew.

He has recycled the same costume he wears every year: thick glued-on sideburns, white studded polyester bell bottoms he found in his parents' attic, and a pillow stuck under a wide-collared silver shirt. Andrew is the King, but the potbellied and sweaty later version. Last Halloween I asked him why he chose to go with that incarnation of Elvis instead of the hip-swinging one the world fell in love with. I didn't expect a real answer, but I got one: "He was who he was, Emily. Wouldn't it make you sad to only be remembered for who you were in your twenties, even if it were for something this great?" Andrew then did Elvis's signature lip curl, which was so charmingly asymmetrical, I kissed it right off his face.

Tonight, he saves his best imitation for Carisse. She gets a curl and a leg gyration.

When Jess sees what I see, she leads me directly to the elaborate bar set up in the corner.

"Tequila?" she asks.

"Nope. Vodka. I try not to make the same mistakes

twice." She pours me a shot, which I throw back fast and clean. I barely feel it burn as it goes down. Jess mixes a vodka and tonic for me next and drops a lime into it. She hands it over wordlessly. I scoot over as a man dressed in what appears to be a hamburger costume sidles up to the bar and reaches for the bottle of gin.

"It looks like we are a match made in heaven," he says, and nudges me in the ribs with his plastic patty. He pours himself a drink.

"Excuse me?"

"You're a prom queen, right? Well, I'm Burger King," he says, pointing proudly to his head, and, sure enough, he too is wearing a tiara, but his looks as if it is made of tarnished gold.

"Clever," I say, because I can't think of anything clever to say. My eyes keep returning to Carisse and Andrew, who are now chatting in an opposite corner.

"Nice tiara," Jess says, pointing to the guy's head.

"It's not a tiara. It's a crown," he says, and rubs his hand against the gold spokes.

"It's a tiara. Crowns go all the way around. Tiaras go only halfway. That's a tiara," Jess says. I look at her, unsure why she is picking a fight with a hamburger. He looks at her, confused too, like we are more than he bargained for.

"Yeah, whatever," he says, taking his drink and walking away, bumping Jess with his bun as he passes by.

"What was that about?"

"I wasn't going to stand by and let you get hit on by a guy wearing an ugly tiara. You're above that. Anyhow, I wanted him to leave us alone. Now, please stop staring at them. You're embarrassing me."

"I'm not staring," I say, and turn my gaze to look at Jess, because of course I'm staring.

"He won't go home with her, you know?"

"I know."

"He's probably just talking to her to make you jealous."

"I know."

"You should probably go over and say hello. Play it cool."

"I know."

"Just remember, you broke up with him."

"I know."

"Why'd you do that again?"

I look at her and take a slow pull from my drink.

"I don't know."

"Yeah," she says. "That's what I thought."

It doesn't take too long for some of my discomfort to get washed away by the alcohol. I don't stop staring at Carisse and Andrew, who now look even chummier than before, but I no longer feel enough shame to try to hide it. I reason that she is asking for people to stare, since her breasts look like they may eject from her tank top at any moment. Andrew, despite the fact that he is dressed up as an aging Elvis, looks fantastic. His hair is mussed into a cross between a pompadour and a fauxhawk. He has crinkles around his eyes, more brackets than commas, which get exaggerated every time he smiles. I am tempted to go over there and lick them, stick my tongue into their soft grooves. I am not sure why it has never occurred to me to do that before.

Carisse leans into him as they talk, both of them clearly flirting, and I wonder how I could have let him go. Andrew had wanted to marry me. Me and not her. Me. And I had been the one to walk away. Who does something like that? I could have said yes. It is just one word after all. A whole path would have unraveled then, and I could have followed it, let it lead me somewhere, anywhere, really. And now it would have been us over there in the corner, not them.

People say yes all the time. It is a choice, like anything else. *I am going to be one of those people who says yes*, I decide. Like they teach in twelve-step programs, that you should act "as if" you are a person who does the opposite of what you do naturally. Alcoholics should act "as if" they don't want a drink. I should act "as if" I am someone who says yes. It seems so simple. Three letters.

I intentionally ignore the thoughts that sound like Jess. *You are not ready for an Andrew*. And the ones that sound like me, the ones that hurt the most. *Andrew would have been the one to eventually walk away. You did what you had to do. You left first*. But the words are fuzzy, like white noise, and I don't have the energy to parse them out. Instead, through the haze of four vodka tonics, and a few shots, it's becoming clear that I have to talk to Andrew. Right now.

I tell myself that I have no reason to be nervous. The man in the corner is someone who has seen me naked more times than I could ever count, someone who used to take up half of my bed, and possibly even more of my life. Never mind that he is now a man in the corner who pretends like he didn't see me walk into the party, a man who would rather talk to a Hooters waitress.

I cross the room and make my way through the costumes. *Static cling, the avian flu, the Mona Lisa, a Wonder Woman Pez dispenser, a pair of dice, another fucking cat.*

"Hey," I say to the two of them.

"Can I talk to you alone for a minute?" I ask Andrew, and tilt my head toward the hallway that leads to the bathroom. It is the only place in the entire loft that has any semblance of privacy. The rest of the apartment feels like one big stage.

"Sure," he says. "See you later, Carisse." I see Andrew take one last peek at her boobs before he follows me down the hallway.

"What's up?" he asks. "How have you been?"

"Okay," I say. "Okay. You?" I am not sure how to stand and suddenly feel ridiculous in my costume. I want to appear relaxed, which is next to impossible in a gown. I am wobbling on my high heels, the product of nerves and too many drinks.

"Good," he says. "Glad to hear you're feeling better. You looked rough on the subway."

"Yeah." I am no longer capable of making small talk. I need to say what I want to say.

"Listen, Andrew, yes."

"What?"

"Yes, I want to say yes." I look up at him and see he has no idea what I am talking about. I can tell he is wondering if I am drunker than I seem. I am.

"Yes? Yes to what?" He stares at me, but he's smiling. He finds me amusing when I am drunk. I give myself a quick pep talk. *You can do this.*

"Yes, I want to marry you." I say it. Straight and to the point. I feel a flush of pride for getting the words out.

"Excuse me?" Andrew takes a step closer and looks down at me. He feels even taller than usual, almost menacing. His dark hair falls onto his forehead, a large clump just above his eyes, but he doesn't push it away. "I don't think I asked you to marry me. In fact, I know I didn't. What the hell are you going on about, Emily?" I feel the weight of his use of my full name. No Em, but Emily. He does not look relieved or loving or even kind.

He looks mad as hell.

"I, I just . . . I wanted to let you know that I made a mistake. I want to tell you yes." I put my arm on his shoulder, my way of saying *Please don't be mad, we can fix this.*

"You are a piece of work, you know that? What makes

you think after the shit you pulled these last two months that I would ever want to marry you? The thought makes me sick." Andrew's voice gets louder, but then he notices the volume and lowers it.

"You are out of your fucking mind," he says, and takes a step back. Though he is speaking in a whisper now, his tone is hard. He breathes in deeply, and exhales slowly, controlled, like they do in yoga class.

"You know what? I don't need this right now. You are drunk. Fortunately, I have enough sense for both of us. I'm going to pretend like you didn't just insult me like that. I'm going to pretend like this never happened." Andrew turns away.

"Bye, Emily. Good luck to you," he says, a couple of meaningless words thrown over his shoulder. An afterthought.

"But, Andrew—" I don't get to finish my sentence, because he is already down the hallway, and has slipped back into the party, lost in the throngs of the costume bazaar.

I find Jess and tell her we need to go home. Now. She takes one look at my face and runs to get our coats. When she gets back, she grips my elbow and steers me toward the entrance.

"You okay?" she whispers to me, under a fake plastered-on smile. She knows enough not to draw any attention to us.

"No. Not okay. Not even fine," I say. So far I have held back the storm of tears. I can't hold out much longer, though, and am grateful once we reach the front door.

I take one quick look back on the way out. I can't help myself. I see Andrew is again talking to Carisse, and their heads are bent forward, a caricature of flirtation. In the other corner, I notice the guy with the tiara is kissing someone, his fake lettuce pressed up close against a white body. I point them out to Jess.

"No way," she says. "I can't believe it."

And it is then, when I see the simplicity of it all, the culmination of choices that has brought me to this moment—the Burger King making out with a woman dressed as the Dairy Queen—that my tears begin to fall.

# Twelve

Emily, dear? Hello? Hello?" A gravelly voice echoes through my apartment and breaks through my dreams. "I am not sure if this machine is working. Is this working?" There is a loud knocking sound; the person on the other end is hitting the phone against something hard.

"It's Ruth Wasserstein here. I left you a few messages already, and I can't get ahold of your father. I know it's early, but please call me back. It's . . . well, it's important."

"Ruth? Hi, it's me. What's wrong?" I say. My emergency instincts kick in and supplant my hangover. Instead of nausea, I feel uprooted by fear. My answering-machine light is blinking furiously, and my pulse begins to match its beat. *Blink. Blink blink blink blink. Blink.*

Grandpa Jack. *Something has happened to Grandpa Jack.* There is no other logical explanation for Ruth to be calling at eight a.m. on a Saturday morning. *Grandpa Jack is dead. This is how these things happen. With unexpected phone calls and blinking answering-machine lights. This is how these things happen.*

"It's all right. Take a breath. He should be okay," Ruth says. "It's just that he's . . . well, he's missing. Jack is missing."

"Missing? So he's not dead?"

"Dead? No, he's not dead," Ruth says, laughing and then stopping herself. "Well, at least I don't think so."

"So what you are saying is Grandpa Jack is not dead, right? That's what you're saying."

"Oh, dear, I didn't mean to scare you like that. He's wandered off, that's all. I'm sure he's okay. But I think it would be best if you came up here. I've already called the police."

"I'm on my way. Ruth?" I take a deep breath, willing the oxygen to stop my body from shaking. "Thank you so much for calling me."

"Of course. And don't worry, Emily, he's probably just lost." She hangs up the phone. *Just lost*, I tell myself, like she means it figuratively.

I run out the door and don't take the time to brush my teeth or comb my hair. I need to find Grandpa Jack. *Please, God, don't let him be dead*, I say over and over again, under my breath, my new mantra. I have no time for positive thinking.

When I sprint through the front door of my building and

fly past Robert, I take a quick look at my doorman, remember he is an older gentleman too, probably just a few years younger than Grandpa Jack and with grandchildren of his own. A sick jealousy washes over me, a feeling not dissimilar to what happens in department stores when I see mothers and daughters shopping together, sharing the two-by-two feet of dressing-room space. *Why isn't Robert missing instead of my Grandpa Jack?* I wonder. *Why does it always have to be the people I love? Why does it always have to be the people I'll miss the most?*

I'm bitter and angry above all else. Even above the fear.

"Where are you off to, princess?" Robert asks, unaware that I am thinking hateful thoughts about him. His kindness shames me.

"Sorry, Robert, gotta run," I say, as I step into a taxi. *Why my Grandpa Jack?*

"Have fun, princess," he says again, and whistles. *Princess?*

Five minutes later, only after I am in the cab, only after I have shouted "Riverdale" at the driver, I realize I'm still wearing my costume from last night, tiara and all. I take my hands to my head and press my fingertips hard against the metal spokes. This is the scary part of the fairy tale, the part before the happy ending. When Cinderella loses her slipper, or Sleeping Beauty bites into the poisonous apple. I feel the sharp edges of the tiara dig into my skin. I don't stop pressing until I draw blood.

* * *

When I get to the retirement home, Ruth is waiting for me in the lobby with two police officers. They are all polite enough not to comment on my gown.

"Hello, I am Emily Haxby. Jack Haxby is my grand-father." I put out my hand to shake each of theirs. I use my lawyer voice; maybe the seriousness of my tone can erase the sequins. My eyes immediately start scanning the lobby, hoping that this is all a big misunderstanding and that Grandpa Jack will be sitting down somewhere reading a book. Perhaps they just don't see him, like when you don't notice the glasses on your face.

"We have sent out two patrol cars to scan the streets, Ms. Haxby. I'm sure we'll find him soon," one of the police officers says, his hand resting casually on his hip, just above the holster for his gun. *He could shoot me right now*, I think. *Swing the pistol with his pointer finger, like they do in old westerns, and shoot me right now. What would I need to do to provoke him? Would screaming until my lungs gave out be enough?*

"Have you spoken with your father, dear?" Ruth asks.

"I left him a couple of messages on the ride over here, but I got his voice mail. He might already be on his way. That's what I'm hoping, anyhow." I am tempted to apologize that I'm the only family representative. I feel wholly inadequate for the task.

*I can deal with this*, I tell myself. *I went to Yale Law*

*School, for God's sake. I can deal with a missing octogenarian. You can do this.*

"Okay. What should we do? Should I start looking on foot? I need to do something." My voice holds steady. I sound in control. *Grandpa Jack is going to be okay. Everything is going to be okay.*

"Ma'am, I think it is probably best if you wait here with Ms. Wasserstein. She gave us a recent photo, and some of the nurses have volunteered to help us out. They have some ideas about his favorite places. Don't worry, I'll call you when we find him." I notice he says "when," and not "if," which provides a bit of relief. *They are going to find him.*

"I have my cell phone. You can call me while I look," I say, and turn to leave, but Ruth puts her hands on my arm, both gentle and forceful at the same time.

"Let me come with you," she says, and in my half-second delay in responding, she sees that I am worried about her slowing me down. "Please."

"Sure. Yeah, of course."

I examine the two cops before we leave them behind to do their own search. They look capable, with their guns and their graying hair.

"Come on, dear," Ruth says, and we link arms as we walk through the automatic doors and back out onto the street. She leads.

"What happened?" I ask, once we are moving. It feels a little better to be moving, doing something, though my voice still has that edge of anxiety. Ruth tells me only the important facts with the precision that comes from having practiced law for fifty years.

"When I stopped by his apartment this morning, he was gone. I figured he was in the breakfast area, so I came downstairs to look for him, but he wasn't there either. So I started asking around, and nobody had seen him. I asked the nurses to search the building, which they did, and no luck. And, well, now here we are." She pats my hand, in a way that is comforting and not patronizing, in a way that makes me miss my grandmother and my mother and Andrew and Grandpa Jack so much I think I might explode with emptiness. "He probably wandered off and got lost. He gets confused sometimes."

"I know." I run away in my head for a few moments, thinking of last night and then back to Grandpa Jack.

I look for a way to comfort myself, a best-case scenario for the situation, and I can't come up with one. The best case is what Ruth described—he got confused and wandered off—but this does little to ease my anxiety. This means I will be losing Grandpa Jack soon, perhaps slowly, but in the only way that matters, and I am not sure if I can do that. I am not sure I can lose both Andrew and Grandpa Jack in one year.

Ruth and I turn left from the retirement home and take my grandfather's and my usual route. We walk with an affected casualness, as if this is a typical Saturday morning stroll, and pretend that we are excited about the baby that waddles by or the puppy peeing on a small patch of grass. Our eyes crisscross in front of us, though, dart from side to side, and soak up the visual cues. We peer into shop windows and see hanging meats. Fresh-baked breads. Toilet-paper pyramids. No Grandpa Jack.

My spine feels stiff and alert, and my head hurts from my laser-like focus. I do not let a single detail pass by undigested. I picture worst-case scenarios; I can't help it. We will stumble upon his body on the curb, tossed aside and still, his wallet emptied, a baseball bat nearby. We will find him disheveled and scared and alone and at first we won't even recognize him. We will never see Grandpa Jack again.

I buy Ruth a hot chocolate at a coffee shop. It has only one table and two chairs. I feel disappointed when we walk out, partially because my grandfather is not in there but more because they didn't give me any space to look for him.

"Emily," she says, breaking me out of my reverie. "How's work?"

I give Ruth a wry smile. She is trying to distract me, and I appreciate the effort.

"Work sucks."

"Yeah, I know how that can be. Long hours, right?"

"Yup, and lecherous partners." While we scan the streets, I tell Ruth the story of my Arkansas case, about being on the wrong side and about Carl propositioning me. I even describe his open boxer shorts and seeing him in the flesh.

I am not sure why I share this, dirty details and all, but there is something about her warmth that makes me feel like she can handle it. I know none of this reflects well on me either, but I am okay with her seeing that too.

"I guess things haven't come as far as I had thought," she says. "I thought we women had moved past that."

"Yeah, I did too." We stick our heads into a pawnshop, an antiques store, a Rite Aid. No one has seen Grandpa Jack. *Where the hell is Grandpa Jack?*

Ruth keeps me talking as we walk, and I explain why I don't want to report Carl to the firm. I am surprised when she understands. Jess didn't get that, didn't understand the humiliation involved, the potential destruction of my career. Jess thinks staying quiet is an act of cowardice, which it might very well be.

"I guess you have to decide if it's worth the fight. You pick your battles in this life," Ruth says. "You've got to decide what it is you want."

"I have no idea what I want." *Other than to find Grandpa Jack. That's all I want right now.*

"You'll figure it out. You know, I think in some ways we had it easier in my day. I had to fight every battle. There wasn't really a choice, at least not for me. You guys are sort of the hungover generation."

"The hungover generation?" I look down at my wrinkled prom dress and my cup of coffee; I pat down my bed head.

"I mean, it is almost like the next morning after the last

146

wave of the women's movement. There isn't the energy left over to keep up the momentum. Where are we now? Postfeminism? Post-postfeminism?"

"I don't know. Just postfeminism, right?" We check the bank. The long aisles of the shiny new Whole Foods. Though organic is not my grandfather's style, all bets are off today. We will look everywhere if we have to. "I just think *I* don't have the energy. Please don't look at me as representative of anything."

I wouldn't want Ruth to indict the women of my generation just because I can't seem to get my act together.

"I'm not. I think we're all falling behind. I don't know why, but there is a pandemic phobia of intellectual thought in this country. We have only one woman on the Supreme Court. It's crazy. Did you know that even Liberia has elected a woman president? We are so freaking regressive." She slaps her hands together with force, pure aggression. I wish now that I had had the opportunity to see Ruth in action, in her heyday, on the bench, issuing judgments and taking names. I bet when she was younger, people called her a "spitfire." I bet that used to piss her off.

"Back to you, dear," Ruth says, recovering her composure. She smooths out her pants, a physical act to transition the conversation. "Have you thought about quitting?"

"Yes and no. I mean, I don't know what I would do if I quit. It is sort of who I am, if that makes any sense," I say.

"When people ask me about myself, I tell them that I am a lawyer. It's an identity thing, I guess. I don't really have anything else."

"Yeah, I know what you mean. I'm a judge, that's what I say. Even though now I really am just an old lady living in a retirement home. Even though the only thing I judge now is the monthly senior talent show. You know Jack did stand-up a couple of months ago?" Ruth smiles, which rearranges the lines on her face. She inverts her parentheses and transforms commas into apostrophes. The pattern is that of a woman who has no regrets.

I try to remember Grandpa Jack's comedy routine, but I can't think of a single joke. I only hear the rhythm and picture him standing up at the diner, in the narrow aisle between the tables, performing for Andrew and me, as practice. We gave him a standing ovation.

"Yeah. Ruth, how did you figure out who you wanted to be?" I ask, but this is not exactly what I want to know. What I really want to ask, but don't, is when I will become who I am supposed to be.

"I haven't yet figured out who I want to be, dear," Ruth says, answering both my questions, and then throws her head back in a hearty, unselfconscious laugh. "I'm not kidding. I haven't figured it out yet. But don't tell my daughters that. I lie to them every day. I tell them they will figure it out, with time. To just keep doing what they are doing. But let me let you in on a little secret, because I think you can handle it." She leans in to whisper in my ear.

"All parents lie to their children. It's our duty. But the truth of the matter is, I don't think many of us know what we are doing. We all walk around much of the time confused and very much alone. Probably how Jack feels right about now."

The mention of my grandfather and the fact that he is missing, or lost, or whatever he is, feels like a light fist to the stomach, a reminder of what I have and what I haven't and what I will likely lose. We are wandering through a small park now, and though I am still scanning for him, I am not sure what I am looking for. Do people look different when they get lost? Could he somehow camouflage with the swing set, the patchy grass, the homeless laid out on park benches?

"Emily, you have to realize that we are all making it up as we go along," she says, and swings her arms about to explain that she means this too, our roundabout search. I nod and tuck the advice away somewhere I can take it out again, later, when I may need it. *We are all making it up as we go along.* Ruth takes a breath and stops talking for a moment, as if to decide something, and pats her hands around her circle of hair. She looks up at me, with a smile on her face now.

"But there is one thing I must, must tell you." She leans in again, as if preparing for an important speech. *She can see the hungry look in my eyes,* I think. *She knows I need her help.*

"Yes," I say, eager for the morsel of guidance.

"1985 called, and they want their dress back."

We laugh so hard, a couple of people on the street glare at us, as if the noise we are making is noxious, one more pollutant to the Bronx air. But it feels too good to release some of the tension and to forget our mission for just a minute.

At the end of the park we turn left again, "securing the perimeter," as they say in cop shows. As we look, I try not to keep checking my cell phone, though neither the police nor my father have called. We talk some more about work, and I even say a few things about breaking up with Andrew. I don't mention what happened last night, though. That wound is still too raw, my presumptuousness embarrassing. All I can do is plead drunk. That's the only defense I can come up with for my idiocy.

I spot a diner on the corner, not *our* diner but one similar, with the same greasy smell and fluorescent lighting and cake case. I take Ruth inside, praying that Grandpa Jack is in here somewhere, that he decided the streets were too empty, perhaps took refuge in the restaurant noise. *This is where I would come*, I reason. *This is where I would come to be found. A place with banging plates, and a jukebox, and crying babies who spit up on their high chairs. This is a place to be found and lost.*

And sure enough, tucked into a booth with his back to us, his newsboy sitting atop his head, is a man who, at least from behind—plaid shirt, white thinning hair at the nape of the neck—looks just like my grandfather. Only much, much smaller. I point him out to Ruth.

We walk up to Grandpa Jack slowly, so as not to startle him, but when we approach, there is not a hint of relief on his face at having been found, only happiness to see us. My first thought is *Thank you for not being dead.*

"Well, hello. My two favorite ladies. Have a seat," he says, and motions to the booth beside him. Ruth and I look at each other, wordlessly debating how to handle this, how to handle him. We slide onto the opposite side so we can both face my grandfather.

"So, what did my girls do today? Did you get the Caddy washed, Martha?" he asks Ruth, looking straight at her but somehow seeing my grandmother. Ruth just nods along, a little shocked maybe, but mostly defeated, I think.

"And you, my dear, how are things going? Please tell my son that he better hurry and knock you up. I want some grandbabies," Grandpa Jack says, as he looks at me and chuckles. He thinks I am my mother.

I want to laugh with him, but of course that feeling fades as soon as it comes. Only a momentary aside from the overwhelming uncertainty that comes from being a part of someone else's delusion, the overwhelming sadness that comes from having your existence forgotten by the one you love. To watch as he, too, is erased by a trick of the imagination. Right now he is living in a time before I was born.

"Grandpa?" I ask. "Are you okay? We've been looking for you." I figure the best route is to ignore his words and coax him with mine. "We were really worried." I scrunch my eyebrows together, an exaggerated expression to demonstrate that anxiety he may not hear.

"Ah, don't be silly, sweetheart." He waves me away, like I am the one not making sense. I am not sure if he recognizes me as me now, and I am both desperate and afraid to find out. In a way, there is comfort in his vagueness. Maybe I can pretend that he is fine, that this morning was just a temporary loss of his grip on sanity. People bounce back.

"Jack, we had the police looking. You can't just walk away like that. I was worried. The nurses were worried." Ruth uses her eye contact as a tool to bring him back. It doesn't work. My grandfather just looks at her and shrugs her off. A casual, almost comical, lift and drop of his shoulders.

"Aw, come off it, Martha. You are always worrying about nothing. I'm fine. Just went for a round of golf is all." His accent has changed too. Deepened, more New York. "See here, Charlotte, your mother-in-law is always on my back for no reason. You let my son out once in a while, don't you?" I have nothing to say to this, nothing at all, since my heart is broken by the fact that Grandpa Jack appears to be broken. I may not be a doctor, but I know enough. We all do. Ruth and I are both thinking the same thing. *So this is what Alzheimer's looks like.* And then, another silent prayer, not so different from the one this morning: *Please let him come back. At least for just a little while.*

Two hours later we are sitting in the emergency room; Grandpa Jack looks tiny, with his skinny limbs poking out of his hospital gown. He sits up, his feet dangling off the side of the rolling cot, and looks around, bewildered.

"What are we doing here?" he keeps demanding every fifteen minutes or so. He goes in and out, well, more like back and forth, between a time long gone and now. When he disappears, Ruth and I just ignore it and pretend like he is making sense in the context of our conversation.

We talk to the doctors away from my grandfather; he is tucked behind an area cordoned off by a curtain. I tell them this seems sudden. Last time I saw him, at the diner, he was fine. Perhaps a little confused at the end of the visit, but overall he was fine. Ruth steps in, though.

"Emily, I hate to say this, but he's been getting worse for a while. I tried to tell you last time you were here, but you didn't seem to get it," she says gently. My face gets hot, the shame sharp and painful.

"So what happens now?"

"Unfortunately, we don't have any real way to treat him. He should see a specialist soon, but more importantly, we have to up his care," the doctor says. His words feel like a second slap in the face. He is absolutely right, this man in the white coat, who looks to be only a couple of years older than me. I wonder if he has seen relatives disappear. I wonder if he can see my shame.

"He's in a great facility now, but I think it is time he switches floors to what they call the 'constant-care' wing," the doctor says. I want to scream that I know what the constant-care wing is, that my Grandpa Jack has told me that that's the final tollbooth on the way out.

"He needs more consistent attention, where there are nurses who check in on him regularly. Listen, I don't know how much you understand about Alzheimer's . . ." the doctor says.

"Not much," I tell him. "Only what I've seen on TV and I guess today."

"Your grandfather is likely to deteriorate mentally, and eventually he'll be unable to do many basic things. Like dress himself. But most people don't die from this. They usually die from something else, you know, as they get on in age." The doctor looks at Ruth apologetically, but she doesn't seem offended in the least.

"So how does it work with him recognizing us? He seems to be going in and out," I say. "Will it be like this from now on?"

"It's hard to tell. He seems to be having a severe episode today, but tomorrow he may wake up and be much closer to normal. It's a tricky disease. I imagine what happened has happened in some form before?" The doctor looks over at Ruth for corroboration, and she nods her head yes.

"Not like this, though. Not this bad. Nowhere near. I mean, if I had known, I would have . . ." She doesn't finish her sentence. She looks ashamed, complicitous. I want to tell her not to feel bad, that this is not her fault.

I am carrying enough guilt for both of us.

Much later, after I bring Grandpa Jack back to the retirement home, after I arrange for his floor switch, after I hire an additional private twenty-four-hour nurse, after I thank the police officers and the doctors, after I hide in Ruth's bathroom and cry, after I hug her multiple times, after I order a huge bouquet of flowers to surprise her tomorrow morning, after I borrow a T-shirt and shorts and take off my dress, after I sign all of my grandfather's medical forms and consents and find out just how much Blue Cross Blue Shield covers for "constant care," after I say my good-byes to Grandpa Jack, I come home to an empty apartment and my answering machine. *Blink. Blink blink blink blink blink. Blink.*

There are three messages from Ruth, from before my day started. Before, when I was an Alzheimer's virgin. There is also, finally, a message from my father.

"Hey, Em, got your messages. In D.C. at meetings all week. I'm sure you have everything under control. I'm sure he just wandered off. You know how independent Jack is. Call my assistant if you need anything." I am too tired to react to my father's obvious denial, which is as reflexive as it is convenient.

The first message is from sometime last night, what feels like a million years ago now, while I must have been asleep or on my way home from the party. Andrew's voice is drunk and aggressive, but he is short and to the point. His message is one word, two letters, repeated three times.

"No, no, and no."

# Thirteen

The first time Andrew said "I love you," we were sitting in a movie theater, about three quarters of the way through an action film. It was about gangs in L.A., or corrupt cops, or a serial killer, or something like that. I just remember it was graphic and stupid, and Andrew had picked it out. We had agreed on a system that for every action film I went to with him, he would see a romantic comedy with me, which we both thought was a pretty good deal. I remember sitting there before he said it, enjoying the warmth of Andrew's shoulder against mine and feeling sticky and high from too much candy and soda. I was watching the movie but not really watching it, more observing it, I guess. Movie-watching as a spectator sport.

I have no idea why Andrew picked that moment, why he turned to me just after a tangential character lay on the sidewalk with a gunshot wound to the head and chest, brains and heart spilled out onto the sidewalk. A bloody show for the rubberneckers and the audience. But that's the moment he chose, and I guess I'll never know why.

He turned to me and whispered, and at first I couldn't make out his words. I just felt the steam of his breath tickling my ear. So I leaned back again, as if to say *I didn't hear you*, and also because I wanted to feel that tingling again.

And that's when I heard it, on his second try. "I love you."

I didn't know what to do at first. I got trembly and hot and nervous and wet. I thought about saying it back, right then. And I did to myself a few times; practiced it in my head. *I love you too. I love you too. I love you too.* But I couldn't bring myself to say the words out loud, because those are words that you can't unsay. I wanted to take my time with it, to make it a decision and not a reflex, and so I didn't say anything at all. I just took his hand and squeezed it. And, when that didn't feel like enough, I leaned in and gave him a passionate kiss, eerily similar to the one we would see later at the end of the movie, just before the credits rolled.

The second time Andrew said "I love you," we were lying in bed on a Sunday afternoon. It was about two weeks later, one of those humid summer days where it made much more sense to lie naked on top of our sheets with the air conditioner cranked up to high than to go outside. We lay facing the same direction, my back against his chest, and Andrew traced his fingertips up and down along my sides, making invisible doodles on my arms.

He started writing sentences on my body with his

fingers, which I read aloud as he wrote. First cute ones, like *E. smells* and *E. is a sex goddess. A. rocks E.'s world* and *A. is a hunk of man meat.* We were both laughing hard, our shoulders shivering as if it were too cold. And then Andrew abruptly stopped laughing and took his fingers to write again. This time the tips tingled my right shoulder blade.

*I love you.*

I didn't say anything back and didn't read it out, like I had with his other messages. I just took his fingers to my lips and kissed them. I wasn't sure if I had to say anything, really, because he hadn't said the words out loud. But apparently he wanted my echo, because there was no more laughing after that. We lay there for a few minutes more, each of us suddenly unplugged from the other. I thought about saying it aloud then, when it was clear Andrew needed to hear it, but instead, I just practiced again and again in my head, frozen by fear, by doubt, the words never making it to my lips.

Shortly thereafter, Andrew got up, picked his jeans and T-shirt off the floor, and got dressed in the bathroom. He left me there, naked and alone on the bed, and walked out the door and into the heat, without either of us saying another word. Not even an easy one, like good-bye.

We never discussed that Sunday afternoon. When I next saw him, two days later, he looked me in the eyes and said, "Let's just drop it." And I did, because I got to put off doing something that couldn't be undone. So Andrew didn't say "I love you" again for a long time, and the words went unspoken, both of us recognizing that they would not be reintroduced into our lives until I said them myself.

A year later we were in a coffee shop, the kind taking a last stand against Starbucks with its thrift-store chairs, vegan cookies, and over-promising teas with names like Serenity or Inner Peace. I was curled up with a stack of cases, trying to get in a few extra hours of work over the weekend, and Andrew sat with one hand gripping his mug, his nose in *The New York Times*; the two of us a parody of the yuppie couple of the new millennium. We sat silently that way, though there wasn't silence at all. On top of the typical coffee-shop sounds—the whir of an espresso machine, the click of the cash register, the bell above the door—Andrew was making his noises, an occasional snort at something he read in the paper, the jangle of his keys in his pocket, a sniffle since he was getting over a cold, a clearing of his throat. And as we sat there, all I could do was listen to those Andrew-specific noises, the rhythm of his breath, the in-out in-out, its low whistle. Snort. Jangle. Sniffle. Clear.

Hypnotized. I wanted to buy his soundtrack.

*This must be what love is*, I thought. *Not wanting his noises to ever stop*. And I said it to him then, out of the blue, without any premeditation or prompting. Before I could stop myself and think about the consequences.

"I love you."

Andrew just smiled and nodded and went back to reading the paper. He didn't say it back just then, because he knew I wouldn't want it to be a reflex. Later, in bed, he said it again, for his fourth time, and I said it back, my second. And then, only then, were the words made part of our lives, a couple of new beats we added to our other noises in the nighttime.

On Sunday morning, when I wake up to an empty apartment, I realize I need to take back control of my life. I first call Grandpa Jack, and he recognizes my voice. Since I somehow found religion yesterday, I talk to God again. *Thank you, I say. All I need is a little more of this.*

Pre-yesterday, Grandpa Jack and I would have long conversations on the phone, especially on the weekends, when I would often be too lazy, or too busy with work, to make the trek to Riverdale. We would talk about everything and nothing, really, movies we had each seen (never the same ones), the politics of the residents' association (until recently he was the president), restaurants (both of us vicarious eaters), and my father (an endless enigma and an object of fascination for us both).

Today we talk about the weather.

"What's it like out?" he asks.

"I dunno. Fifties probably. Partly cloudy. Wear a jacket."

"Not my winter coat."

"Nope, that would be overkill."

"Umbrella?"

"I don't think so, Grandpa. But you might want to bring your cap."

"Okay."

"Why, where you going?"

"Out. Outside. For a walk."

"Bring a nurse, please."

"Emily."

"Please."

"Cap, check. Jacket, check. Nurse, check, got her stuffed in my pocket. Okay, I'm off."

I hear one of the nurses from last night in the background, the one with the heavy Jamaican accent, telling me not to worry, that she's going with him.

"Emily?"

"Yeah?"

"You okay over there?"

"I'm okay, Gramps."

"Wear a jacket, okay? But not your winter coat."

"I love you," I say, just before we hang up.

"Love you too, kid," he says. "Bundle up."

Next I need to make amends for my big screwup the other night. I know I owe Andrew an apology, but I don't want a do-over conversation. Instead, I just want to erase my ever having humiliated myself, and him, with my aggressive presumptuousness.

E-mail is the best route, I think. Perhaps the easy way

out, but there it is. The virtual equivalent of a note on the pillow after a one-night stand.

> To: Andrew T. Warner, warnerand@yahoo.com
> From: Emily M. Haxby, emilymhaxby@yahoo.com
> Subject: Sorry
>> Hey, A. Want to apologize for the other night.
>> Apparently, seeing the King got me "All Shook Up."
>> Seriously, though, I am sorry. About everything.
>> Good-bye, Andrew.
>> XO,
>> Emily

I don't hit send right away; instead, I let it sit on my computer screen for a while. I come back to it every few minutes and read it as if for the first time. *What do you want to say, Emily?* I wonder if it is too flip, if a joke is inappropriate. Is the *Good-bye, Andrew* too melodramatic? Should I mention his message? No, he was drunk, and I deserved it. I have erased it already in the only way I can.

I have trouble deciding how to sign it too, whether I should say *Love* or *Best* or *Regards*. I settle on *XO*, though I spend a lot of time with *XOXO*, and then *XOXOXO*, and then just with *X* and then just an *O*. I forget which means hug and which means kiss, and I am not sure if I want to give Andrew both or just one. More than one of each seems excessive, desperate even. One without the other, weird. *Love* is too warm, too confident that he will forgive me.

I finally just hit send on my original draft, tap the key hard so I can't take it back. And my e-mail is off somewhere, out of my control, en route. I picture it like a tangible thing, the letters pushing through wires under the city in a neat row, making suction sounds; as it goes from my apartment to Andrew's uptown, it moves faster than the 6 train.

People like to say that the opposite of love is not hate but indifference. There tends to be a whispered reverence around the expression, as if it has magical healing powers. Better to be hated than ignored by that angry ex of yours; better to be hated than ignored, generally.

Otherwise, you may spend your life staring straight down the barrel of the opposite of love.

But I think that's bullshit. Nonsense print copy for a paper towel. A sound bite to needlepoint on a throw pillow. Could indifference really be worse than hate? How depressing to think we could be spending most of our days surrounded by people who feel something worse than hate toward us.

I can't believe it. I won't believe it. Because if I did, I wouldn't be able to pick up the phone right now. Instead, I would have to deflect indifference with indifference and not call my father back.

But, of course, I do. Of course, I pick up the phone and dial his cell for probably the sixth time in twenty-four hours and wait for the click over to voice mail. As I practice my message in my head— something slightly angry, but not overtly confrontational—I hear my dad's clipped voice pick up.

"Hello, this is Kirk Haxby."

"Hi, Dad," I say. "It's Emily." I clarify as if he has more than one child.

"Hey, sweetheart. How are things going over there? You find my father yet?" He chuckles at his joke, as if Grandpa Jack gets lost all the time, as if I were making a fuss over nothing. I feel myself start to lose it, my body letting me down as usual by producing tears when I am just angry.

"Dad?" My voice starts to shake, and I fold myself over. I rest my head on the kitchen table, feeling its coolness against my forehead. I can't decide if I should ask my father to come to the rescue, to make sure I'm doing all the right things by Grandpa Jack, or if I should go it alone and tell my father to go to hell. Leave him to run Connecticut instead of our tiny family.

"Dad, yesterday was really serious."

"Excuse me a second, Emily." I hear my dad cover the phone and talk to someone in the background, something about a fax and six copies. His tone is harsh, and I imagine the people who work for my dad find him intimidating. I wonder if some of them have murderous fantasies about

165

him, like I do about Carl. "I'm back. Sorry about that. I'm all yours. What happened?"

"Grandpa Jack wandered off. Ruth and I found him in a random diner. He was disoriented, Dad." The tears start now, one by one, a slow progression down my face. I don't wipe them away. And I don't let them creep into my voice. "He didn't recognize us."

"Damn it," he says. I hear him brush another aide away, saying in a warning tone "Not now.

"Tell me exactly what happened," he says to me. My father has switched over to political mode, his voice in control and in charge. In a way it is a relief, and I feel my body surrender the responsibility.

"Apparently he has been getting worse for a while. Last time I visited he seemed fine, but I don't know. Ruth tried to tell me, but I didn't listen." I say this like a confession, though I know my father is as guilty as I am. He hasn't been to Riverdale in months.

I tell my father everything in detail—Ruth and I looking for hours, my grandfather not recognizing us, the doctors saying he will only get worse; I leave out that Grandpa Jack mistook me for my mother.

"Okay. Well then, we are going to have to get him nurses, full-time care, move him to that other wing. We need to check into his insurance. Let me get my assistant on the line. She can help." As usual, detail before emotion.

"It's all done. You didn't call me back yesterday, so I did

it myself." That is my only dig, a small one, but I can tell by the pause that follows, he notices. It might be cruel of me, but I hope he feels the impact of his absence.

I give my father the rundown. The Blue Cross Blue Shield, the floor switch, the PCP's telephone number. I, too, stay with the details. Like my father, I find them soothing, one of the few ways in which we are alike.

"He has a neurologist appointment next Thursday. I'm hoping to go, but I may get stuck at work," I say.

"I'll go," my father says, surprising me. "Of course I'll go." I hear some more noises in the background, as my father tells his assistant to rearrange his schedule. He is coming to New York.

I lift my head up and rest my neck on the back of my chair. I close my eyes and don't say anything for a few seconds. My tears leak horizontally now, bleeding into my hair.

"Emily?" he says. "You still there?"

"I'm here, Dad."

"Emily, I'm sorry. I'll be there soon."

"I know, Dad."

"I'm glad you were there yesterday. I . . . I didn't know."

"I know, Dad." *Better late than never*, I think. A cliché for a belated birthday card, but I hold on to it nonetheless.

"I love you, you know."

"I know, Dad," I say, which is, of course, a lie. What I want to say is *I know, Dad. I know you don't hate me.*

# Fourteen

I do not say good morning to Marge when I pass her at the security turnstile on my way into the office. For the first time in my five years at the firm, I don't say "Hello," or "Good morning," or "How are you," or even nod. *Fuck you, Marge*, I think instead. *Fuck. You.* I direct all of my rage at her, by not even glancing in her direction, by not acknowledging her existence, revenge for every time she has ignored me. Today, Marge is everything that is wrong with my life, and I feel all of it at once, a rush of anger aimed at an impenetrable target. I hate Marge for a million reasons, but mostly because I know she won't notice my slight. And so my hate just slides to the floor like a puddle at my feet, a fucking yellow puddle that I step in as I walk by. *Fuck you, Marge*.

As I get into the elevator, an ugly man in a beautiful suit runs to catch the door. Carl. I immediately press the close button, but Carl is too fast for me. He sticks his hands between the doors as they slide shut, and when they reopen, he shuffles into the glass box. He flashes a triumphant smile, and it is clear to me that, as with everything else he does, he sees this as a victory. *Fuck you, Carl*, I think, as he takes up space in my elevator. *Fuck. You.* But I don't say that, and when Carl says, "Good morning," I don't have the luxury of ignoring him. He is still, dick notwithstanding, my boss.

"Morning, Carl." I leave off the "good" intentionally, my tiny act of rebellion. I don't want him to have a good morning, and in fact, I'm not so sure he even deserves to have a morning at all. I know plenty of people who deserve it more.

"Emily, I'm glad I ran into you. We got some boxes in on the Synergon matter, and I need you to do the review."

"Some boxes?" I keep my voice calm, though I already know what's to come. I can tell by his mock casual tone that he is about to drop a shitload of work into my lap. A document review, no less. Which means a shitload of the most tedious work you can imagine, work that can drive you to drink or to masturbate in the bathroom, work that is normally done by someone far more junior than me. Work for someone who has yet to pay their dues. I have paid my dues. For five fucking years. *Fuck you, Carl.*

"Yeah," he says, prolonging the agony on purpose. "Six hundred and seventy-eight boxes, to be exact. And they need to be reviewed by next Monday."

"Impossible," I say. "We need to bring in some juniors, then. There is no way I can look at all of that stuff by next Monday. Six hundred and seventy-eight boxes?" I cross my arms in defiance, which has the unintended effect of drawing Carl's attention to my breasts.

"Nope. Emily, I want you to do this. You know this case better than anyone else. I don't want a stupid junior associate screwing this up. I trust you." I know Carl is attempting to spin this assignment as a compliment, and although it may have worked on me a couple of months ago, today I'm not biting. I refuse to spend twenty hours a day for the next week in a conference room, doing nothing but reading page after page for Synergon.

"No way, Carl. I can't do it," I say, proud of myself for standing up to him. *Maybe I can change*, I think. *Maybe I can finally be someone who gets the right words out.*

"Yes, you can do it." Carl looks me up and down, seemingly evaluating my worth, evaluating whether he wants to be sharing this elevator with me after all.

"And what's more, Emily," he says, as he steps off at his floor, "you will." His timing is perfect. The doors close behind him, like a period at the end of his sentence. And when I respond, I am left talking only to myself, my image reflected in the mirrored doors, half of me on each.

"Fuck you, Carl," I say, out loud this time, anger forcing me to enunciate each and every sound, my mouth enjoying the sharpness of the letters. But what I really mean to say, again, is not what comes out. What I really want to say is *Fuck you, Emily. Fuck. You.*

When I walk into my office, the first thing I do is check if Andrew has emailed me back. He hasn't. I tell myself that he will, that eventually words from him will be on my screen. At this point, I don't think so much about what he might say. I only worry a response may never come.

"Where were you Friday night?" Mason says, as he walks into my office without knocking. He sits down in my guest chair, crosses his legs, and peeks at me through sleepy eyes.

"You look like crap, darlin'," he says, before I have a chance to answer his question. His voice is tender, and I can tell he does not mean it unkindly.

"Fuck you, Mason," I say, but without any force behind the words. I smile at him to show that I'm kidding. I make a mental note to work on improving my language, because you never know when there might be children around. That's just what I need to add to my conscience these days. *Corrupting a minor.*

"Seriously, you okay?" Mason asks, though his tone sounds more curious than concerned.

"Hanging in there. Rough weekend."

"Wanna talk about it?" Mason leans forward in his chair, as if to say *You can talk to me*, but then he sits back again, as if to say *Or not*.

"No, not really. Sorry, I had to leave the party early. I would have liked to hang out."

"You missed my fantastic costume," he says, as my phone rings. The caller ID tells me that it's Carl. I ignore it and pull some tape from the dispenser and start wrapping it around my finger. I make a transparent Band-Aid.

"Really? What were you?"

"I was a prom king." *A prom king?* I stop fidgeting for a moment and take a long look at Mason. He has always been handsome, of course, but today I notice for the first time his long eyelashes and how they curl upward at the end, like the special effects in a mascara commercial. Perhaps Mason and I were meant to be, like the Burger King and the Dairy Queen. Maybe he has been in front of me all along.

"Seriously?" I visualize Mason's latest girlfriend, Laurel, and try to remember if, the one time I met her, they looked happy together.

"Nah, I'm kidding. Heard your costume was great, Em." Maybe not. I banish the thought of Mason and me having sex wearing matching tiaras.

"I would have liked to have gotten a good look at your purple dress, though," he says, and winks at me. My phone rings again. Carl, a second time.

"Do you need to get that?"

"No, it's Carl. Maybe if I ignore him, he'll go away. What were you really, Mace?"

"Ah, nothing special. I took the easy way out. I wore my

172

old Texas gear. The cowboy hat, the cowboy boots, my too-tight-for-New-York Levis. I looked hot."

"I'm sure you did, darlin'." I give him my best Southern drawl.

"You have no idea, sugarplum." He winks at me again, and I laugh, because only Mason can pull off winking at a girl twice within five minutes. "So, I saw Andrew and Carisse chatting up a storm at the party. They seem to have become fast friends."

"Yeah? I didn't notice."

"Really? Because I thought that's why you rushed out."

"I didn't rush out." He gives me a look that says *Come on, I saw you, I saw you and your purple dress*. "All right, I rushed out. But not because of that. To be honest, I don't really want to talk about it."

"Fair enough. But just tell me this, are you okay, Emily? I'm starting to get a little worried. You're like a walking zombie these days."

"I know. I'm fine, though."

"Promise?"

"Promise."

"You swear on your mother's life?" One question is all it takes for me to realize that Mason doesn't know me very well.

"I swear," I say, and he leaves my office, satisfied.

Ignoring Carl does not make him go away. He leaves me three messages and sends me six e-mails over the next half hour. I need to leave my office to take some time to consider my next move. I refuse to review Carl's six hundred seventy-eight boxes. I can't do it. I won't do it. I think about getting back onto the elevator, imagine pressing the button for the ground floor and walking out of this job and into the anonymity of Park Avenue. Letting my body feel the fall weather, its crispness a welcome slap in the face. Maybe I don't even have to clean out my desk. I can leave the old me and its stuff behind. The Synergon files. The picture on my desk. Start over. Maybe I can take on a new name, an alias, one with transforming powers. A better, stronger, articulate me. *Just keep walking*, I will tell myself once I hit the revolving doors. *Just keep walking*.

But I don't have the courage to walk away like that, and I actually quite like my name, to tell you the truth. Instead, I take a left out of my office and go straight to the ladies' room, keeping my head down as I walk. Once inside, I feel an immediate sense of relief, even before I empty my bladder. I love the APT restroom, with its black marble countertops and platinum faucets that reach up and over in an elaborate arch. The sink basins come out of the walls in defiance of gravity. And the best part of all, the stalls are huge, larger than the dressing rooms at Bloomingdale's. It is the kind of place, barring the attack of unpleasant smells from a coworker, where a girl can go and get away for a moment. I hide in here often, in the second stall from the right, and watch the parade of indistinct black high heels move under the door.

I sit on the toilet and squeeze my eyes shut. Maybe if I can't see anything, I will be able to block out the images that keep flashing in my head. Andrew's eyebrows crunched together in confusion when I broke up with him and then spread out again in a tight straight line at the party. Carl's plaid boxers in the hotel room. Carisse's triumphant smile. Grandpa Jack looking right through me. Grandpa Jack seeing my mother instead.

I feel my body begin to relax, and I let my head roll to the side. I conjure up the *Sounds of the Ocean* CD I sometimes play late at night, and I find it easy to recreate, because, after all, I am in the ladies' room. I listen to waves crashing and receding away, picture hot sand between my toes. My mind wanders away, and I drift off.

I'm not sure how long I sit like that in the stall, but based on the stiffness of my shoulders and the drool on my face, it's been a while. I wake up to the sound of my secretary calling my name and knocking loudly on the door.

"Emily, are you in there? Are you okay? Emily?" she asks.

"I'm fine. I'm fine. I'll be out in a second," I say, and prepare myself to leave the safe confines of the stall. *You can do this.*

"Carl is looking for you. He's been calling every five minutes, and he swung by your office a couple of times. Not for nothing, but you should probably call him back."

"The man is out of control." I pull myself together and try to make it look like I wasn't just sleeping in the bathroom. I straighten out my pantsuit, pray that I don't have marks on my forehead from resting it against the metal toilet-paper holder, and walk out of my stall.

As if on cue, I hear myself being paged over the loudspeaker.

"Emily Haxby. Emily Haxby. Please dial extension 670. Please dial extension 670. Emily Haxby, please dial extension 670." Carl's extension.

"He is going to be the death of me," I say to Karen. Her eyes are sympathetic, and she reaches over and touches my head. A maternal gesture, and I feel a rush of love for her and lean into her hands. At least I have Karen. *At least my secretary loves me.*

"Honey, you have a little piece of toilet paper in your hair."

I stomp down the two flights of stairs to Carl's office. The clacking of my shoes against the cement creates a loud drumbeat. *I can't even go to the bathroom in peace. How dare you, Carl?*

I don't knock when I enter Carl's office. I just push the door open and walk in, like I own the place. I am livid. *Fuck you, Carl. Fuck. You.* I sit down in his guest chair, and he looks up at me, surprised at my impolite entrance.

"You rang, you stopped by, you paged. What can I do for

you?" The sarcasm drips from my words. I cannot force myself to be civil. I take a couple of breaths, hoping it will take the edge off, but the oxygen only inflames me further. I want to hurl my legal pad at Carl's head. I want to punch him. I want to poke him in the eyes. I want to knee him in the nuts.

I hate Carl. More than Marge, more than Carisse, more than my father. I fucking hate him.

"Um, well. I wanted to discuss the boxes that need to be reviewed. A. Sap," Carl says calmly. His eyes are curious, and I can tell he is not used to fielding anger from associates. Things are usually the other way around. The way he says "A. Sap," like they are two different words, pisses me off. *A.S.A.P.* I want to scream at him. *The term is A.S.A.P., acronym for "as soon as possible," you dipshit. Not A. Sap.*

"No." I don't meet his eyes, because I am worried I will lose control if I do.

"Excuse me?"

"No, I am not reviewing those boxes. I am a fifth-year associate. That is first-year work, and if you want it to get done, I suggest you find a couple of juniors to do it." I say it quickly, rushing the words into one another. But the anger fuels me on. *I will not do it. Repeat after me, Emily, I will not do it.*

"I am sorry. That is not a decision for you to make. You will do it because I asked you to." *Does that mean I should have let you eat me out because you asked me to?* I almost, almost say these words out loud but realize I can't. I have walked pretty close to the ledge, but that would be jumping off.

"Carl, I'm not doing it. You can fire me if you want to, but we both know that wouldn't be very wise on your part. Given what happened in Arkansas." The threat comes out before I've even formulated the thought, and I can't believe that I had the nerve to actually say it. Carl's shock, too, is palpable, and he pauses to regain his composure. *What have I done?*

"Okay. I get it. I'll find someone else to review the boxes. But I will not accept this kind of behavior in the future from you. Tread carefully, Haxby. Tread carefully. Consider this your one get-out-of-jail-free card." For a moment I am impressed by Carl, his ability to give a little but to still cede back total control. To gently remind me that, at the end of the day, he has all of the power.

"You know what? I quit." And the words are out again, without my knowing it. Without planning. Without even a moment's consideration of the consequences. *So this will be the day I quit*, I think to myself. *I will remember this day. It will be distinct from all the others, yesterday and tomorrow, because this is the day I walked out.*

Carl looks calm, serene even, and does not seem bothered in the least that I have resigned.

"Come on. I will not accept that. You're not quitting.

You're a valued member of the APT team. You have repeatedly shown your *dedication* to this firm. And just because you're angry right now is not a reason to throw away your career here. So this is what is going to happen." Carl leans forward, and he almost looks kind, like somebody's father.

"You are going to go back to your office and think this through. I will not accept your resignation. In fact, I will pretend like you haven't quit at all. We will get some other associates to do the review, and you will take some time to regroup. Okay? Go on vacation or something."

And there it is, the opportunity to take it all back, to undo this whole thing. *How often in life do you get the chance to rewind like that? He is throwing out a lifeline. Emily, take it. You can unquit.*

"Carl, I'm serious, I quit." I say the words again, and I can tell I mean them. Even though my conscious thoughts tell me to undo what I have done, someone else is now running the show. The thought of having to work at APT for even just one more second is overwhelming. *I am done*, I realize. *I am done here.*

"I already told you. I will not accept your resignation. Now, please get out of my office," he says, and shuffles around some papers on his desk. "Some of us have work to do."

I leave Carl's office, and on the walk back to mine, I think about my options. In the eyes of APT, I still have not quit.

I can still come to work tomorrow and collect my paycheck on Friday. I still have health insurance. This can be just another little secret between Carl and me, one that lives in my bottom drawer with my *Kiss My Arkans-ASS* shorts. But I also know I cannot turn back now. I do not want to grow up to be Carl MacKinnon or any of the other partners, even the ones I actually admire. This is not the life I want. I don't know what I do want, but I know enough now to say this is not it. It is time to walk away.

When I reach my office, I call the managing partner of APT. If Carl won't listen, I will get someone else to take my resignation. Not surprisingly, I get Doug Barton's voice mail, and I leave him a message saying that I need to speak with him urgently. I also leave a message for the head of the litigation department, James Slicer. I don't tell either Doug or James that I am quitting, because for reputational reasons this is something better not said on a machine.

"I quit," I tell Kate in person at her office a few minutes later.

"What?"

"I quit. Well, actually, I'm quitting. Carl refused to accept my resignation, so I have left messages for Doug and James. I'm quitting. Today."

"Get in here," she says, and she leads me to her guest chair. Kate closes her door and sits across from me, behind her large wooden desk. She looks like a real lawyer, sitting there among neat stacks of paper and leather-bound treatises and one of those little green lamps.

"Are you okay? You seem a bit ... a bit ... frazzled. Or—" She pauses, deciding whether she wants to say what she actually thinks. "Well, you seem a bit hysterical."

"I'm fine. I'm quitting. So I'm a bit jumpy, yes, but please don't try to talk me out of it."

"Why?"

"Why am I quitting or why don't I want you to talk me out of it?"

"Why are you quitting?"

"I'm done here, Kate. I hate it. Everything about this place. Except, of course, for you and Mason. But I hate everything else. I'm done. I feel like I am not only not making the world a better place, I am making it worse. That's not why I went to law school." I take a deep breath and then I keep going.

"And Carl wanted me to review six hundred and seventy-eight boxes for Synergon, and I told him I wouldn't do it. I threatened him, because he hit on me in Arkansas. So he said I didn't have to review the boxes. But that's not the point, is it, Kate?" I start to cry now, lines of tears rolling swiftly down my cheeks. I wipe them away with my sleeve, and Kate hands me a tissue and some hand sanitizer.

I know she wants to ask me questions about what happened with Carl, but I am not done. The words keep tumbling out. *Today is not only the day I quit*, I think, *today is the day I got verbal diarrhea.* I wonder if I will ever be able to control my mouth again.

"And I just feel horrible. Grandpa Jack has Alzheimer's. I found out this weekend. He got lost, and it was just awful. And I miss Andrew. Though Jess was probably right. I am not ready for an Andrew. But it still sucks. And if he ends up with Carisse, I deserve it. I think he hates me now, and that's probably the worst feeling of all." Kate attempts to break into my monologue, probably to say something like *Andrew doesn't hate you,* but I don't let her get a word in.

"You know what else? Want to hear the kicker? I fell asleep in the women's bathroom today. In my favorite stall. Kate, I got toilet paper in my hair."

Somehow this breaks the moment, and Kate and I start laughing, gut-gripping laughter, until tears are falling down her face too. She dabs at her eyes furiously with a tissue to keep her mascara from running, but she's too late. For the first time, I see what Kate looks like underneath the perfect make-up. She looks freer somehow.

I spend the next hour in the safety of her office and tell her exactly what happened with Grandpa Jack. I give her all of the explicit details of sharing a hotel room with Carl too, and she blanches at the thought.

"I think I would have kicked him in the balls," Kate says.

Eventually we move on to her wedding plans, and, surprisingly, I enjoy talking about the details. Her color scheme. The flowers. The band. The invitations. I find comfort in picturing Kate's to-do list, with items carefully checked off once she is sure they are exactly right for her and Daniel. I can see she views the wedding as a jumping-off point. If that day goes well, so should the rest that follow.

I imagine how her wedding could have been for me had the last few months been different. It would have been a jumping-off point for me too. Andrew would have stood behind Daniel at the altar, looking handsome in his tuxedo, the perfect best man. I would be across from him, in formation with Kate's bridesmaids, a line of pale pink. Andrew would have caught my eye and smiled at me, smiled one of those knowing smiles, a smile that said something like *This will be us soon*. And if I was someone different, someone *ready*, I would have smiled back, a smile that said something like *I love you too*.

And then I think about how it will likely go now that I have ruined everything. Andrew and I will both look steadily ahead and make sure not to catch each other's gaze. He will bring Carisse as a date and look over at her in the audience. And when they exchange those smiles, I'll stand mutely on the sidelines, like in a bad dream, when you scream and it doesn't make a sound.

Although my decision to quit today seems final, the powers that be keep me from following through. Neither the managing partner nor the litigation-department head returns my calls; apparently, any emergency I may have cannot be important enough to stop billing for a few minutes. I consider going to the receptionist and bribing her to use the firm's loudspeaker. I picture myself, the microphone in hand, announcing my resignation to all of APT via a page.

*Ladies and gentlemen*, I would say, and everyone in the office would stop what they were doing and listen.

*This is Emily Haxby*, I would say. *I quit, you fuckers.*

Or perhaps I could go simpler, subtler, more polite. Do it the way I imagined this morning. Walk out the front door and never come back. Leave behind APT, leave behind Emily Haxby.

As I walk out for the day, I pass the main conference room near the elevators. I glance through the door, and I see that it's filled with boxes. Six hundred seventy-eight boxes, to be exact. The floor-to-ceiling view down Park Avenue is blocked out by the towers of cardboard.

At the table, Carisse is bent over a document, reading each word carefully. After a few seconds she puts it down and reaches for the next sheet in a stack about two feet high. I knock on the window and wave as I walk by. I smile when I see that she is only on box number one.

# Fifteen

My big moment comes at eleven-thirty on Wednesday morning, when I finally get summoned into Doug Barton's office. As managing partner of the firm, he gets the corner office, a boss's office, and its two walls made of windows. The double view gives the impression that we are suspended above New York City, dangling over Midtown, and unrooted from solid ground. Although my office is on the same floor as Doug's, it feels higher up here. I get dizzy before I even sit down.

"So, Emily, what's up?" Doug asks, after we shake hands and I steady myself in his guest chair. His voice is friendly and casual, as if we are longtime friends, although until today I was unsure if he even knew my name.

"Well, I wanted to talk to you about something important." And then, in the spirit of his relaxed tone, I add, "Doug."

His desk is completely clear of all paper and books and

legal pads. Since it's apparent he does not busy himself with actual work, I wonder what he does in here all day. Maybe I should wash my hands after the meeting is over. Just in case.

I glance out the window and am startled to see a man on the outside looking in at me. He smiles, like we, too, are long-lost friends, and then takes out a squeegee and moves it up and down, rhythmically cleaning the transparent glass. He swings fifty stories above-ground to make sure our views remain unsmudged.

"Okay." Doug coughs, his polite way of saying *Get to the point.* He looks like he plays a lawyer on TV, with his silver-streaked hair and manicured cuticles and commanding glare.

"I'm here to give you my resignation. Slightly less than standard notice, but I couldn't reach you on Monday. My last day will be next Friday."

"I'm sorry to hear that. I've always viewed you as a valued member of the APT team. You have shown continual *dedication* to the firm." He clears his throat. I get the impression that compliments do not come naturally to him, that they are an inconvenience that comes with the office. He adjusts his cuffs under his suit jacket, and I see that they are monogrammed, like Carl's. The grown-up version of a camp label.

"Thanks, Doug." I am having fun using his name. I am half-tempted to push this buddy-buddy thing as far as I can and try to high-five him.

"May I ask where you are going?" He grabs a pad from the drawer to jot my answer down. He rests his pen on its tip, expectant.

"Actually, I don't know yet. I'm going to take a little time off to clear my head, but I'll have to start looking for a new position relatively soon. For financial reasons." He nods his head at this, as if he can relate. Though based on the Rolex on his wrist, I would imagine financial concerns don't come up much for him.

"That's very unorthodox. Usually our associates leave for another job. Perhaps go in-house at a company. Very rarely do we have associates leaving to do . . . to do . . ." He pauses and clears his throat again. "Nothing."

He utters it like it's a dirty word, like I said I was quitting to rape small children.

"Yeah, the decision was sort of sudden. But I need some time off. I haven't taken more than a handful of days since I started with the firm five years ago. I don't think I have taken a single real vacation." His face registers the implications of this. When associates leave, the firm is required to pay out for vacation days that haven't been used. This is the only reason I am able to quit without having another position. APT owes me more than three months' salary.

"We always like to learn from departing associates," he says. "So it would be great if you could discuss with me some of your reasons for moving on." He surprises me with his next question. Until now, I thought he was following a script.

"I see you have been working a lot with Carl MacKinnon lately. How has that experience been?"

His question is subtle enough that I am given the option to either take the bait or to ignore it. I pretend to be fascinated by the view to buy a few moments to consider my answer. I had assumed the firm had adopted a "don't ask, don't tell" policy in regard to sexual harassment, so I am thrown off guard by his prompting.

I am unsure how Doug will react if I tell him the truth about Carl. I find that men like him, professional men in their late fifties or early sixties, often dismiss what I have to say, as if whatever comes out of my mouth can't be all that important. I think they don't know how to relate to a woman who is too young to flirt with, too old to be treated as a child, and too female to mentor. Or maybe many of them have daughters around my age whom they have grown accustomed to tuning out. I check the bookshelf behind him for family photographs, but there are none.

"Working for Carl is challenging." I pause again. "And I do think he has trouble creating a healthy working environment for women." I am not sure if I want to say more, to be responsible for telling on Carl; but at the same time, I hate the idea of him preying on the new class of associates—the women who are fresh out of law school, the ones who are still figuring out how to survive at APT. I want to preserve their naïveté, their optimism, just a little while longer.

"Let me put it this way. I have heard from others, and have seen from personal experience, that he can be inappropriate." I realize this is an incredible understatement, that Carl's antics go way beyond inappropriate, but I can tell from the look on Doug's face that I don't need to elaborate. He is listening to me, and he gets it. He does not have to know the specifics about messing with hotel reservations and the offering of cunnilingus. It's still sexual harassment even when they offer to do all the hard work.

"Do you intend—" Doug stops, and I realize he likes to deliver his questions like a cross-examination, intentionally timing his beats for maximum impact. "To sue?"

"I haven't really thought about it. It's not a fight I particularly feel like having, though I've got to tell you, I have a great case." This is true. Carl not only hit on me but took away the summary judgment motion right after I said no. I am surprised he would be so careless; it's so clearly a retaliatory strike.

"I wouldn't want to see the firm destroyed because of one incredibly irresponsible partner," I say, and uncross my legs so that my feet are planted firmly on the ground. I take a deep breath before I continue. "But I do think it's time you cleaned house. If you don't, I make no promises."

Doug jots down a note, and I see that he is taking my threat seriously. He knows that there must be many more women like me out there and that by keeping Carl around he is opening up the firm to millions of dollars in liability. I don't know whether he thinks my suing is a real possibility, but I am not sure if that's important. If I don't, it's only a matter of time until someone else does.

"Thank you. I appreciate your candor," he says.

"No problem." I feel like I have taken back some control of the situation. In less than two weeks I will never have to see Carl again.

"I wish you the best of luck with your future endeavors." He stands up and shakes my hand good-bye, indicating that our conversation is over.

"Thanks." I decide to go for one last shot. "Oh, and I assume I will be receiving a bonus check at the end of the year, considering I already surpassed my billable-hours target."

"Absolutely. I will see to it myself." He smiles and looks proud of my having asked. I wonder if he now wants to give me a high-five. "Please keep in touch."

"Thanks." And just for fun, and because I can, I add, again, "Doug."

I leave his office and close the door behind me. I wait until I am halfway down the hall, well out of view, before I do my first victory dance at APT. A mean, mean Running Man.

# Sixteen

To: Emily M. Haxby, emilymhaxby@yahoo.com
From: Ruth Wasserstein, yourhonor24@yahoo.com
Subject: Thank you!
Dear Emily,

   I am now on e-mail! (I want to put a smiley face here. My granddaughter taught me how, but now I forget. So please insert smile here.) I know I am about a decade behind on this stuff, but I got a new laptop for my birthday. It is tiny, tiny, tiny. I don't know how such a little machine can do so much.

   First of all, I wanted to thank you so much for the flowers!!!! They were beautiful, and my apartment still smells lovely. I hope you don't mind, but I clipped one of the roses and brought it to Jack's new room. I know you've been checking in with the nurses but thought you would want to know from me that he seems to be doing a bit better. He has

been having more good moments than we saw last
weekend, and we even played a few rounds of
poker!!! (Insert smiley face again.) Don't tell him I
told you, but I kicked his you-know-what.

Anyhow, I am excited to be part of the Internet
superhighway conductor. My penmanship was never
any good, so I feel like this finally levels the
playing field. And it moves so fast. I am going
to type this and then you are going to get it. It's
amazing!

I look forward to seeing you soon.

Your friend,

Ruth Wasserstein


To: Ruth Wasserstein, yourhonor24@yahoo.com
From: Emily M. Haxby, emilymhaxby@yahoo.com
Subject: Re: Thank you!

Ruth! Welcome to e-mail!!! I am glad you enjoyed
the flowers.

I have big news for you: I quit my job! ☺

What do you think? Feel free to lie and tell me this
is the best decision I have ever made. By the way,
love your e-mail address. Do you think I should
change mine to unemployed@yahoo.com?

To: Emily M. Haxby, <ins>emilymhaxby@yahoo.com</ins>
From: Ruth Wasserstein, <ins>yourhonor24@yahoo.com</ins>
Subject: Re: Re: Thank you!

I think you should change it to
<ins>funemployed@yahoo.com</ins>.

Congratulations! Seriously, I am very proud of you.

Now that you are going to have a lot of free time, do you have any interest in joining my new book club? Hope you don't mind, but you will be the only one under seventy-five.


To: Ruth Wasserstein, <ins>yourhonor24@yahoo.com</ins>
From: Emily M. Haxby, <ins>emilymhaxby@yahoo.com</ins>
Subject: Re: Re: Re: Thank you!

I am honored that you thought of me. I would love to join. What are we reading?


To: Emily M. Haxby, <ins>emilymhaxby@yahoo.com</ins>
From: Ruth Wasserstein, <ins>yourhonor24@yahoo.com</ins>
Subject: Re: Re: Re: Re: Thank you!

A biography of Margaret Thatcher.

Just kidding.

We are reading *Bridget Jones's Diary*. We all saw the movie last week and fell in love with Colin Firth. There is just something about barristers, isn't there? I should have retired to London.

To: Jess S. Stanton, jesssstanton@yahoo.com
From: Emily M. Haxby, emilymhaxby@yahoo.com
Subject: Still no word
   Haven't heard anything from Andrew, and it's been a few days. What do you think that means?

To: Emily M. Haxby, emilymhaxby@yahoo.com
From: Jess S. Stanton, jesssstanton@yahoo.com
Subject: Re: Still no word
   It means he hates you. (Just kidding.)
   It means he loves you. (Just kidding.)
   I have no idea what it means.
   Maybe it means he's busy.

To: Ruth Wasserstein, yourhonor24@yahoo.com
From: Emily M. Haxby, emilymhaxby@yahoo.com
Subject: Re: Re: Re: Re: Re: Thank you!
   Ruth, I sent Andrew an email a few days ago and still haven't heard from him. What does that mean?

To: Emily M. Haxby, emilymhaxby@yahoo.com
From: Ruth Wasserstein, yourhonor24@yahoo.com
Subject: Re: Re: Re: Re: Re: Re: Thank you!
   It means he still loves you, dear. That's what you want to hear, right?

# Seventeen

My answering-machine light is blinking. *Blink. Blink. Blink. Andrew.* I walk across the apartment and pretend to be nonchalant—drop my keys, kick off my shoes, put down my bag—but then I find myself right back in front of the machine. Moth to light.

Embarrassing, this anticipation to hit the button, embarrassing that I am circling around, hawkish, hungry. It's so cliché to get excited by a silly blink.

No, not quite ready to press play yet. Must shower first. Must clear my head. As I strip off my clothes and turn on the water, though, the anticipation overwhelms me.

I run back. I cover my eyes. I press play.

Of course, it's not Andrew. In fact, it's *better* that it's not Andrew.

"Hey, Em. Can you take Jack to that doctor's appointment? If not, I'll arrange for a car service and a nurse to take him. Sorry I got tied up. I know I promised, but you know how it is. Busy running Connecticut. Please call me back to confirm. Thanks. I owe you one."

If I had the opportunity to erase three little words from the universe, ban them from ever being strung together again, I would, without a doubt, pick "busy running Connecticut." Not "I love you," not even "no offense but," though everyone knows that's a thinly disguised insult. Instead, I would pick "busy running Connecticut," because although my dad uses these words as an excuse, they are nothing more than a choice. Apparently I can't compete with the good people of the Constitution State. This is nothing new; my dad missed my thirteenth birthday party, the first birthday party to which I invited boys and the last one my mom ever threw for me, because he was too busy with important legislation changing the official fossil of Connecticut to *Eubrontes giganteus*.

I listen to my dad's message four more times. The repetition helps to reduce its sting. I guess it doesn't matter, really, whether he comes with me or not. I was planning on taking Grandpa Jack to his appointment anyway. *This is probably a good thing*, I tell myself. *He would have just gotten in the way. So what if he let you down a little bit. Grow up, Emily. Be a grown-up.*

I attempt to reason with the sadness that seeps over me. A mute, numbing sadness that deadens your fingertips. The sort that's the hardest to fight because it feels very much like nothing. It feels like reasoning with a refrigerator.

I throw a frozen meal into the microwave and eat from the plastic tray compartments, as if I am on an airplane. Though I usually ignore the vegetables on the far right side of the container, I force myself to eat them today, because this is what adults do. We eat green beans. I lie on the couch and numb myself with a marathon of reality television. Tonight I make sure to watch only those shows in which someone gets eliminated. I find it soothing to see people care so much that they have lost, to watch the mistaken belief that their world only stretches as far as the cameras can reach.

"I can take him," I tell my father over the phone a few hours later.

"Thanks, kid. I'm sorry about this," he says, and rustles some papers in the background. "Things are crazy here with budget stuff."

I hear more crinkling sounds, and I recognize the trick; it gives the impression that you are so busy that you can't stop working for even a quick phone conversation. I use it all the time on partners at APT.

"No problem. I was planning on going anyway." I throw on my Yale Law School sweatshirt, but wearing it makes me feel younger and studenty, so I take it off again and put on a cardigan instead.

"Will work give you a hard time for sneaking out early? I don't want you to get in trouble," he says.

"It shouldn't be a problem." My father doesn't need to know that I quit; quitting will be viewed as nothing less than failure.

"Well, thanks, Em, I owe you one." *Owe me one what?* I want to ask. *Owe me one parenting occasion? Next time I find myself unemployed and lonely and devastated about Grandpa Jack, I'll remember to cash in.*

"By the way, we need to talk about Thanksgiving," he says. My stomach twists. No, I feel like my father just stuck his fist down my throat and squeezed my bowels. I had conveniently forgotten about Thanksgiving and the exhausting marathon to the other side of January.

"Okay."

"Well, how about we go to my club in Connecticut? The food will be good, and you'll see some people from the neighborhood that you haven't seen in years. It will be fun." He tries to sound enthusiastic, but it rings false. My father knows I am not a big fan of his "club." It's the kind of place in which Groucho Marx and Woody Allen would have been happy to claim membership, because, of course, they couldn't. Well, not until very, very recently, and even now they might feel a bit "ethnic."

"What about Grandpa Jack?" I ask. "We can't let him spend Thanksgiving alone." The rustling of papers in the background stops, and my father clears his throat.

"Of course. You didn't let me finish. You take the train out here and we'll lunch at the club; then I'll drive us back to Riverdale and we can spend the evening with my dad. I'll have my assistant arrange to get a small dinner catered there for the three of us. What do you say?"

"Sounds fine."

"And, of course, Andrew is welcome to join us. I haven't seen him in ages."

"He can't. He's going home for Thanksgiving." I add another lie onto the pile.

"Too bad. I would have liked to talk to him about the new health-care plan we're kicking around."

"Yeah, well, some other time. Listen, I've got loads of work to do, big motion due in a couple of weeks, so I gotta go, Dad."

"Me too, sweetheart. Bye."

And my dad and I both hang up to the sounds of the other rustling papers.

# Eighteen

Today is my last day of work. My desk has been emptied. Its guts upended and labeled and sent off to the records center. The walls are now bare, except for a few protruding nails where my degrees once hung. My pictures and mugs and books are all packed neatly into two cardboard boxes. Seems weird that I have so little to take with me after five years that the sum total of my experience here can be carried home on the subway. There should be more somehow.

I wonder if I am carrying those five years on my body. The lines that are etched into my forehead and sprout from the corners of my mouth. Wrists that now get sore when it rains. A few extra pounds, some of which sits in packets under my eyes. Perhaps, for a while at least, it will be the mirror that triggers memories of my time at APT.

Before I head downstairs, I check my e-mail again for the tenth time today and about the hundredth time this week.

The screen tells me I have new mail, and I take a deep breath before opening my inbox. *Please don't be spam.* I cross my fingers; I click.

To: Emily M. Haxby, emilymhaxby@yahoo.com
From: Andrew T. Warner, warnerand@yahoo.com
Subject: Re: Sorry
   Hey, E. I am so sorry to hear about Grandpa Jack. (Kate told Daniel . . .) If there is anything I can do, please let me know. He has been like a grandfather to me these past two years, so if how I am feeling is any indication, you must be hurting right now.
   As for the party and particularly for my voice-mail message, I'm sorry too. Neither of us is very good at saying what we really want to say, I guess. I wish I knew what I wanted to say. That would make everything easier. Wouldn't it? But I don't. Have been trying to figure it out for the past two weeks, or maybe since Labor Day, and have come up dry. Instead, I think it is probably time I just said good-bye.
   Peace,
   A

At first, just the fact that Andrew took the time to write an e-mail back is enough to bring waves of relief. *He doesn't hate me.* It feels almost intimate seeing his words on my screen. Words meant only for me. I like being the *E* to his *A*. I picture him sitting at his black Ikea desk, a relic from college that has seen him through final exams, the MCATs, and now a farewell e-mail to me; he carefully crafts each sentence and considers its implications. His sign-off is perfect, really, though I would have preferred an *XO* or even a *love*. I know I haven't earned either. But Andrew has, and I wish I could rewrite my original e-mail and resign it *Love always, Emily*. I am not sure why I think this would have made any difference, but to me it matters.

I read through the e-mail again and again and end up memorizing it by accident. My instinct is to write back immediately, if only to prolong our contact. I would almost rather the agony of waiting for a response from him than having nothing to wait for at all. I don't feel ready to let go. Andrew is right; I was never any good at saying what I wanted to say, or even knowing what it was I wanted in the first place.

I realize his words contain an implicit decision. *Instead, I think it is probably time I just said good-bye.* I hold out hope for a few minutes on the word "probably," as if this suggests some wavering on his part. But after I read the sentence out loud to myself, I know I'm mistaken. I asked for a good-bye, and I got one. The stillness of my office feels suffocating, and I try to fill the void by tapping a pencil against my desk. *Good-bye, Andrew*, I say to myself, like a chant to the beat. *Good. Bye. An. Drew.*

Though I want to send him a new message, I hold back. Because I still don't know what I want to say. I just know that there are words out there I wish I could take back, words that I wish I could unsay. Words like "yes" and words like "good-bye."

"You're going to be missed," Carl says later, at the farewell party Kate has organized for me in one of the conference rooms. There are about forty or so people here, all eating jumbo shrimp and sipping wine in my honor. I recognize only about half of them. Lawyers can't resist free food.

"Thanks. I have a feeling this place will go on without me." Though, to be honest, I feel uncomfortable imagining Monday. I don't like that everyone here will shuffle back into work and go about their business, not giving a second thought to the fact that my office now sits empty. I will be forgotten the moment I get on the elevator tonight.

"Your leaving doesn't have anything to do with . . . well, it doesn't have anything to do with any misunderstanding in Arkansas, does it?" he asks.

"There was no misunderstanding, Carl. I think you were perfectly clear, actually. And you know what? I'm sure Carisse did a great job on writing that motion. She has shown her *dedication* to the firm." I raise my wineglass in a half toast, ceding victory to Carisse and Carl. For once, I am saying exactly what I want to say.

"I am not sure what you mean by that," he says. I shrug my shoulders and let his statement hang there, unanswered. I realize with a rush of excitement that I have no obligation to talk to Carl anymore; I can derive no benefit from kissing his ass.

"Bye, Carl," I say, and I walk away.

I wander through the party and find that it's less awkward than I expected. I had pictured small talk and uncomfortable good-byes. The kind where you internally debate whether you should shake hands or hug, and whether it is worth pretending like you're planning to keep in touch. I spend most of my time talking to the people I like, the ones whom I'll actually miss.

My favorite litigation partner, Miranda Washington, comes over to say good-bye. She is a black lesbian, the sort of attorney who sends human-resources directors into orgasms over how many boxes they can check off on diversity surveys. Because of her, the APT brochures boast about its multifaceted partnership. *We have black lawyers! Gay lawyers! Women lawyers!*

Despite the diversity P.R., though, the partnership wasn't thrilled about the prospect of her joining their ranks at first; they didn't quite know what to make of her. But in the end, as always, they voted with their pockets. Miranda is a former investment banker and brought APT a huge book of business from her Wall Street days.

"Doug told me you took Carl down. I just wanted to say

I'm proud of you. It's about time someone spoke up," Miranda says.

"Thanks," I say, and look down at her feet. She is wearing pink Converse sneakers with a conservative pin-striped suit. "Not sure if I took him down, really. I didn't fight the good fight, if you know what I mean."

"That's not true. Between you and me, you got what you asked for vis-à-vis that asshole over there. It will hopefully be official at the next partnership meeting. I've been trying for years, and no one listened. So thanks."

We both look over at Carl. He is talking to Carisse in hushed tones, and his hand rests on her shoulder. They look like they might break into a waltz. For a moment I actually pity Carisse. I pity both of them.

"Hey, can I ask you a question?"

"Anything," I say.

"Why did you come to work here to begin with?"

"I don't really know. Partially to pay off my student loans. But that's not the whole truth."

"What is?"

"Lack of imagination, I guess. Taking a big-firm job was what everyone else was doing. The sad part is, and I know this is going to sound embarrassingly naïve, but I started out wanting to do something else. I used to want to change the world. At some point, I actually thought it was possible."

"I can tell. You look like you have do-gooder blood."

Julie Buxbaum

"Thanks, I guess. Not so much anymore."

"Well, maybe it's time you started."

"What? Changing the world? Come on."

"Yeah. Seriously, if I hear that you end up taking exactly the same job from some firm across the street, I'm going to personally kick your ass. Go do something real. Go change the world. Why shouldn't you be the one to do it?"

"I don't know," I say.

"Okay, maybe not change the world. That sounds like hard work. But how about a little tiny corner of it? Promise?" she says, and holds up her little finger. "Promise you'll at least try?"

"Okay," I say, "I'll try." And I pinkie-swear on it.

A couple of hours later, I say good-bye to Kate and Mason. It is an airport good-bye, the kind with tears and hugs and dramatic sniffling. I feel silly, since I know I will be seeing both of them next week. But I can't help it. For the three of us, this is an ending of sorts, and though it is time for me to go, it's still sad to leave. It's like saying good-bye to my war buddies. They are the ones who crouched with me in the foxhole. The ones who lit my cigarettes and shielded me from enemy fire.

When I walk out of APT for the last time, I have a box tucked under each arm. I get the impression, as I ride downstairs on the elevator, that I look like I was fired. There is something demeaning about the cardboard, my stuff poking out of the tops and the wetness around my eyes. The other people back away into the corners, as if getting laid off is contagious. I feel like telling them that I quit, announcing it with relish, but I know that would be weird. Instead, I hold my head up as high as it will go, straighten out my back, and walk off the elevator with as much dignity as I can muster.

At the security gate, I see Marge standing guard in her blue suit. I want her to congratulate me, to tell me good luck, to give me closure, but I know that is too much to ask for. As I slide through the turnstile, it clicks behind me, and the number etched on the side increases a single digit. One more nameless person has left the building.

"Good-bye, Marge," I say as I pass her. And maybe because of the boxes, maybe because it's clear that this is the last time I'll ever bother her, Marge answers.

"Good-bye," she says. Her accent, it turns out, is British after all, but not posh like I imagined, more cockney and down to earth. I look at her, shock and glee pasted on my face. *Marge just spoke to me. She actually spoke to me.* She meets my eyes but doesn't crack a smile. She just looks over, thoughtfully, as if taking stock of this woman and her cardboard.

And then, like a flash, she winks.

# Nineteen

I feel crazy sitting here in my striped pajama pants, eating toast and jam with sticky fingers and brushing off the crumbs that cling to my sweatshirted breasts. This is something that just last week would have sounded fun and novel, something I used to long for, but today seems pathetic. *What happens now?* I wonder. *Do I just sit here all day and pray for some sort of reality show marathon?*

I promised myself two weeks off before I started looking for a new job. The idea was to give me a chance to clear my head. But now that it's Monday morning, and I have woken up and not gone to work, and the only shows on television are soap operas and the local news, and all of my friends are busy at their jobs, I have no idea what the fuck "clearing my head" actually means.

I consider the possibility of getting some exercise, seeing if my legs still work and can take my body places, but decide against it. I am too tired to change, and then to sweat, and then to shower, and then to change again. To be honest, I feel too tired to do anything at all. Too tired to sleep, even. I lie down on the couch, my feet propped up with pillows. I flip on the TV and let my eyes stare blindly at the screen. *This is how people relax*, I tell myself, as I lay here and quickly slip into something resembling a catatonic state.

Though I can't follow the story lines, I watch soap operas continuously. There is something comforting about the way these beautiful, glossy-haired people talk, and move, and kiss, and yell at one another. I like that much of the story is implied from meaningful looks, most often just after closing a door. I mean that literally, of course. The actors constantly close these huge mahogany doors and then look at the camera, as if to say *I love him*, or *I am going to kill him soon*.

To avoid any subtlety, the music fills in the gaps, deepening if someone is dangerous or in danger, lightening up when the characters are about to kiss.

I come up with elaborate backstories to make up for the years I have missed. Evil twins and the resurrected dead. Siblings newly discovered and reunited. Backstabbing, in both senses of the word. Loves lost, gained, lost again. In my imagination, the characters get lots of do-overs.

By Friday I consider the possibility that there might be something wrong with me. Without my noticing, I have seamlessly moved beyond relaxation. There was no sinister transition and no musical accompaniment. I have not left the couch in five days. I even sleep here. I tell myself that I like the feel of the nubby material against my back, that it takes too much effort to move across the room to my bed. There doesn't seem much point.

Sometimes I don't even get up to go to the bathroom and just wait patiently, hoping the need to pee will subside. It usually does.

I don't call anyone, and though the phone rings a couple of times, I don't get up to answer it. My answering-machine light is on, but I don't have the energy to count its blinks, to push its buttons. I wonder if this is what depression is and try to think back to the warning signs described on television commercials. I don't feel like hurting myself, so that's good. I don't feel sad or irritable. Check, check. I don't feel happy either. Maybe it's the flu, I wonder. But my head doesn't hurt, and I don't have a fever. I consider taking Tylenol, but I don't know what for.

I just sit here and watch television, and sometimes fill in the backstories, and sometimes not. Sometimes I sleep. Countless hours go by, and because I can't account for them, I assume I have spent them sleeping the sleep of the dead. The kind unmarred by nightmares or the need to turn over. Just empty, still sleep. There doesn't seem to be anything I am supposed to do next, so I just stay here. Where it's warm and not scary in the least. Work, I realize now, was mere background noise, a way to fill my empty days. Without work, it is as if all the sound has been turned off.

I think about Andrew a lot of the time. I pretend he's sitting here with me, not saying much but watching the television too. He might hold my hand or get me a glass of water. He would come up with better plots than I can. His would involve more passion. More sex. Maybe revenge.

I even let myself imagine my mother here also, hanging out on my couch. I don't let my mind go there too much, but sometimes I picture her putting her cool fingers against my forehead and checking for a fever. She would probably make me eat something, because I haven't ventured much beyond bread these last couple of days. I am almost at the end of the loaf now, but my fridge is empty, and I can't be bothered to order delivery. Too much work to find some cash.

In my imagination, my mother sits quietly, but that's mostly because I can't remember her voice. But I'm distorting things, because when my mother was alive, she never sat quietly—she always talked, talked, talked right through whatever we were watching, even *The Cosby Show*. She always thought real life was so much more interesting than television; she never understood the need to escape.

I give my mother story lines too. Hers tend toward science fiction. Medical miracles and the like.

This is the opposite of love, I realize, when I look over and see my empty couch, see right through my imaginary companions. The opposite of love isn't hate; it isn't even indifference. It's fucking disembowelment. Hara-kiri.

Taking a huge shovel and digging out your own heart, and your intestines, and leaving behind nothing. Nothing of yourself to give, nothing, even, to take away. Nothing but a quiet pulse and some mildly entertaining soap operas.

If to love is to hand over self and heart, then this, my friend, this—to self-disembowel—is its opposite.

I wish I knew how to needlepoint so I could stitch it onto a fucking pillow.

# Twenty

I wake up to the sound of loud banging. I open my eyes, and at first I'm unsure of where I am. The view is unfamiliar. I see blond wood, sharp corners, and oatmeal-colored carpet. It comes back to me slowly. I am still lying on the couch. The heat must have kicked on during the night, because my clothes are sticky from sweat and my hair is damp at the neck.

I hear a key in the lock, but I'm too groggy to turn to see who it is. I'm not sure that I care. If it's a robber, they can help themselves to my belongings. I don't think there is anything of real value here. Other than my television. They will have to kill me before they take that.

"Emily? What the hell?" Jess walks into my apartment and sets her keys down on the kitchen table as if she owns the place. She stares at me lying on the couch and takes a long look around. I can see her mentally calculating the days since we spoke last, see her trying to figure out how long I have been lying here. I would make things easier and tell her, but I'm not sure what to say.

"Why haven't you been answering your phone? I must have left a hundred messages." Jess crosses the room and stands in front of me, blocking my view of the TV. I wonder if I have to answer her. Maybe I can close my eyes again and pretend to be asleep. I don't want to hurt her feelings, but I'm too tired to listen, too tired to do the talking thing. I am even too tired to be embarrassed of her seeing me like this.

"Are you sick?"

"I don't know."

"How long have you been lying here?"

"I don't know."

"Emily," she says, not a question or a demand but a sigh. A tired sigh, and I wonder for a moment if I've made the noise. No, it was definitely Jess, because after she sighs, I see her take control of herself and then of me.

"Get up," she says, and rips off my blanket. She has no mercy.

"But I'm tired, Jess. Just a few more minutes." I want more of this sleep, of the sleep that I have never known until now, the kind of sleep that sets deep into your soul, the kind you would inject into your veins if you could.

"No."

"But—"

"Get up and get into the shower." She grabs my wrists

and forces me upright. I get light-headed; I don't remember the last time I was vertical.

"Now," she says, and points the way to the bathroom, as if I don't know how to get there myself.

"Fine," I say, because I don't have the energy to fight with her and because she has been known to use her long nails as weapons. Jess follows me into the bathroom and turns on the water.

"Jesus, how long has it been since you've had a shower?"

"I don't know."

I start to take off my clothes, slowly, like a retarded stripper. My hooded sweatshirt smells like a teenage boy's bedroom.

"When was the last time you ate?"

"I don't know. Had some bread. Lots of it," I say. And then, to win some points, "It was whole wheat." Jess walks out of the bathroom, leaves the door open.

"I'm getting in now," I call out, to show that I am here too, that I want to help her help me. But Jess ignores me, because she is already on the telephone.

"Two extra-large pepperoni pizzas, please," she says, and then gives the delivery guy my address.

"Hurry," she tells them. "It's an emergency."

About an hour later, we are both sitting at my kitchen table. I find out it is Saturday, a full week since I left my job. It is also four-thirty in the afternoon, though I would have sworn it was morning. I am wearing the clean clothes that Jess picked out and left for me in the bathroom. A white T-shirt and my favorite pair of jeans. Before we talk, I eat five slices of pizza, one after the other.

"I came close to my personal record," I say. "Remember in college when I ate seven?" I am trying to get Jess over to my side, to win her over with our happy memories. To make her forget what I looked like just sixty minutes ago. I feel the shame of it creep over me slowly. Someone has borne witness to my unraveling.

"Yup. Drink some water too," Jess says. I lean forward and down the glass she sets in front of me. She refills it, and I down it again.

"Thanks. I'm sorry. I didn't mean to not call you back." I look at her, and she looks at me and then away. She seems unsure of how to talk to this new incarnation of me, whether to treat me lightly or to give me the kick in the ass I deserve.

"I'm okay now." This is true; somehow, the exhaustion has broken. I feel awake and alive. I wonder if Jess snuck something into my pizza.

"Here." She hands me a piece of paper with the name and address of her therapist. "You have an appointment on Wednesday.

"While you were in the shower," she says, before I even ask the question.

"Thanks." I realize I am in no position to protest. I have

not gone that far off the deep end that I don't realize what is happening is not normal.

"I didn't mean not to call. I mean, I just got really tired and felt like sleeping. And I just lost my grip a little, you know?" Jess nods but doesn't say anything. I know she knows. She once had a love affair with a couch too, back in college.

"You're going to be okay, Em. People just fall apart sometimes. We are going to fix you," she says. "Actually, you're going to fix you."

She takes the empty pizza boxes and stuffs them into a full garbage bag. I notice that the hood of my sweatshirt is sticking out of the top, but I let it go. Maybe it's time.

"Yeah," I say, taking a moment to let her words echo in my head. *People just fall apart sometimes.*

Jess and I take a walk to get some fresh air, and it turns out that it is one of those spectacular autumn days in Manhattan, where the trees have turned to yellows and reds but most of the leaves still cling on. Not yet ready to litter the streets, not yet ready to surrender the fight to winter. The sun shines brightly, and its rays cut as deeply as the chill in the air. We walk slowly, arms linked, around the West Village, and all of the other people on the city streets feel like extras or backup dancers to our two-woman show. Jess does most of the talking as we walk and points out architectural details on the brownstones we pass, her favorite bagel place, her dry cleaner, and the corners on which she has had special kisses—all things I already know but enjoy hearing again. Over there at the corner of Eleventh and Sixth Avenue, right in front of PS 41, she kissed her ex-boyfriend from high school, again, just once, before he got married to someone else. It was afternoon, at the tail end of recess, and the kids in the playground cheered, ignoring their teacher's attempt to usher them back inside.

The next morning, when I wake up, I head straight for the shower. I do not go near my couch or the television, which is now facing a wall, unplugged. I figure that we could both use some time apart. I shave my legs, tweeze my eyebrows, put on clean clothes straight from the dryer, even wear some concealer, because though I have done nothing but sleep for the last week, I look sapped. Since it is time to resume the role of functioning human being, it seems only logical to look the part.

As I leave my building, Robert wolf-whistles at me, long and drawn out. Probably inappropriate of my doorman, but I appreciate the compliment.

"I don't know where you're going," Robert says, "but you're going to knock them dead."

"Thanks," I say, and decide it's better to keep to myself that I am headed to the constant-care floor of the Riverdale Retirement Home. The one place where that's a real possibility.

# Twenty-one

I won't let them stick a kaleidoscope up my ass. I'm not going to do it," Grandpa Jack says, as he hands me the letter from the doctor. I am not sure which one this is from, because Grandpa Jack has been on a medical tour lately. Since our trip to the neurologist a few weeks ago, he has seen a psychiatrist, a cardiologist, an internist, a urologist, a gastroenterologist, and now finally what appears to be a colorectal specialist. He throws the paper at me like a cranky child, even though today he is perfectly lucid. We can almost pretend everything is all right when he is like this, when he looks exactly like the old Grandpa Jack, when we are not in another stupid waiting room. I am tempted to ruffle his white hair and to pinch his sinking cheeks, but I know that will only make him angrier.

We are in the diner again, this time *our* diner, and my mouth tastes both sour and sweet, the remnants of a meal consisting solely of sugared coffee and pickles. The place is more crowded than usual—there is a children's party in the back—and our conversation keeps getting interrupted by a noisemaker. When they sing "Happy Birthday" to a boy named Steven with a bib full of spaghetti, Grandpa Jack and I chime in.

"It's not a kaleidoscope. It's just a microscope, or a camera or something. And it says here that they need to look at your colon. It's important." I glance at the note and feel the burden of our role reversal. I am in charge of his medical decisions. I sign the permission slips now.

"I am eighty-nine years old. Who gives a shit what my colon looks like?" I look up at Grandpa Jack and notice he is smirking. "No pun intended, doll."

We laugh at his joke for longer than it is funny.

"Can I be honest with you?" he asks, and pushes the straw of his milk shake away.

"Of course."

"I know what's happening to me, Emily. I can see it. Would it be so terrible if there were some dangerous stuff going on in my colon?"

I don't answer him. I stare at the letter in my hands, and the intensity makes the words bleed together into a Rorschach inkblot, into the shape of a stain.

"Seriously. It would be a good thing."

His voice is soft; he is singing me a lullaby. I am tempted to rest my head on his shoulder and hand over its weight.

But, instead, I cross my arms around my stomach and grip my sides.

"There is something . . . I don't know, right about letting things just be, isn't there? Letting things happen the way they are supposed to happen." He says it like that would be easy, to sit back and let cancer cells, or whatever else might be lurking, ravage him. I picture his insides in my head. Angry ants rip, feast at his sacks of organs. They leave behind nothing but deflated balloons.

"It's better this way. You don't want to admit it, but it is. I may be the first person in the history of the world who can say with one hundred percent sincerity that I hope I have cancer. In fact, I am going to start eating more of that fake sugar crap right now. Emily, I *pray* that I have cancer. Please, God, give me cancer!"

His voice grows louder as he drops to his knees on the diner floor in mock prayer, his hand clutching a pile of pink packets.

"Lord, give me the big C! Come on. You can do it. I want the big C!"

"Stop it." I grab his elbow to lift him back up, but Grandpa Jack ignores me.

He is too busy genuflecting.

"Big C! Big C! Big C!"

"Stop it, you're making a scene. People are starting to stare. This is not funny."

"Come on, say it with me. Big C!"

"No."

"Which way is Mecca?"

He starts bowing furiously.

"What are you doing?"

"Covering my bases."

"Okay," I say. "All right. I get it. No colonoscopy."

"Say it."

"What?"

"You know what. Big C!"

"Okay. Big C! Now please sit down." Grandpa Jack stands up and drops himself into the booth next to me, satisfied.

"Cheer up, kid," he says, and puts his napkin back on his lap. "I promise you that if I live past ninety, I'll let those doctors rip me a new asshole if they want to. I'll be so confused by then I'll be running around with a diaper on my head."

"Grandpa, you know that's a load of crap."

He looks over at me, and his grin stretches slowly from one side of his face to the other. When he gives my hand a little squeeze, I know he has never been prouder.

"No pun intended, doll. No pun intended."

# Twenty-two

Dr. Lerner's office building is in the West Village, tucked into a street filled with charming New York brownstones. It stands about four stories above its neighbors, ugly and oppressive. The kind of building that you assume houses one hundred dentists (and at least one therapist and two cosmetic surgeons) and makes you wonder what might have been there before; whose home gave way under the burden of commercial enterprise, and how the plans were snuck by the zoning commission. Maybe someone got free braces or rhinoplasty out of the deal.

Based on the replacement building, it looks like the destruction and construction occurred sometime in the 1970s. The lobby's fluorescent lighting makes the white interior look dingy and forgotten. A security guard watches a tiny TV on a foldout table and doesn't even look up when I get onto the elevator without signing in.

I am happy not to leave behind a paper trail.

When I enter Dr. Lerner's office, I am ready for an audience. For people to stare and wonder about what must be wrong with me. I picture a waiting room full of people, one or two of them overmedicated and drooling. As it turns out, I am the only person here. I am not sure if this is a relief or a letdown. I have already practiced my serene facial expression in the mirror, one that says *I am only here because I am complicated*.

I take a seat on a battered plaid couch and wait. There are magazines on the coffee table, a choice between *The Economist* and *Cosmo*, both at least two years old. I assume this is some sort of psychological test, and I decide to go with *The Economist*. I hope this will make me look like I care about world affairs and the spread of democracy. Like my life is bigger than the problems I intend to dump and leave behind in Dr. Lerner's office.

I turn the magazine pages slowly. Though I can't seem to concentrate on the words or even understand the graphs, I pretend to read. I am anxious; the idea of paying someone to listen to me feels somehow immoral and illicit, like paying for sex. It seems fundamentally opposed to the WASP code. I like to think of my people as mute optimists—leave the elephant alone and, eventually, perhaps with the help of a couple mimosas, he will disappear from the room on his own accord.

After about ten minutes, two women come out of the

closed door on my right, one of whom walks briskly out of the waiting room. I acknowledge therapy etiquette by not staring at her departing back. Instead, I focus my attention on the woman who stays behind, the woman I presume to be the doctor.

Though, on closer look, Dr. Lerner doesn't look like a doctor. She looks like a tarot-card reader. Gold gypsy bracelets dance up her arms, and she wears a hot-pink sari. Though the lights are dimmed in here, I am about ninety-five percent sure she's not Indian.

"You must be Emily," she says to me, and reaches to shake my hand. "I'm Dr. Lerner." She leads me into her office, which is even darker and cavelike, and has stacks of books lining the walls. The smell of incense is heavy in the air. It reminds me of my college boyfriend's apartment, where my eyes would water from candles burned to hide the smell of pot and where the lighting was kept so dull I couldn't see his acne.

"Have a seat," she says, and points me to another couch, also plaid. She sits down across from me, in a folding chair with a cushion, and arranges herself into a lotus position. She looks too old to be able to manipulate her body that way comfortably. I sit down too and wonder if I am supposed to copy her. I decide against it when I remember I'm wearing a skirt.

"So, what brings you here today?" she asks in a cheery voice, like she is a saleswoman ready to show her wares. She rests her arms on her calves, palms up, and her bracelets provide tinkling background noise.

"I've been going through a rough time lately." Dr. Lerner doesn't respond, and I immediately recognize the technique. I have used it often with reluctant witnesses. Nothing gets people to talk like awkward silence. I take the bait, mostly because I am paying a hundred bucks an hour for this.

"I recently went through a depressive episode."

"I see," she says. "And what makes you say that? What does that mean, exactly?" Her tone is casual, not clinical or clipped like a doctor's. It's like we are girlfriends chatting over coffee.

"Put it this way, I couldn't get off of my couch. I slept. A lot. For like a week straight."

I fake a yawn, a bizarre attempt at emphasis.

"And now?"

"Not so much. I mean, I snapped out of it. But now I feel sort of sad. Before I just felt numb. In some ways it was actually better before. Does that make sense?"

"Absolutely. It's a very common defense mechanism. Lots of people shut down emotionally when they don't want to deal with whatever is going on in their lives. Some people shut down for years," she says, which makes me think of my father.

"Why don't you tell me what's been going on with you until now? Anything happen or change recently?"

"Nothing much. I mean, I broke up with my boyfriend, Andrew, on Labor Day, but that was a few months ago, and I broke up with him, so really I should be over it by now. And I quit my job, but I think that's probably a good thing. I hated it there. The only other thing I can think of is that my grandfather has gotten sick. He was just recently diagnosed with Alzheimer's. But it has been a long time coming, so it wasn't too shocking." I rush the words, since now that I am here, I might as well get the most out of my hour.

"Emily, do you notice that you put caveats on all of your feelings? Emily, it sounds as if you don't feel entitled to be upset or have a reaction to anything." I wonder if repeatedly using my name is another technique.

*What is Dr. Lerner's first name? I wonder. She looks like a Peggy. Or maybe a Priya?*

"Let me suggest something," she says. "After I speak, I'd like you to take a moment to think about what I said. To concentrate on it. I can tell your mind is churning, and I want to make sure you hear me."

*Does it look like I am not paying attention? Am I paying attention? Focus, Emily, focus.*

*Do I put caveats on all of my feelings?*

"Why don't we start with Andrew. What happened there?" she asks, and the question feels violating. I want to tell her to mind her own business, but then I remember that I am paying her to mind mine.

"I broke up with him. We had been dating for two years, and I was worried he was going to propose. So I ended it." I say it matter-of-factly, like I am a nonchalant heartbreaker.

"I see," she says, though I am not sure what she sees. "Why did you end it?"

"You tell me," I say. Dr. Lerner doesn't dignify this with a response, and her silence is chastening. Her look says *Work with me here*.

"To be honest, I'm not sure. At the time I felt like I had to. I knew I couldn't marry him."

"Why not? Why couldn't you marry him?"

"I don't know. I just couldn't. I felt like a fraud."

"That's an interesting word choice."

"I guess."

"What is a fraud to you?"

I take a deep breath to forestall my annoyance. I am not here for a vocabulary lesson. "Okay, you know, a fraud. Like I was pretending. Like I was there but I wasn't there."

"Did you love Andrew?"

"Yes. I did. Love him."

"And now?"

"Now?"

"Now."

I take a moment, though I know the answer to this one. I'm just not sure I'm ready to say these words out loud.

"Yes, I still love him. Yes."

"And the sex?"

"Excuse me?"

"And the sex? How was it?"

I pause again.

"I ask because it tells a lot about the relationship. So, how was it? The sex."

"Fucking fantastic."

Somehow talking about sex breaks the ice, and I am more comfortable with Dr. Lerner. I feel sort of like we *are* girl-friends chatting over coffee, except we talk only about me.

"Let's discuss your family," Dr. Lerner says, when we are about halfway through our session. I want to giggle, because I knew somehow it would come to this. The therapist expecting me to rehash all of my childhood traumas.

"I don't have all that much family, so there's not that much to tell. I am an only child. My dad lives in Connecticut. He's a politician. And I have told you about my Grandpa Jack. That's about it."

"And your mother?" I knew she was going to ask, of course. And for a moment I consider lying. I could answer that she lives in Connecticut too. I have done that before, since people don't know how to respond when you say your mother is dead. After the "I'm sorry"s and the "I didn't know"s, it's hard to get the conversation back on track. I sometimes lie implicitly and say, "My family lives in Connecticut," because it is simpler than having to explain. It's not that I'm uncomfortable saying that my mother is dead out loud, it's just that everyone else is uncomfortable hearing it.

"She's dead." Lying in therapy is a bad idea.

"I see." This time I know what she sees. She sees that my mother is dead and that this has irrevocably fucked me up.

"Yeah, well, cancer. When I was fourteen."

"Cancer. Fourteen," she repeats, as if these are foreign words that sound interesting to her. "Well, that really sucks."

I laugh, because she's exactly right. It does really suck.

The rest of our hour together flies by. I forget that we are on the clock, so I spend much of my time talking about random things. Like Marge, and Carl, and what it's like to take a deposition. Occasionally, I worry that we are getting too off track from the reason I am here—my stint on the couch. I ask Dr. Lerner about that, but she just tells me to "relax and trust the process." And because I am surprised when our session is over, and because I decide to trust her and the process, whatever that means, I make another appointment with Dr. Lerner for next week.

I take the long way home and circle the neighborhood. The leaves have started to fall and collect in small heaps under the carefully spaced trees. I kick the piles, enjoying the sounds my feet make as I scatter them along the side-walk, adding a small bit of extra chaos to the city. Every once in a while, I sniff the sleeves of my sweater. I kind of like that they stink of patchouli.

# Twenty-three

For me, the calendar can be a minefield. Each year I can expect certain days to be more difficult than others. Most major holidays. Mother's Day. The anniversary of my mom's death. Her birthday. Mine. If you were to mark those days out with a black indelible X, it would probably come out to about one crappy day every two months or so. Not particularly bad odds. But toward the end of the year, with the Thanksgiving–Christmas–New Year's clusterfuck, it's a grand slam; I barely catch my breath with the first before I get hit with a second, then a third.

By the time January rolls around, I am so emotionally exhausted that I make the same resolution every single year: Get more sleep. As if closing my eyes in a dark room for multiple hours in a row can replenish the little bits of my soul that get eaten every year around this time.

If anything, my week on the couch debunked the myth of the redemptive power of sleep.

231

I have been dreading today, Thanksgiving, ever since my dad and I made plans, or maybe since this time last year. Let me be clear here. I realize I have much to give thanks for, and I know that relatively speaking, especially on a global scale, my life is pretty damn good. But Thanksgiving for some reason has the inevitable effect of making me take stock of my proverbial half-empty glass. There is only one source of unconditional love for each of us, and I lost mine at fourteen. I don't mean this in a self-pitying way. I just mean that Thanksgiving reminds me that most of the love I will get going forward is going to have to be earned. And it takes a hell of a lot of work to earn love. I'm not sure I have that kind of energy.

My dad picks me up at the train station, and we head straight to the country club. We don't stop at his house, because there is no reason to go there anymore. I don't like to see its transformation: the slow decline in displayed photographs and the replacement of furniture. A testament to the gradual erosion of memory. It is Grandpa Jack as a house.

My father's country club, or just "the club" as he likes to refer to it, looks like an old plantation estate, with sprawling, impossibly green lawns, multiple porches, and a long circular driveway. High hedges skirt the property, an effort to separate it from the mean streets of Greenwich, Connecticut, and to thwart all of those hooligans just hoping to get a peek at Shangri-la. When you pull into the driveway, after being cleared by a man at the security gate, valets with black faces and stiff uniforms welcome you. Open your car door. Bow. And then whisk your vehicle away to a distant lot.

The entryway is lined with tennis and golf plaques. The winners listed have pretentious names followed by numerals, names better suited for yachts than for people. There are some group photographs of the tennis teams: all white, and, as if to emphasize their uniform whiteness, they wear white collared shirts, white shorts, white socks, and white sneakers, the blinding white you see only in detergent commercials, the kind of white that says *We are whiter than you.*

The dining room is mock casual, like a lodge and a ball-room smooshed together and decorated with autumnal flower arrangements. A couple of stray pinecones litter the place to add authenticity. When we walk in the room, my dad does a quick visual sweep for faces he recognizes and then nods and smiles and waves like a pageant winner at a local parade. The place is filled with his "constituents," the people he hopes a few years from now will elect him as governor. Since I have never mastered the long-distance hello, I avoid eye contact and dutifully follow the maître d' to our seats.

"Do you have anything smaller?" I ask when he places us at a table for six.

"I'm sorry, no. We usually accommodate only large

groups on Thanksgiving," he says, and hands us our menus before walking away.

My father and I sit diametrically opposed, and the four empty chairs stare back at us. We both mentally fill them with our dead. My grandparents on my mom's side, my dad's mom, my mom, and soon, possibly, my Grandpa Jack. My dad signals a waiter over and demands the extra chairs be taken away. He doesn't say it, but his gesture, his gruffness and impatience, are transparent: *We don't dine with ghosts*.

"Mr. Haxby, so nice of you to join us today. And this must be your lovely daughter you are always talking about. Emily, right?" The waiter speaks in a clipped British accent, which has the effect of making our meal seem even more formal, like we flew to London to celebrate the conquering of the New World. I am surprised that he knows my name, and I wonder if they keep a guest roster to make the club appear friendlier. My dad smiles at him, and I reach over to shake the waiter's hand.

"And will Miss Anne be joining us today?" the waiter asks. Anne is my dad's personal assistant, the woman he jokes he can't live without. I am surprised that the head-waiter knows her by name as well.

"No, she will not," my father says, and his tone scolds the waiter for his indiscretion. But it is my dad who gives himself away. He must be dating Anne, a woman only a few years older than me. She can't be more than thirty-three, tops. Anne is a compact brunette who decorates herself along party lines—pearls around the neck, small studs in the ears, slim watch, slim phone. I take a moment to process this new information, my father and Anne, and I find that I like the idea. It makes my father seem more human somehow.

The waiter leaves quickly after that, with the extra chairs but without our drink order. He walks away with his head down, like we banished him from our two-man island.

"So you and Anne come here a lot?"

"For business lunches. It's not too far from the office. I think I see the Pritchards. Shall we go over and say hello?"

"Come on, Dad. I'm not stupid. Are you dating her? It would be fine if you were. She's a great woman." In truth, I admire Anne. She turns up the volume on life; her voice, her gestures, her presence manage to command attention without asking for it, to be loud but not crass. If she didn't work for my father, if she wasn't sleeping with my father, under different circumstances, I could see us becoming friends.

"Don't be ridiculous, Emily. I'm her supervisor. It would be inappropriate." He dismisses the subject with a flick of the wrist. A signal for the waiter to get us drinks. Two martinis, straight up, with extra olives.

"How's Andrew these days?" my father asks.

"He's fine. He's been pretty busy at work." *So we Haxbys just continue to lie to each other. That's how we do business here.*

"Good," he says, and rubs his hands together. "Let's order." Since there is a fixed menu this afternoon, what my father actually means is *Let's get this thing started, so we can be done sooner.* We are uncomfortable sitting at this large table full of small untruths; we have left ourselves little room for conversation.

After we place our order, the meal comes out quickly. The staff makes a big show of presentation with our food, placing it in front of us with much fanfare and the elaborate lifting of clattering lids. One of the busboys even says "Voilà" when he opens mine.

Before we dig in, my dad says grace, which is something he does only when we are out in public. Hands steepled in prayer, eyes shut, more-salt less-pepper hair left a little long in the front tucked behind his ears. He looks earnest—schoolboyish, younger than his fifty-eight years—when he gives thanks for the food and that we can share this wonderful meal together, amen.

Our plates are filled with the quintessential Thanksgiving elements, turkey and mashed potatoes, stuffing and gravy, except the food is brought out in individual portions. I find this depressing, my single-serve meal, compartmentalized neatly into carefully scooped circles.

"Would you like some of my cranberry sauce?" I ask.

"I have the same thing, Emily," my dad says. "Why would I want some of yours when I have my own?"

*   *   *

I guess it doesn't matter that we don't have much to say to each other over lunch, because we are interrupted constantly. I'm sure this is why my dad wanted to come here to begin with; it is a prime opportunity to mix business with obligation. Serious-looking men and women come over to shake my father's hand and pat him heartily on the back. We keep friendly smiles plastered onto our faces, our job as heads of the networking brigade. A few families approach also, people from the neighborhood whom I have known for years but think of rarely. Their names come up now only when my dad has some piece of gossip to report, mostly births and deaths.

A few divorcées stop by, one at a time, on their way to the "powder room." They brush my father's cheek with kisses, showering him in cleavage and perfume and hints like "We should grab that drink." He accepts their offerings graciously, as if surprised by the attention, as if he doesn't notice their hunger, though since my mother died, my father has been the most eligible bachelor in Greenwich. He is attractive, successful, and widowed—which means he lacks both a pesky ex-wife and the baggage of the perennial bachelor. To his credit, he has never been particularly interested in exploiting these opportunities, friendly to these women partially to preserve their dignity, partially to preserve their vote.

I think the old family friends are the ones who remind me most why I never liked it here. The self-promotion is shameless. We hear about daughters marrying into "families in hedge funds," eight-thousand-square-foot vacation homes, and graduation from various Ivies. I compliment one woman's bag, and she says, "Oh, this little thing?" and then quietly, "Marc Jacobs, Barneys," as if she is embarrassed that it is so readily available to the masses. We hear in exaggerated, gleeful whispers about other people's misfortunes—bankruptcies, cancer, divorce.

It is not the wealth, per se, that I find uncomfortable. After all, I used to work at APT, where the partners make millions each year. It is the culture of competition stirred with schadenfreude that I find disheartening. Afterward, I feel like I spent the last hour getting one-upped by Carisse. Like I am getting my ass kicked in a game I am not even playing.

I somehow avoid the subject of work until we are eating our pumpkin pie. We are not given slices of pie, mind you, but individual mini-pies with a round mini-crust. I think they are supposed to be cute, these midget pies.

"So, how's work?" my dad asks, reverting to what used to be our safe topic. I knew this was coming, of course, but I hadn't yet decided how I was going to answer. If I tell the truth, the worst thing that can happen is that my dad will get upset with me. If I lie, nothing will happen.

I lie.

"Good," I say. "Busy."

"And the Synergon case? How's that going?"

"Fine. Can't really talk about it, though. Attorney-client privilege."

"Oh." My dad's face falls. I'm not sure if this is because I don't let him go down the one avenue in which we connect or if it bothers him that I am part of a club in which he can't be a member. His look makes me feel guilty, though, and I second-guess myself. Maybe I should come clean? But this seems impossible now that I have lied straight to his face. I decide to throw him a different bone and change the subject to politics, his other favorite topic.

"And how's work for you? Any big news in the governor's office?"

"I'm glad you asked. I am proud to say we added fifteen thousand new jobs this year alone." My question is all it takes. We spend the rest of the meal and the entire car ride to Riverdale discussing Connecticut politics, a subject I have learned through osmosis. Since we are card-carrying members of different parties, though, we have become adept at side-stepping all discussion of ideology.

"So, say you are on Fox News and you have to fend off Bill O'Reilly. What would you do?" he asks.

"Vomit on his shoes."

"Be serious, Emily. If you have strong opinions you need to learn how to sell them. It is no longer just about the idea anymore. It's the packaging. It's the ability to communicate the idea."

"I know how to argue," I say. "I went to law school."

"You are missing the point. It is not about arguing. It's about P.R. It's about the spin. For example, you should start your sentences with things like *I am sure you would agree that, blah, blah, blah*," he says. "It makes the other side have to articulate an opposition to something that it's impossible to be against."

"So what you are telling me is that it is all about oppositional force," I say. "It's much harder to argue against nothing than against something. There is no give and take without the give."

"Exactly. I am saying it's all about talking without talking. That's the skill."

"Talking without talking?"

"Yup, talking without talking."

"I can do that."

"What took you guys so darn long?" Grandpa Jack asks when we walk into his room on the constant-care floor. He is sitting on a chair, flipping through an old *National Geographic* magazine filled with bare-breasted tribal women. There are few nurses around because of the holiday, and the place is desolate. Everyone here has given up, packed it in, and gone to either home or heaven. My grandfather's abrupt welcome doesn't portend well for the visit. Maybe it was overly optimistic of me to hope for a good day.

"Hey, Grandpa Jack," I say, and give him a kiss. The aide I hired to keep my grandfather company jumps to her feet, looks at her watch, and then at me. I nod back that she can leave, but I am too distracted to remember to thank her until she is already out the door.

"Hi, Dad," my father says, and shakes Grandpa Jack's hand.

"Where the hell have you guys been?" my grandfather asks, waving away our greetings. "Our reservation was for five-thirty."

My father takes a step back and turns his head away, unable to look me or my grandfather in the eye. It is immediately apparent that he has not been here to visit in a long, long time. This Grandpa Jack is new to him, the one with skin too taut over his mouth and paper-thin over his cheekbones, the one where he is reduced to delusion by the snap, crackle, and pop of a synapse, by a neuron misfire. Grandpa Jack now has mottled flesh, and swollen eyelids, and the haunted face of someone who has lived too long.

"Sorry. We got tied up. It's okay, though. We can have Thanksgiving here," I say. My tone is overly bright, and my fake enthusiasm only seems to heighten the tension in the room.

"What about the show, Martha?" Grandpa Jack says. My dad's head falls into his hands at the mention of his mother, who has been dead since I was in diapers. Her reappearance makes me question reality for a split second; could we all be laboring under a gross misunderstanding? But, of course, this is nothing but my own chemical spill of hope.

"We're not going to the show, Grandpa. But we're going to eat turkey. It's all laid out downstairs." My father catches my eye and signals toward the door.

"We'll be right back, Grandpa." This is so he doesn't get scared that we have left him behind. It doesn't matter who he thinks we are; I don't want him to think he's alone.

My father and I step outside into what looks like the hallway of a hospital. It is white, and smells of antiseptic, and electronic gadgets are strewn about. Disembodied sounds echo against the walls, the groans of old people shifting positions in their beds. A woman in blue scrubs sits alone behind a Formica arc at the nurses' station, rifling through a greasy paper bag from McDonald's. I make a mental note to invite her to the feast we have set up downstairs. I plan on doing this, not for her benefit, but for ours.

My dad leads me by the elbow farther down the hall and steers me into a little nook with two chairs and a vending machine. It is the sort of nook where people deliver bad news.

"What's up?"

"Are you fucking kidding me?" my dad asks, and points his long fingers in my face to show his distress. *He bites his cuticles too*, I think absently. *I've never noticed that he does that too.*

"Are you fucking kidding me?" he screams, this time his tone unmistakably violent. I am too shocked to answer. I have never heard my dad use the word "fuck." Not once in my entire life. My father has also never yelled at me, despite my having tried to provoke him for the entirety of my adolescence. The experience is so foreign, I'm not sure if it's unpleasant. It's definitely confusing, though, and I can tell that he, too, is surprised by his harsh words. *Have we all lost our minds? Has there been some sort of Haxby collective short circuit?*

"What?"

"Why didn't you tell me he was going to be like this? Why didn't you tell me it had gotten this bad?" My dad bangs his fist against the white wall, and his bare knuckles scrape against the plaster.

"I did tell you." A wave of exhaustion rushes over me, competing with the anger gearing up just below.

"I did tell you," I say again, but this time it comes out like a whisper.

"No you didn't. You didn't tell me he was like this." His tone is now that of a petulant child. He's no longer the powerful guy I had lunch with, the one who was glad-handing every person at the country club. Right now he looks haunted and lost, like a kid who wants his mommy to tell him everything is going to be all right. Funny that I feel exactly the same way.

"What the fuck do you think Alzheimer's looks like, Dad? You could have seen for yourself the day Grandpa went missing. If you had bothered to call me back. Or maybe you could have come to the neurologist and talked to the doctor yourself. Oh, I know, you could have taken time from your busy fucking schedule running fucking Connecticut to visit some other time." I stop to catch my breath.

"Or maybe, maybe you were just too busy fucking Anne." I scream at him with such force that my father takes a step back, absorbing my words like a physical blow. But I am not done. Not yet. My fury comes spilling out, brutally throwing up words, like I have some bizarre strain of the stomach flu.

"And why is this my fucking fault? Why is this my fucking responsibility? He is your father. He is your family too. You think this is easy for me?" I yell as loud as my voice will go, until it feels harsh in my throat. Until it hurts.

"Well, it's not. It's not easy. How dare you?" I demand, because I can't think of anything else to throw at him. I am shocked by the power of my outburst, and just as quickly as it comes over me, it dissipates. It leaves no residual anger behind, only overwhelming tiredness. I slide down the wall until I am sitting in an upward fetal position. I cradle my knees and rest my head against them. I hear weeping sounds and don't immediately realize that they are coming from me. This sort of encounter, the tears and the yelling, is unprecedented, and it feels bizarre for my dad and me to be so off script. Neither of us says anything for a little while, letting the break take some of the heat out of the moment.

My dad eventually sits next to me on the floor, both of us mopping up dust with our black suits and neither of us caring. He folds into exactly the same position I am in and then takes his arm and puts it around my shoulders.

"I'm sorry," he says, and I notice his face is wet too. "I'm so, so sorry." My dad grabs me into a hug, and my running nose leaves a mark on his sleeve.

"I wasn't expecting this, for him to be like this," he says.

"I know," I say.

"I just sort of freaked out," he says.

"I know," I say again. Although my dad may be my parent, I know he is still Grandpa Jack's child.

My father and I walk slowly back to the room, each step taken deliberately, like we are the ones in need of "constant care." When we pass the nurses' station, I notice that the woman is no longer sitting behind the counter, and I am relieved. I don't want to invite her to our Thanksgiving after all. I want it to be just the three of us.

For the second time today, I stuff myself with turkey and potatoes and cranberry sauce, somehow making extra room in my stomach for another round. My grandfather, my dad, and I sit around a small oak table in one of the private rooms downstairs. The food is set out family style, and since the caterers forgot to leave serving spoons, we dig our own utensils into the aluminum pans. Our forks leave track marks in the mountainous glob of mashed potatoes.

My father, though subdued, takes a second helping of food and offers to refill each of our plates. He keeps staring at Grandpa Jack, as if he is trying to visually pinpoint where everything went so wrong. Or maybe he is just looking for evidence that the person in front of him is still his father.

"Your son came to visit the other day," Grandpa Jack says to my dad when he gets up to dish out another serving of apple pie. Until now the delusions have taken the form of a sort of time travel; if Grandpa Jack is not talking to us here and now, he is talking to his wife and kid fifty years ago. I wonder if this is what we all have to look forward to. Complete disassociation with anything concrete or real.

"He is such a fine young man. And a doctor!" My grandfather claps his hands together at this, pure joy about his imagined grandson.

"Dad, I don't have a son. Just Emily, remember?"

"Don't be silly, Kirk. He was here just two days ago. He's gotten so tall, you know? And he let me win at poker."

"What are you talking about?"

"Ask Ruth. She was so happy to see him. We both emptied the poor kid's pockets."

"Andrew?" I ask. *Andrew came to visit Grandpa Jack?*

"Andrew!" My grandfather repeats after me, and claps his hand again. "I won four games in a row. Such a nice young man."

"Why would Andrew visit without telling you?" my dad asks, and I feel my stomach bottom out.

"He did. Tell me, I mean. I just forgot," I say. My dad looks confused, but lets it go. *Did Andrew really come to visit Grandpa Jack? Or is this just another delusion?*

"We played a lot of poker," Grandpa Jack says, and takes a wad of cash out of his pants pocket.

"See, I won thirty bucks."

After dinner my father drops me in the city on his way back to Connecticut. We don't say much on the ride, both of us too tired to speak. Despite the fact that my father and I have made what Dr. Lerner would call "progress," I am relieved that this day is almost over.

"About Christmas," my dad says, when I start to climb out of the car.

"Yeah?"

"What do you feel like doing this year?" he asks.

"I don't know."

"In light of what's going on with Jack, what do you say we skip it?"

"Skip it?"

"Yeah, I don't really feel up to celebrating, and I'm sure you don't want to either. So why don't we just, you know, ignore it."

"Okay."

"Yeah, it doesn't seem right to celebrate. Don't you think?"

"I guess."

"It would just be wrong."

"Right," I say. "So we'll just skip it. I'll just pretend—"

"Right. Like it's not—"

"Like it's not Christmas."

# Twenty-four

When Kate knocks on my door at two-thirty in the morning the day after Thanksgiving, she interrupts a disturbing dream in which Grandpa Jack and Andrew are playing strip poker. She wakes me, mercifully, just before they are each down to their tighty-whiteys. Kate, on the other hand, is dressed in flannel pajama bottoms, a Columbia sweatshirt, and slipper socks. She doesn't say anything to me, though I haven't seen her in weeks. She just stands at my door, with puffy eyes, a leaking nose, and no shoes. But it's only when I see that her hair is curly that I know this is a real emergency. I immediately move into action, and within thirty seconds she is seated on my couch with a wad of Kleencx in one hand and a Jack and Coke in the other.

"The wedding is off," she says, staring into her drink as if it contains the tea leaves to her future.

"What?"

"The wedding is off," she says again. This time her voice cracks, and I can see she is fighting back another round of tears.

"What happened?" I sit across from her on the couch and rub my eyes to wake myself up. I consider pouring myself a stiff drink too. I'm not sure I can handle the disintegration of Kate and Daniel; there's comfort in knowing that there are people in this world who not only believe in "the One" but actually find them.

"I think our relationship was like communism," she says, which makes me wonder if this isn't her first drink this evening.

"We were good in theory. Not so much in practice." She snorts at her own joke and spills some of the drink on her sweatshirt.

"But what happened?" I ask again, but Kate doesn't respond. Instead, she just stares at the empty television screen. "What caused the Berlin Wall to fall? Who took the first sledgehammer? Kate?"

"It was all a sham. That's it. We were a sham," she says, and crosses her arms. She leans back, as if amazed by a sudden breakthrough. "I mean, imagine if the Berlin Wall was made of Legos. No, what's that game where you take a log from the bottom, and you put it on the top, and whoever makes the tower of logs fall loses?"

"Dominoes?" I ask. I have no idea what she's talking about.

"No." Kate slams her drink down on my coffee table.

"Uh, Boggle? Clue?"

"No! Jenga!" she says, and throws her hands in the air. "Thank God, that was going to drive me crazy. Anyhow, the point is, we were like that. Built on nothing but a couple of moving logs."

"But you were built on more than logs or bricks or whatever."

"If it looks like a duck and acts like a duck, then it must be a duck, right? But we weren't a freaking duck." Kate's hysteria creeps up a notch as she pellets me with metaphors. "We looked like one, and we acted like one, but we weren't one."

"What were you, then? If not a duck."

"Jenga. We were Jenga." She says this calmly now, like it makes perfect sense and like I am an idiot for not following. "The game with the unstable logs."

Instability I get. In fact, we are sitting at the very place I had my own mental breakdown. I briefly wonder if there is something about this couch that makes people go insane and whether a trip to Ikea is in order. Then I remember I am unemployed and can't pay for a new one.

"Okay, so you and Daniel were like Jenga and not ducks. I kinda get it. But what really happened? What's going on, Kate?" I ask her, because it is time to cut the bullshitting. We need to talk about this.

"I just realized I was marrying him for all of the wrong

reasons. I thought if we looked and acted like the real thing, we'd become the real thing. But we didn't. We weren't like you and Andrew. We weren't meant for each other."

"But Andrew and I broke up."

"I know, but that's not because you weren't meant for each other." She blows her nose loudly into her tissue. It sounds like a bell.

"We're not?" I am lost again, but this time it's a grammatical problem. That damn double negative gets me every time. *Is she saying Andrew and I are meant for each other? Or is she saying that we're not? And the Berlin Wall was symbolic of the fall of communism, right?*

"You and Andrew broke up because you're screwed up and probably a little bit crazy, not because the two of you aren't meant for each other," she says matter-of-factly, and then pats my hand. As if I am the one who showed up at her apartment at two-thirty in the morning ranting about children's toys. "And I mean that in the nicest way."

"This is not about me."

"I mean, on the surface we have so much in common, and Daniel has all the qualities I've always said I wanted. You know, he's funny and smart and stuff. But really, I'm not sure that I even like him that much. The guy waxes his eyebrows. How can I marry a man who waxes his eyebrows?"

"Well, think of the alternative. You don't want to marry a unibrow."

"True," she says, as if she is reconsidering the entire breakup. She shakes her head to release the thought.

"But it's not about the hair, Emily. I guess I figured I should marry Daniel because he showed up at the right time. I'm thirty-four, and I'm supposed to want to get married, especially because if I want to have babies I need to get started soon. But I guess I just realized that doesn't mean I should settle for the wrong man."

"But you both like lofts," I say, apropos of nothing. I realize I am grasping at something to hold on to here, but I had thought Kate loved Daniel. I never considered the possibility that their relationship was a carefully constructed facade.

"Listen to this. Tonight he didn't get home until after midnight. Didn't call or anything to say he was going to be late. It turned out he had drinks with some clients and didn't have cell reception in the bar. Totally not a big deal, right? But here's the point. While I was sitting at home waiting for him, I was convinced he was cheating on me, and you know what my first reaction was?"

I shake my head.

"Relief. Can you believe that? I felt relief because if he was cheating on me, as horrible as that would be, it would have made everything clear. I would have no choice but to leave him. I actually wanted to have no choice. And that's why I finally ended it. I realized today that it's exhausting to be a coward."

"Kate, I want to tell you something. You are my fucking hero."

"But you're not listening to me. It's all over. I'm going to grow old alone and have a zillion cats. I'm not a hero. I'm a loser." Kate starts to cry now, deep sobs into the tissues.

"No, you're my fucking hero. Because you're brave. You actually have the courage to go after what you want. You're not settling just because the rest of the world tells you to. You know how few people can actually say that they live by their own rules? The rest of us just walk around afraid all of the time and do things because we assume we have no other choice." She looks at me, with a half smile on her face.

"Yeah?"

"Yeah. Let me ask you this. Do you love Daniel?" I want to make sure this is not just premarital jitters.

"Yes and no. I mean, I care about him a lot. He is a huge part of my life. But do I love him, love him? Death-do-us-part love him? I don't know. I don't think so." Kate rests her head on the arm of the couch. "Maybe I am just crazy. Maybe I've gone bonkers."

"Is this because he's not perfect? Because no one is."

"No. Other than his stupid eyebrows, there isn't anything I actively dislike about him. He is sort of perfect," she says, and shrugs.

"When you come home and he's there, are you happy to see him?"

"Sometimes, but most of the time I kinda wish he would go away."

"If he needed one of your kidneys would you give it to him?"

"Absolutely not." She says this without a moment's hesitation.

"If I needed one of your kidneys would you give it to me?" I ask, taking advantage of the fact that she is in no condition to lie.

"Absolutely," she says, and then starts to cry all over again. "Does that mean you and I should get married? Am I a lesbian? I never considered the possibility. Maybe I am. Damn it. Is that what this is all about?" I try to keep a straight face.

"Kate, you're not a lesbian, not that there's anything wrong with it."

"Do you think being a lesbian will help my chances or hurt my chances of making partner?" I can't suppress the laughter, because for the first time tonight, I see some semblance of a Kate I recognize.

"You are not a lesbian, so I don't think this will affect your partnership chances one way or the other. And thanks for the kidney, by the way. Seriously, that means a lot to me." And it does. I realize that although I may be an only child, I have some sisters in this world. *I'd give you a kidney too, Kate*.

"You did the right thing. Calling off the engagement, I

mean. You shouldn't spend the rest of your life with some-one you don't really want to come home to every day." I say this with authority, like I know what I'm talking about. I don't think Kate should marry Daniel. Not anymore.

"He doesn't pass the kidney test," she says, as if the matter is settled. "Giving him my kidney doesn't even sound good in theory. Our relationship is actually worse than communism."

"What did Daniel say when you told him?" I ask a couple of hours later. We are still on the couch, and I have replaced Kate's Jack and Coke with a cup of tea. She is going to have enough to deal with tomorrow without a hangover.

"He got really concerned about all of our deposits. You know, like how much money we put down to rent the hall, and the band, and the flowers. He actually took out a pad and started adding it up."

"How does that make you feel?" This is a line I picked up from Dr. Lerner, and I'm curious to see if it works outside the psychologist's bat cave.

"Better, to be honest. It makes me feel like he was in it for the wrong reasons too. I mean, if his biggest concern when I told him we're not getting married was how much money he was going to lose, then he couldn't really want to spend the rest of his life with me, right?" I wish I had an answer for her. *I don't know. I don't know how this works.*

"I wish I could tell you, but I am not the best judge of character. I thought you guys were happy."

"We weren't unhappy. Just not *happy* happy, you know?"

"I know." I close my eyes for a minute and think about how much of our lives are wasted pretending.

"I'm scared to death."

"Yeah, but maybe sometimes you need to do what's scariest in order to get to where you need to be."

"I know you're right." I see that Kate is starting to get sleepy. She asks me to wake her in a couple of hours because she has to go home and change before going into the office. Her inexorable march to partnership will continue tomorrow, right on through the holiday weekend, and I hope that work will provide her with a welcome distraction. For just a little while at least.

"Hey, Emily," Kate says, after I kiss her good night on her forehead.

"Yeah?"

"Thanks for being here."

"Anytime. It's a small price to pay for a kidney."

When I finally get back into bed, I no longer dream of Grandpa Jack and Andrew playing strip poker. Instead, I dream I am in a hospital bed, my arms black and blue from an IV drip. I look up and see a bunch of people crowded around me, a circle of heads around a hanging lamp. I can't make out their faces because it is too bright, but I can hear voices talking about me.

"Her organs are no use to us after all," the doctor says. "I have never seen a patient with so few parts. There aren't even spares."

"What do you mean?" Andrew asks. He is dressed in his scrubs and has a stethoscope around his neck. He looks like a doctor, not a boyfriend.

"I mean, she's, uh . . . well, take a look for yourself." The doctor pulls off my gown with a dramatic sweep of his hand, and I feel my skin exposed to the crowd. I want to ask what is going on, but when I open my mouth nothing comes out. Only the desperate silence of nightmares.

"She's hollow," Andrew says excitedly, as if he doesn't know me and I present an interesting medical mystery. "Look at those marks. I think she must have done it to herself."

I hear the high-pitched screech that means that I am flatlining, the sound of death on every *E.R.* episode. *Well, that's it, then*, I think. *I am dead. Death by disembowelment.*

But, of course, I'm not dead. And when I wake up and realize that the terrible noise is coming from my alarm clock, I am disappointed. I wanted to find out what happens next.

# Twenty-five

The dream haunts me for the rest of the day, the week even, and makes my insides ache. I can't handle the idea that I have become nothing to Andrew, just another slab of meat on a surgical table. I can't handle that I've brought this all on myself, that I've lost him for good. Before, when I thought of us, I felt only an emptiness—a low electric hum— but now, suddenly, it's like a buzz saw, an ocean in my veins, the splitting of stitches. I never wished he wasn't there when I came home, never thought we could be reduced to mere artifice. We lacked durability, maybe, but not real intimacy.

It hurts to realize he must be moving on with his life. Though Kate claims she doesn't know if he is dating again, I imagine he must be. Andrew is a guy who operates in absolutes. His good-bye was good-bye for real. And his proposal would have been for life.

I am not sure if writing to Andrew is a smart idea and consider waiting until next week's appointment with Dr.

Lerner to talk about it. Last time, we were so busy deconstructing Thanksgiving, we ran out of time before we could get to Andrew. But since I don't want to be the type of person who can't make a decision without her therapist, and mostly because I don't want to give her the opportunity to tell me not to, I sit down at the computer and write Andrew an e-mail.

To: Andrew T. Warner, warnerand@yahoo.com
From: Emily M. Haxby, emilymhaxby@yahoo.com
Subject: Hey There
    Hey, A. Grandpa Jack said you visited him last week. If you did, I just wanted to say thank you. I know he appreciates the company, and the fact that he remembered at all says a lot. Hope you had a good Thanksgiving.
    Also, thought you should know that I think about you all the time and that I miss you.
    Love always,
    E

I don't stop to consider whether I sound like a stalker or to read it over for typos. I just hit send and let my e-mail fly across Manhattan, and this time I picture it like a ball in a massive pinball game, dodging cabs and people to make it uptown, all that work just to score a point. Maybe Andrew will bounce it back, spurred on by its kinetic energy, and we will go back and forth like that for a while, the machine buzzing, the two of us finally communicating, connecting. But, instead, I hit the ball and it sinks right into the back left pocket, and I see that the game-over light is flashing. I already know that with Andrew, I am out of chances.

Five minutes later, I see I have new mail.

> To: Emily M. Haxby, emilymhaxby@yahoo.com
> From: Andrew T. Warner, warnerand@yahoo.com
> Subject: Re: Hey There
> Went to visit Grandpa Jack for me. Not you.
> Thought I should say my own good-byes.
> Emily, I don't know how to say this nicely, I am not sure there is a nice way to say this, so I will just say it:
> Please stop contacting me. Please just leave me alone.
> —A

I deserve this. I realize that. I deserve tears, and pain, and loss, because I did it. I broke us. And so all I can do is write Andrew a one-sentence reply on my screen:

*I would give you my kidney.*

All I can do is not hit send.

# Twenty-six

Today, Dr. Lerner wears a kimono. It is woven from pink silk, and the sleeves hang long and loose. Her office is dark again, but I have seen Dr. Lerner enough times now to say with certainty that her ethnicity has never once matched her costume. Her features, though, are still indistinct and shifty. Sometimes, when her hair is pulled back and covered, I am convinced she is old enough to be my grandmother. Right now, it hangs in brown waves around her face, and I wonder if she might be still shy of forty.

"I saw my mom today," I say as soon as I sit down on her couch.

"And tell me about that." Dr. Lerner doesn't take the bait. Instead, she waits patiently for a response, as if I could have a perfectly good explanation for seeing my mother after she has been dead for fifteen years. Like I am perfectly sane.

"Okay, I didn't actually see my mother. What I mean is,

I thought I saw my mother, which happens fairly frequently, actually. I will be on a subway or in a store or wherever, and I'll think I see my mom."

I attempt to fold my legs in imitation of Dr. Lerner. I settle on a half lotus, because my left side won't cooperate.

"Go on," she says.

"Well, it's usually something small that triggers it. Like some woman's hair or an ear or the way pants fall, and for a moment, just one moment, I am convinced that that woman is my mother. And then I churn out an elaborate story about how my mother could still be alive. So that it makes sense that my mother is on the Six train with me or something. Fucked up, right?"

"Totally fucked up," Dr. Lerner says, as if she doesn't think it is fucked up at all. "Tell me what happened today."

"I was standing on a corner at a stoplight—the northeast corner of Twenty-third and Third, to be exact—and I noticed this woman standing just in front of me. And for some reason there was something about her eyelashes or the shape of her eyes, and I thought, for just a second—it couldn't have been more than a second—*Could this be my mother?* I mean, maybe after fifteen years she would look different, right? I came up with some stupid story to make myself believe it. And then I stopped, because I realized I was being ridiculous, and the moment passed and I went and bought myself some new underwear because I hate doing laundry."

"Tell me about the stupid story you came up with and how it made you feel," she says, putting air quotes around "stupid story," and hands me a tissue box even though I'm not crying. I take it just in case she knows something I don't.

"It's really embarrassing. But this time I came up with the idea that maybe that day in the hospital when I saw her die was all an elaborate hoax. Maybe my mother got mixed up in some nasty Mafia business or something and is now in the witness-protection program." I feel silly—worse, pathetic—as soon as I hear the words out loud. Somehow, for just a millisecond, they had seemed plausible in my head. "You know, because there are tons of English teachers in Connecticut who are secretly mixed up in the Mafia."

"But how did it make you feel? That's the interesting part, that's the part we can learn from, and you seem to want to avoid it."

I start tossing the tissue box in the air. Catch and release. "Okay, how did it make me feel?" I toss the box up and down a few more times, watching its vertical spin.

"Yes, Emily, how did it make you feel?" She catches the box mid-toss and sets it back down on the couch next to me.

"I guess it made me feel good. Because I think the hardest part about her being dead is the finality. I'll never ever get to see her again. I mean, it's over. It's been over for fifteen years. That's really scary." As soon as the words are out, I feel my insides shift. The tears begin to fall down my face, too fast to stop them. I grab a tissue, angry that Dr. Lerner was one step ahead of me.

"So coming up for a way for that not to be true, even with something as stupid as the Mafia, gives me just one second of hope. Or possibility. Or something. And before I realize how screwed up it all is, it felt like, I mean, I guess it feels . . . It feels like relief," I say.

"I don't think it's screwed up, as you say, to look for that kind of escape every once in a while. It makes perfect sense, and I imagine it's very common. But I want you to think about other ways in which you find relief," she says, putting another set of air quotes around "screwed up" and "relief." If I weren't busy crying, I would laugh at the gesture. "Basically, what we are doing here is unraveling your defense mechanisms. Because, over time, normal defense mechanisms can hold us back from living our lives."

"I live my life," I say.

"Let's go back to your mother for now," she says, ignoring me. Dr. Lerner has mastered the art of ignoring me. "What do you miss the most?"

I almost laugh again, because it's like I'm watching one of those oops-cancer movies, a manipulative tearjerker that shows shiny bald heads and dying children despite being billed as the "feel-good film of the year." The trailers should come with a warning: *This movie will leave you bawling and dehydrated.*

Dr. Lerner is guilty of that same false advertising. She

looks kind, like an earth mother, sitting lotus-style in her hand-woven kimono, but she's diabolical.

"You know what I miss the most? This is going to sound horrible, but I think I miss the idea of her more than anything else," I say. "I'm not so sure I miss *my* mother. I just miss having *a* mother."

"What does that mean? Having a mother?"

"Sometimes it's just really hard not to have a mom. When everyone else goes home for the holidays, for example, they have this person, and I probably romanticize the notion a bit, but they have this person who wants to take care of them, who loves them unconditionally. I miss having that person—you know, *that* person who, no matter what happened, no matter how much I screwed up my life, would love me."

"There are lots of people who love you, Emily."

"I know, but that's not the point, is it? Not with that unconditionality. I may barely be able to remember her, but I do know she gave me comfort in a way no one has or can since. I can't remember ever feeling alone or unloved as a kid. I may have been a bit of a loner, but I never felt lonely."

"What do you remember about your mother, about her specifically?"

"Random details, mostly. Like how she was always so much smarter than everyone else. She just seemed to know everything. She could explain how batteries worked or photosynthesis."

Dr. Lerner nods. She doesn't state the obvious: *How can you not remember all the times your mom tucked you in and said "I love you" and stayed up late gluing pasta elbows to your art projects? How can you not remember that but remember that she knew how to explain photosynthesis?*

What kind of person doesn't remember their own mother? I remember when she was dying and who she was then—brave, defiant, and sick, so unbelievably sick—but that wasn't who she was. That would be like judging a book on the last sentence. I didn't take the time to memorize her when I had the chance. None of the important stuff, like the rhythm of her laugh or the texture of her voice or the feeling of her fingertips against my forehead. It never occurred to me that I might need those memories one day.

When I picture her now, I have to rely on the cheapest form of nostalgia. A photograph. I think of one that used to live on one of the bookshelves in our living room, though that has disappeared into the ether also. It was taken in the early '70s, and in it my mother sits directly on the beach without a towel to protect her bathing-suit bottom from the sand. But it's her hazel eyes that have stayed with me, unguarded and bright, alive enough to burn through the static of the photograph. It was taken long before I was born, so when I picture my mother, I picture a woman who never knew me, and a woman whom I never knew.

"Yeah, it's the idea I miss. Because I forgot to meet the person behind the idea."

"Bullshit."

"What?"

"That's bullshit, and you know it. You just told me exactly what you remember about your mother. That she made you feel less alone. That she was smarter than everyone else. Don't take that stuff away from her, and don't take that away from yourself."

"But that's my point exactly. There's nothing to take away from myself. She's long gone."

"Let's talk about some of your other defense mechanisms," Dr. Lerner says later, after she tells me she has a free back-to-back hour and that I need to stay.

"What other defense mechanisms? And please don't say anything about Andrew. I can't handle it right now." I am tempted to walk out the door and into the mouth of New York City. Get swallowed and chewed up into another faceless, nameless person trudging down the block.

"Let's come back to the present, shall we," she says, and steeples her hands, the way a lawyer would just before an opening statement. After seeing me twice a week for almost a month, Dr. Lerner is about to present her case.

"I'm not even sure where to start." *A real lawyer would have come prepared, I think. Am I that screwed up that she doesn't even know where to start?*

"Well, Grandpa Jack for one. You chose not to read the signs about his illness. I am not assigning blame here. I understand why, but you need to see the pattern. Your father. It takes two not to communicate. You think it makes life better to just stay quiet about what you want. And Andrew—I know you said that I shouldn't talk about him, but let me just say this. I could write a whole book on your defense mechanisms with Andrew." Dr. Lerner takes apart the steeple with her hands and puts them in a pile on her lap. She looks pleased with herself for saying it like it is. The same look people use after they say "No offense, but . . ."

"Oh, and I almost forgot. Your career. How long can you ignore the fact that you are unemployed? Have you even taken the time to consider what you actually *want* to do with your life? Your days? Don't you get it? Don't you get bored of denial?" she asks.

"I see what you mean," I say, though that's a lie. I don't see anything at all except the box of tissues, which is now just an empty cardboard box. This, it seems, is how therapy works: Dr. Lerner throws something out there, and now it is my job to take her words and lend them credence with real-world examples. I could tell her how I haven't told my dad that I'd like to spend Christmas together. Or how it took me over a year to tell Andrew I loved him. How I was so scared of losing him, of feeling anything, that I left him first. But I don't say any of this out loud.

I can't do it. Maybe because I don't believe her, because her explanations are too simple, too shrink-wrapped. When I think of defense mechanisms, I think of a little boy hitting the girl he likes the most on the playground. I don't think of me. I don't think of couches, and dead mothers, and ex-boyfriends, and Alzheimer's, and unemployment, and absentee fathers, and sexual harassment, and everything else that is confusing in my life.

Nope, I don't think of me at all. So, instead, I say nothing and stew in the awkward silence and wait Dr. Lerner out. Two can play her game.

"I love when you prove my point for me," she says a few minutes later, and smiles at me—not in a happy way but in an *I-win* kind of way. "I mention defense mechanisms, how you clam up and stonewall your own life, and how do you react? What do you do? You shut up."

"But—"

"But what? Emily, wake up. This is your life, for God sakes. It's time to face up to it. You can't get anywhere, can't get over anything, if you don't let yourself feel anything in the first place. It's time."

"Okay."

"Stop looking at the tissue box. It doesn't have any answers for you."

"But . . . I just . . . I don't know."

"What don't you know? That your mom has been dead for fifteen years and finally, finally you are just starting to deal with it? That you are sabotaging your own life because you are too afraid to actually live it?"

"It's just . . . I don't know, I—"

"Speak up," Dr. Lerner says, gently now. "I can't hear you. No one can."

# Twenty-seven

It's been twenty-four hours since my last session with Dr. Lerner, and I find myself on an Andrew binge. A torturous exercise of recounting him, the nuances and the details, with the specificity of a documentary filmmaker. I realize now that during our two years together, I spent much of that time—not enjoying, no, that would have been too easy—but memorizing, saving those best bits for later. To savor after he left me behind. Dr. Lerner is right. I've been living a life of delayed gratification—the cigarette after sex.

But someone has ripped off my bulletproof vest. Someone has forced me to watch, over and over again, the life I shed with barely a glance backward.

*Not someone, Emily, you.*

*Watch it*, I tell myself. *Watch it.*

And so I do. I watch all of it, on a loop, everything I miss, everything I deserved to lose:

I miss the way he used to kiss my shoulder whenever it was bare and he was nearby. I miss how he cleared his throat before he took a sip of water and scratched his left arm with his right hand when he was nervous. I miss how he tucked my hair behind my ear when it came loose and took my temperature when I was sick or when he was bored. I miss his glasses on my nightstand. I miss watching him take Sunday afternoon naps on my couch, with the newspaper resting on his stomach like a blanket. How his hands stayed clasped, fingers intertwined, while he slept. I miss the cadence of his speech and the stupidity of his puns. I miss playing doctor when we made love, and even when we didn't. I miss his smell, like fresh laundry and honey (because of his shampoo) at his place. Fresh laundry and coconut (because of my shampoo) at mine. I miss that he used to force me to listen to French rap and would sing along in a horrible accent. I miss that he always said "I love you" when he hung up the phone with his sister, never shy or embarrassed, regardless of who else was around. I miss that his ideal Friday night included a DVD, eating Chinese food right out of the carton, and cuddling on top of my duvet cover. I miss that he reread books from his childhood and then from mine. I miss that he was the only man that I have ever farted on, and with, freely. I miss that he under-stood that the holidays were hard for me and that he wanted me to never feel lonely.

Never again, for the rest of my life.

I miss Andrew so much that I stop and keel over and put my head between my knees. I miss Andrew so much, I begin to rock back and forth, hugging myself to make it stop. I miss Andrew so much that I throw up in the bathroom, emptying my body into the bowl in one violent motion.

I miss Andrew so much, I flush it all away.

# Twenty-eight

To: Jess S. Stanton, jesssstanton@yahoo.com, Ruth
Wasserstein, yourhonor24@yahoo.com, Mason C.
Shaw, APT, Kate R. Callahan, APT
From: Emily M. Haxby, emilymhaxby@yahoo.com
Subject: Help!

    Okay, troops, I need your input. I need a new job
pronto, and not sure what to do with this stinkin' law
degree. All suggestions and thoughts much
appreciated.
    Love,
    Emily
    PS: Please no jobs that involve food preparation,
sweating, or tassels, or any combination
thereof.

To: Emily M. Haxby, emilymhaxby@yahoo.com
From: Kate R. Callahan, APT
Subject: Re: Help!
   Maybe you should be a therapist. Speaking of
which, thanks so much for your help the other night
and all your support since. You make me feel so
much better. I am starting to feel like calling off the
engagement was the best decision I have ever
made . . .

To: Emily M. Haxby, emilymhaxby@yahoo.com
From: Jess S. Stanton, jesssstanton@yahoo.com
Subject: Re: Help!
   Best friend extraordinaire! Too bad it is a nonpay-
ing position, because you already got the job. I
know this sounds far-fetched, but how about a job
as a lawyer?

To: Emily M. Haxby, emilymhaxby@yahoo.com
From: Mason C. Shaw, APT
Subject: Re: Help!
   I say become a stripper.
   By the way, who is this Ruth friend of yours? Is
she hot?
   Are we still on for drinks on Friday?

Julie Buxbaum

To: Mason C. Shaw, APT
From: Emily M. Haxby, emilymhaxby@yahoo.com
Subject: Re: Re: Help!

Ruth is hot, but way, way out of your league. Still on for drinks. Stripping often requires both tassels and sweating. Next time read directions carefully.

To: Emily M. Haxby, emilymhaxby@yahoo.com
From: Ruth Wasserstein, yourhonor24@yahoo.com
Subject: Re: Help!

Sorry to miss you over Thanksgiving, but had a great time with the grandkids in D.C. Anyhow, it is about time you asked about a job. I have some great ideas, but I will keep them to myself until I make some calls.

By the way, kicked Jack's butt again at poker.
I won thirty bucks!

# Twenty-nine

W hen she says she wants a *fag*, does Bridget mean she wants to have sex with a gay person?" Maryann, a tiny raisin of a woman with a red smear of lipstick, asks the rest of my octogenarian book club. "Because I think that's a very offensive term. My grandson is a gay."

"I didn't know that. We should set him up with my Walter. He just came out of the closet this last June," Shirley says, and grabs a napkin to write down her grandson's telephone number. Shirley is more prune than raisin, wearing her weight squarely in her middle. It looks like her body wanted to hold on to some extra padding just to warm her organs.

There are six of us, five women in their eighties—though I have a sneaking suspicion that Shirley may well be in her mid-nineties— and me, sitting in the diner I usually go to with Grandpa Jack. We have only been here about half an hour, but I am already in love with each and every one of them. Their hair is dyed improbable colors, yellows, reds, and blues, and then sprayed up into tufted balloons around their faces. The group's collective perfume is heavy in the air and mixes with the diner smells, a pungent combination of baby powder and bacon.

So far, the meal itself has not gone smoothly. Three of the women have sent back their soup—two because it was too cold, one because it was too salty. The air-conditioning has been turned down and then up again. The restaurant is too noisy, our waiter too slow, the portions too large. Surprisingly, their fussiness is not annoying; there is relief in sitting with people who have opted out of social politeness. They have long done away with pretense and the filter between thoughts and words.

Although I read *Bridget Jones's Diary* a few years back, I'm not here to discuss the book. Instead, I'm one hundred percent here for the company, cranky though it may be. I want to rest my head in each of these women's laps and ask them to stroke my hair and tell me the story of their lives. Their loves lost and gained. And likely lost again. If they have ever felt too tired to leave their couch. If they have ever vomited from heartache. If they are afraid of dying.

I wonder if the women think it's strange that I'm here, especially since I'm not even related to Ruth, but I'm the one thing they don't seem to mind. Instead, they look to me as the representative of all things young, a spokesperson for my generation. This makes me wish that they had chosen the Margaret Thatcher biography after all. I don't feel like talking about the plight of "singletons," the promiscuity of the women on *Sex and the City*, or even the charmingly sloppy Bridget. My friends and I have rehashed it all before. I want to know what it feels like to be on the other end of your life and to have your choices already made. I want to learn from them, not the other way around.

"A fag is a cigarette," I say. "It's a British expression."

"She sure smokes a lot. Do your friends smoke that much, Emily?" Shirley asks, her raspy voice suggesting she spent years sucking down the Winstons. She takes out her cell phone, flips it open and then shut again. I have noticed each of the women do this, the gadget apparently a badge of honor among the senior set.

"Not really." Which is true, but I think I would have lied even if it wasn't. I want to make a good impression.

"And drinking? Do your friends drink that much?" Shirley says, downing her coffee like a shot of vodka. This woman has stories. I picture Shirley at twenty, hanging out at naval docks, smoking long cigarettes and hoping to seduce a fine young officer in a starched uniform.

"Some of them do. Most of my friends work pretty long hours, so they don't have that much time."

"Sorry to ask you so many questions, it's just that we picked the book to see what it's like to be young nowadays," Maryann says.

"And because Colin Firth is gorgeous," Shirley says.

"I'm so glad that Bridget got herself a happy ending," Maryann says, smiles to herself, and then reapplies her lipstick, which has the effect of holding the smile in place. "I like happy endings."

"Me too," Shirley says, and closes her eyes. She runs away in her head to a better, pre-Riverdale Retirement Home time. Perhaps she sees one officer in particular and makes love to him in the back of a Chevy.

"So, do you have a boyfriend, Emily?" Maryann asks, and the women all turn to look at me, their curiosity pulsing just under their skin. What she is really asking is what category I fit into: Am I looking or am I taken?

I wish it were that simple. *None of the above*, I want to say. I give myself an F on my report card. F for fucked it up.

"Let's talk about the book, girls. Don't put her on the spot like that," Ruth says. She knows most of the Andrew story and that it's still a sore subject. Sore, of course, being the understatement of the century. My seams have come undone and my guts have been spilled out onto the highway. I am still collecting my parts, putting myself back together again.

"It's okay," I say. "I had a boyfriend, but we broke up a few months ago. So I guess what I have now is an ex-boyfriend. It's been hard. But it's my fault. I ended it, so I shouldn't really complain."

"Oh, dear, I'm so sorry. I shouldn't have pried," Maryann

says, and folds her napkin primly in her lap. "So what happened?"

"Maryann!" Ruth says.

"Was he 'the One'?" Shirley asks, leaning forward in the booth.

"I don't know," I say. "Do you guys even believe in the One?"

"I don't," Ruth says.

"You were married for over fifty years!" Maryann says.

"True, but that's *ex post facto*. I know Irving was my One now, because we shared fifty-three years together. But he wasn't some sort of preordained One. And I can't tell you when he stopped being Irving—lovable, reliable Irving, my pharmacist husband from Bensonhurst—and became my One. It didn't happen neatly like that."

"Sure," Shirley says. "My Stan, I loved him more than I ever imagined loving another human being, but it's not like it was clear from the beginning. I mean, I almost left him a few times. Once I put the kids and all of my stuff into the back of the station wagon and was going to drive to Florida. I made it as far as the Jersey Turnpike and called Stan from a pay phone at a rest stop. I didn't have my Razr back then. Funny, I couldn't even tell you what we were fighting about. The point is, anyone who tells you it's easy is lying through their teeth."

"I haven't found a One for me yet," Maryann says, and

her deliberate tone makes me wonder if this is the first time she has said these words out loud.

"But what about what's his name? Your husband," Shirley asks, not in the least bit concerned that she can't remember her best friend's dead husband's name.

"Definitely not. I married him because I was getting older and he asked, and my mother told me I should. He was a decent man, but—" Maryann stops and breaks into a stage whisper. "*Not too bright*. But don't you worry, I haven't stopped looking. So what if we have a two-to-one female-to-male ratio here. I'm still hot stuff."

We all laugh with Maryann, but approvingly, because why should she stop looking? Maybe for her, a happy ending will actually come at the right time, at the end.

"I am my One," says Betty, a woman who has mostly stayed out of the discussion, unwilling to skewer or embrace Bridget as the rest of us have done. "Always have been, always will be. I like it that way."

"I had a couple of Ones," Shirley says, and laughs. "I think anyone who makes you happy counts. A few have made me happy in my day." She closes her eyes again, and I imagine that she is now picturing more than one backseat. After a moment, Shirley opens her eyes and sighs. Her memories bring a rush of pleasure, and her face flushes a deep red.

"I don't know about you," Shirley says. "But I could definitely use a fag."

# Thirty

Though we have spoken almost every day, I have not seen Kate for a couple of weeks, not since she showed up at my door without shoes. Today, in her office, she has shiny hair and matte skin. Her clothes are crisp and tailored and monochromatic. No stains, no wrinkles, no crumbs. She is not a woman who has just called off her engagement. She is not a woman who has been working eighty-hour weeks to forget a man named Daniel. She looks like someone to envy, someone whom you might pass on the street and think to yourself, *I wouldn't mind being her*.

"You are not going to believe this," Kate says, and talks as if we are already mid-conversation. She doesn't seem to notice that I no longer work just down the hall.

"What's going on?"

"Wait a minute. What are you doing here?" she asks, and then stands up to greet me properly. I sneak a closer look at her to see whether this new and improved Kate is just an illusion.

"I'm meeting Mason for drinks tonight, so I thought I'd stop by and make sure you're okay and see if you wanted to come." I try to catch her eye. I hope she's all right. I hope she does not keel over behind closed doors.

"No thanks, I have work to do. But I'm good, really. Not fantastic, but getting there. When you know you've made the right decision, it makes things easier to deal with. And I think Daniel may be relieved too." She looks thoughtful and sad for a minute, and I can see she is telling the truth. Her outside packaging is part real, part aspirational.

"So what will I not believe?" I ask.

"Carl got fired."

"Really?"

"The partnership announced it about an hour ago. I was going to call you but got stuck at a meeting. Anyhow, they didn't say he was fired, exactly. They said that he is leaving the firm, but everyone knows what that means. I am so happy that I never have to work with him ever again," she says, and sits down behind her desk, like now she means business. "So thank you."

"Why are you thanking me?" I ask, and she gives me a look that says, *Come on*, which I return with a half smile.

"So what happens to Synergon? Is Carl taking them as a client?" I remember that it was not so long ago I was taking

Mr. Jones's deposition, asking him about his deceased wife's diet. The thought shames me now.

"Nope. Miranda took it over. She convinced Synergon that since they have had such bad P.R. lately, it would look good for them to be represented by a black lesbian. Shows they support diversity. Anyhow, the best part is she forced them to settle and take a gigantic hit. Somewhere in the high eight figures."

"I can't tell you how happy that makes me. So something good actually came of my leaving? Carl's actually gone? For real?"

"Yup. For real. Carl has left the building. *Adiós, amigo.*" Kate stands up again, brushes her hands together in a good-riddance gesture, and then kisses me good-bye on the cheek. "I would love to stay and celebrate, but I've got a conference call in Forty-six F. See you soon?"

"Of course."

"Love you, Em," Kate calls over her shoulder on her way out the door, rushing out of her office, onward and upward, leaving me behind to sit comfortably in her standard-issue APT guest chair.

I have a few minutes to kill before meeting Mason, so I take the long way to his office and let my fingers trail along the walls as I walk. The place seems exactly the same— the smell of burned popcorn wafting from the coffee room, the hum and tick of the copy machines, partners asking their secretaries to make/cancel/confirm reservations, and the associates, heads bent over endless paper, refusing to look up as the world goes by.

Being here feels good, if only because it reminds me of why I left.

I stop in the women's room, just for old times' sake. A woman in black loafers is using my favorite stall, so I wait and loiter by the sink until she comes out.

"Emily."

"Carisse?" Without heels, and wearing a black long prairie skirt, Carisse looks tiny. Almost meek. "What's up with the shoes? I almost didn't recognize you in flats."

She looks up at me, and I see that her face has the bloated blotchiness of someone who has spent the past hour crying in a bathroom stall. It is a look all APT associates are familiar with.

"Oh, sorry. I mean, are you okay?" I ask.

"I bet now you're happy."

"What?"

"Are you here to gloat about Carl? Looking for a bravo, a job-well-done?" Her matter-of-fact tone suggests she is not being rhetorical.

"No, I just stopped by to say hello to some people."

"You should gloat. Enjoy it."

"I'm not gloating."

"Go ahead. I won't blame you. Just say it."

"I didn't say anything."

"But you were thinking it. How could I be so stupid? That's what you were thinking, right? I mean, seriously, what could I have possibly been thinking?"

"I don't know what—"

"How stupid could Carisse possibly be?"

"You're not stupid."

"Oh, but I am. Want to hear the most ridiculous part? I actually fell for him. I fell for the whole thing. He left me a voice mail last night telling me it was over. Who gets dumped by voice mail? And then today he leaves without even saying good-bye. The jerk. What did I expect from a guy who cheats on his pregnant wife?"

"I'm sorry."

"Such an embarrassing cliché. Take a look at me. This is what a cliché looks like, ladies and gentlemen." She curtsies, and the vulnerability in the gesture, in the pleading in her eyes, makes me pity her.

"You made a bad choice, that's all."

"A clichéd response. How appropriate."

"I don't know what you want me to say."

"Don't say anything."

"Okay, I won't say anything."

"I didn't sleep with Andrew. Just so you know. I wouldn't do that."

"Okay. I mean, that's good. I mean, thank you for telling me."

"Yeah." Her tears have stopped now, and she cleans off her face with a wet paper towel.

"Are you going to be okay?"

"I'll get over it."

"I'm sorry, Carisse. Really, I am."

"Yeah, well, you're right. I made bad choices."

"We all do."

"By the way, I know I should have said this a long time ago, but I'm sorry about you and Andrew. It's too bad. You guys seemed good together."

"Yeah, well, thanks, I guess."

"You know, I think this may be the longest conversation we've ever had."

"Maybe we should do it again sometime," I say.

Carisse's face is wiped free of all defensiveness and sarcasm.

"Yeah, I'd like that."

"Me too." Though I'm not sure I mean it.

"Emily! My long-lost love," Mason says, after I almost topple him over with a running hug. "I'm so happy to see you."

"I'm so happy to see you too, Mace." I grin up at him.

"Yeah, right. I bet you're just smiling 'cause you heard about Carl." Mason kisses my cheek and steers me toward the elevators. As we are walking, I get a sideways view of him. As usual, he looks scrubbed, shaven, and freshly showered, even though it's the end of the workday. Somehow, the hair at the nape of his neck is wet and his collar dry.

When we get downstairs, I see Marge at the security turnstile, standing guard in front of her wooden stool. My heart beats a little bit faster because I know she won't acknowledge me. Her last-day wink seemed like a good ending point, and I wish I could have just left it at that.

"Hello," I say.

"Thank you," Marge says, apropos of nothing, and makes me wonder if I am hearing things. But I am not, because she takes out a metal wand to stop me from going through the exit. *Does she think I am a security risk?*

"What?"

"I want to say thank you for getting that bloke Carl fired." I am left speechless. *Who is this woman? FBI? CIA? MI5?*

"What?"

"That bastard pinched my bum every day for ten years," she says, and lets me pass through. "Two thousand four hundred and thirty-two times in all. I know, because I counted."

"You counted?"

"Yes, I counted."

"Why didn't you say anything?"

"I am putting two kids through college."

"Two thousand four hundred and thirty-two times is a lot. That's a lot of pinching."

"Yes, it is quite a bit. So thank you. And my bum sincerely thanks you as well."

"Well, Marge and Marge's bum," I say, and smile, "it was my pleasure." I walk through the gate, but then I change my mind. I realize I need only one more thing from her. Turns out she is ready for it too, her arm already in the air.

My hand stings for the next hour from her high-five.

Mason and I have drinks at the Royalton Hotel, since it is in walking distance of the APT offices. Though we are smack in the middle of Midtown, the place has a minimalist meets Old Hollywood feel, and it is glamorous to be sitting here, sipping from a wide-mouthed glass in a flirty dress. Every chair in the place is upholstered in white, which adds a hint of danger to the experience; my drink, in contrast, is blood red.

We toast the departure of Carl and my encounter with Marge, and though Mason doesn't ask the specifics about what happened, he says, "You did good." I'm relieved that he's not interested in the details; the truth feels less like a coup and more like the easy way out. We toast ourselves, and then I toast Mason's suit, which is navy, pin-striped, and perfect, and before I know it we are on to our second round and I feel the tingles in my arms telling me I am starting to get tipsy.

"I broke up with Laurel," he says a few minutes later, and

I am not particularly surprised. Mason has relationship ADD.

"What happened?"

"I don't know. I told her I didn't want to see her anymore. She was nice and all, but she just didn't have that fire, you know?" Mason stares at me now, really looks at me, and for the first time this evening I wonder if I am on an accidental date here. We have grabbed drinks before, just the two of us, but it has always been clear that we are just friends. Tonight feels different somehow. We are both single, and dressed up, and flirting. Somehow, sex always works its way into that equation.

"Yeah, I know." I look into my drink. I feel nervous and wonder if I am blushing. *It's just Mason*, I tell myself. *Relax*.

"So what did she say?"

"Put it this way, I don't think I'm gonna get a Christmas card from her this year." The waitress comes over and asks if we want another round.

"A cosmopolitan for me and a martini for him. But please give him extra olives, because he needs 'em," I say in my best Southern drawl. "He's just gone and broke some poor girl's heart."

"See, that's what I need. A bit more fire." He leans in a little closer. I feel my stomach drop out in that way it does when a handsome man is looking at you like he wants to eat you for dinner.

"Yeah?" I say, somewhat stupidly. *Do I want this to be a*

*date?* Mason's not the type you have to worry about "ruining the friendship." And he's definitely sexy, with that overt masculinity—broad chest and hairy knuckles and mediocre manners—that makes me imagine he screws like a cowboy. I get wet at the thought.

I force myself to make eye contact with Mason and continue this game he has begun. Maybe this is what I need to forget Andrew. Wipe him away and fill myself up with someone else. Maybe if I listen and smell and absorb the Mason specifics, I'll forget about the Andrew ones. Do the old bait and switch.

My body will never know the difference.

Mason leans forward a little more, as if to emphasize his intentions. And I lean in too, as if to say *You might be on to something here*. I take a sip of my drink. Mason takes a sip of his. Our eyes stay locked, and I am enjoying being this girl for a change. Someone who lets go every once in a while. Someone who makes unexpected choices. *Just go with it*, I tell myself. *Live a little*.

Mason's knees accidentally brush mine under the table, but he doesn't say sorry. We talk about what I might do next, and how I need to get a job, though the conversation isn't serious. We come up with dream careers: Ben & Jerry's ice-cream taster, luxury travel writer, and Mason keeps bringing the conversation back to stripper.

"It would be in a high-class joint, of course," he says, and I trace my fingers along the top of my glass.

"You'd like having an excuse to put on high leather boots and fishnets every day," he says, watching my fingers move around the circle.

"Those are clothes that breathe," he says, and closes his eyes for a moment and pretends like he is imagining it. I laugh and swat him on the arm. He takes my hand, holds it with both of his for a second too long, then puts it back down.

Mason orders us another round, and I don't stop him. One more drink will bring me over the line from tipsy to drunk. I look forward to crossing.

"Are you trying to get me hammered, Mason Shaw?" I ask, in a voice that I hope is cute and not silly.

"Yes, ma'am," he says. "You know, I've missed you at work lately. It hasn't been the same without you."

"Thanks. I've missed you too. It's been a crazy couple of weeks."

"What have you been up to?" he asks. And I think for a moment before answering. Absolutely nothing and everything. My couch and Thanksgiving. Dr. Lerner and Grandpa Jack. Missing Andrew. The feeling that I might implode at any moment, like my insides will give out and cave in. The grand finale of years of erosion. But, of course, I don't say any of this to Mason. He's not the kind of guy who would understand emotional implosion. He's the kind of guy, though, who would understand having sex to forget somebody else. In fact, he's the kind of guy who would encourage it.

"Nothing much," I say. "Been watching too much television."

After another hour or two, we are both drunk and laughing and making up excuses to touch each other. Mason touches my hair, my fingers, my knee. I touch his shoulder when I leave to go to the ladies' room and again when I come back. I feel both blurry and hyperaware. Like Mason's body is part of the conversation, the punctuation marks adding the beat to our seated dance.

The bill comes and I offer up my half, but Mason brushes my money away, while lightly touching the inside of my wrists. He reminds me that I am unemployed, and we laugh at that, because for some reason it's funny. We leave the Royalton behind, giggling in amazement that we didn't spill on the white chairs. We assume everyone else is sharing in our intoxication, and we smile at people when we leave the bar. I don't look to see whether they smile back.

Mason's hand is on my hip.

We climb into a cab, without discussion of the fact that we live in opposite directions. Mason tells me to tell the driver where I live. I do, and before I know it, we are outside my apartment and Mason holds my hand and leads me into my building.

"Emily, you okay?" Robert asks me, standing guard as usual.

"Fine, thanks," I say, attempting to sound sober. "This is my friend Mason. From work."

"Nice to meet you, sir," Robert says, and shakes Mason's hand. He looks appraisingly at Mason's suit, decides he looks professional enough, and lets us pass.

"Good night," Mason and I say, in unison, and step onto the elevator. And suddenly, within the confines of this box, I am nervous and already morning-after sober. We stand against opposing walls facing each other, and Mason smiles at me, one of those knowing smiles that says *I can't wait to see you naked.* But he doesn't kiss me yet, and I am grateful for that. I need a second to regather my nerve. Something about seeing Robert, who greeted Andrew and me practically every night for two years, makes me wonder if this is a good idea after all.

*You can do this, Emily. Just look at him. He's delicious.*

We walk into my apartment, which means we walk into my bedroom, because I live in a studio. The place feels smaller with Mason here, and though we are still across the room from the bed, I feel like we are too close to it. I want more steps in between.

"Would you like another drink?"

"No thanks, darlin'," Mason says, and moves toward me so that we are barely a foot apart. He takes one of his arms and puts it around my back and draws me in closer, so that our faces are almost touching. *We are going to kiss. I am about to kiss Mason.*

But we still don't, not yet, anyway. Mason tries to catch my eyes first, to see if it's okay, but I can't seem to look up.

Instead, I stare at his lips, which any second will be touching mine.

And then we are kissing, very lightly at first. Mason plays it perfectly. He goes for the tiny kisses, little teasing kisses. His lips brush against mine, and he keeps his mouth closed, so I keep mine closed too, and they tickle, these baby kisses. And like they should, our kisses then get stronger, and the tongues come out. I close my eyes; I don't need to look at his lips anymore to know where they are.

This is a mistake. Not the kissing but the closing of my eyes. It disorients me, and I see Andrew behind my lids. I kiss Mason harder, to make Andrew disappear, the image and the name, bruising my lips against his. I tell myself that Andrew is probably kissing someone else right now, just a train ride uptown, and that I have no reason to feel guilty, or to feel so sad.

He told me to leave him alone. This is me leaving him alone.

And so I keep kissing Mason, but now with my eyes open wide. I look at him as we kiss, up close and clinical. I see his extra eyebrow hairs and a mole under his right cheekbone. *Concentrate on his mole. It's charming. Concentrate on that.*

Mason opens his eyes and sees me staring at him, then the kissing stops and he steps back. He takes a moment to catch his breath, to reclaim his words.

"Do you want to do this?" he asks, not angrily but softly.

I decide to keep going with this, with him—this is the way to go—so I don't answer and just lean in and put my lips against his, and we kiss some more.

"Emily." He takes a couple of steps away. We make eye contact, and his look says it all: *Not like this. I don't want you like this.*

"Is it Andrew?" he asks, though I know he already knows the answer. I nod my head, too disgusted with myself to speak. Why did I have to drag Mason into this?

"Aw, Em," he says, when he sees that I am near tears. He pulls me against him now, into a friendly hug. "I didn't know. If I did, I never would have."

"I know," I say.

"I just thought it would be fun."

"You didn't. I mean, I didn't. I mean, this is not your fault. I'm sorry, Mason. I thought I could. And it would have been . . ."

"Yeah?"

"Yeah, it would have been fun."

A tear leaks out and lands on Mason's suit jacket.

"It's a shame, isn't it?" he says loudly, almost too loudly for the empty room.

"What is?"

"This. I've been hoping to get you into the sack for years, darlin'." He lets out a laugh, and this somehow takes the hint of sex out of the air, and it is just us, my old friend Mason and me, here.

"No kidding. Where did you learn to kiss like that? You're a pro."

"I know. Girls have been telling me that for years. I think I should patent the technique."

"Thanks, Mason. For understanding, I mean." I feel shy and bring my hand to my lips to cover up the evidence.

"No problem. What are friends for?" he says, and tips an imaginary hat toward me, ever the gallant cowboy. "Listen, though, since you got me all riled up, how's 'bout you give me that new friend of yours' number. Ruth, right?"

"Sorry, Mace, Ruth doesn't do booty calls. Wait a second, though. I have an idea." I take the portable phone into the bathroom, make a quick call, and come back with a scrap of paper. "Remember my friend Jess you used to ask me about all the time?"

"Yeah, the tall hot blonde, right?" he asks, and there is excitement in his eyes now. Jess and Mason have both talked to me about wanting to sleep with the other, though the timing has never worked out.

"Go there. Now. She's waiting for you," I say, and hand over her address.

"Really?"

"Really."

"I love you, darlin'," he says, and kisses me on the cheek.

And before I can say anything back, Mason is already out the door, on his way to have sex with my best friend.

\* \* \*

I should make clear that I do believe in casual sex, much the same way I believe in psychopharmaceuticals, and euthanasia, and the right to choose. I want them to be available to me, and the rest of the world, but I would prefer not to have to count on them. And sleeping with Mason tonight might have been a good idea, at the very least statisticswise. My number would have been up to five, which is a bit more respectable and slightly less embarrassing than four (though still countable on one hand) considering I am twenty-nine and have already lived through the years in which I should've had a lot of great sex with a lot of interesting people.

But here's the thing. I know I am no good at casual sex. (Not sex itself, at which I assume I'm about average, no better or worse than the next girl, though probably not nearly as good as Jess, who has had significantly more practice and prepares for it likes it's the bar exam. She has flash cards.) Had I slept with Mason, tomorrow morning I would have woken up and thought about what it all meant, and it would have meant something to me—though I'm not sure what—but probably not all that much to him. In the scheme of the world, or better yet in *my* microscopic morsel of the world, the fact of us having sex does not matter at all. And this is true regardless of how skilled Mason may be, since the event would likely not have made it into my autobiography. If I won't remember it when I am Ruth's age and shooting the shit with some other old ladies at the Riverdale Retirement Home, then it's not worth worrying about now.

But here's the other thing: I am a hypocrite, because even though I know sex with Mason wouldn't mean anything at all either way, I would still think about it, and worry about it, and wonder about Andrew and Mason, and Mason and Andrew, and me and sex, and how I was, and whether we will do it again, and did it really mean good-bye to Andrew, and can I be as flexible the second time around, and did I smell nice. And I don't have that kind of energy. So for me casual sex is a lot like dairy. It's not a good idea, since I don't stomach it all that well.

After Mason leaves, I lie down in the middle of my bed, stare at the ceiling, and make a mental list of the things in my world that I understand. Two minus one equals one. I am in my apartment because I took a cab here and then the elevator and then I opened the door and kissed Mason and then wrote something down which made Mason leave so now I am here alone. Two minus one equals one. That noise is the toilet running because I haven't called the plumber to fix it. Tomorrow I will wake up after I have slept a little, but not all that much or all that well, and I will have a headache, since I'll be dehydrated from the six cosmopolitans I drank. Grandpa Jack is disappearing because the nerve cells in his brain are dying, which happens to one in ten people when they get old. Maybe then Ruth is one of the other nine, the safe nine, but who knows, because percentages don't work like that. Andrew is probably in bed, maybe with someone else, but likely uptown, a whole cab ride or subway trip away. He is far enough that I can't hear him. Two minus one equals one. Carl's wife has twins growing in her belly, because his sperm fertilized her egg, which split, and that can happen regardless of how much of an asshole a person is. I don't know what my father is doing, but I bet it involves budgets and calculations, impossible choices and trade-offs. Two minus one always equals one.

I need to hear someone else's voice—something real and tangible that I can hold on to before I go to bed. I buzz Robert downstairs.

"Good night, Robert," I say, through the static of the intercom.

"Good night, Emily," he says, like he understands. Like people buzz him all the time just to hear his voice.

# Thirty-one

"Dude, I owe you big," Jess tells me the next day over the phone, sounding eerily like a frat boy. "That guy should patent his technique."

"So you didn't mind my whoring you out?" I feel weird for having sent Mason over to her apartment, this, after all, being my first foray into pimping my friends.

"Are you kidding? You didn't whore me out. If anything, you whored him out, and he was worth every penny. I'll spare you the details, considering you passed him along. But let me tell you, you missed out. He might have screwed some sense into your head."

"Consider it your Christmas gift. Speaking of which, do you want to go shopping today?" I cross my fingers. I dread the thought of spending the day listening to pumped-in Christmas carols alone.

"Sorry," she says. "Too sore to walk."

\* \* \*

"Dude, I owe you big," Mason says to me about twenty minutes later, in that same frat-boy tone.

"So you didn't mind my whoring you out either? I felt bad about everything that happened."

"Are you kidding? Best night of my life. Like a rodeo, that one. She's going in the book." He sighs, like he has just eaten a great meal.

"Want to go holiday shopping with me today?"

"Sorry," Mason says. "Got whiplash."

"What are you doing today?" Ruth asks when she calls a little while later. She says it accusingly, as if she can see me right now, sitting on the couch in my pajamas with no intention of leaving my apartment today, or perhaps ever again. Suddenly being outside among the holiday shoppers, and the Salvation Army bells, and the fake department-store snow seems like too much to bear alone. I have heeded the siren call of the television, where the world does not bleed outside its four corners. Everything is safely tucked inside the square and totally irrelevant to my life.

"Nothing much," I say, which is true, although "nothing much" is an altogether different answer than not showering and rotting away my brain with MTV and my teeth with a bag of Gummy Bears, the latter being the whole truth.

"Well, then, I'll see you at Bloomingdale's at one-thirty. We have a group field trip into the city today, and I figure I've seen the Rockettes enough times. Anyhow, I need your help picking out some holiday gifts." My objection is dismissed before I have the chance to make it.

"All right," I say. Maybe I'll be able to handle the holiday frenzy with Ruth by my side. She will be my shield, like a personal Marge, only a lot smaller and eighty-four and Jewish.

"And, Emily, there are some things we need to discuss," she says before hanging up, her voice tender now, like she wants to help me get off this couch. Perhaps she has some career advice, a destination in mind for the pile of résumés I have printed up but haven't yet figured out where to send.

Or maybe Ruth will become my new Magic 8 Ball, the decision-maker in my life, since the one that I have been using for over a decade seems to be defective. It said *Outlook Good* when I asked whether I should accept my job offer from APT, again when I asked if I should break up with Andrew. It has steered me toward here.

Today, when I ask whether Ruth will take its place, it gives me a different two-word answer: *Very Doubtful. Very Doubtful?* I shake it once more, and I get *Reply Hazy, Try Again.* I try again, as instructed, and when I get the same answer the next three times, I realize something is up. Ruth is going to die. That's what the Magic 8 Ball is saying from the safety of its unbreakable plastic window. One day, probably in the next five years, ten if we are lucky, Ruth is going to die, and then I will go to her funeral and maybe shovel some dirt onto her coffin. Do they do that at Jewish funerals? Shovel dirt? And I will wake up the next morn-ing—whether we shoveled or not—in a world without Ruth, a Ruthless world, and go about my business. And pretend that it's all right, that I am perfectly fine, that old people die every day.

"I hate the holidays," Ruth says by way of greeting when we meet in front of Bloomingdale's at one-thirty sharp. I have collected myself, and showered, and put on makeup to hide the fact that I have been crying. I hope Ruth doesn't ask why my eyes are red, because I can't explain that I have spent the last two hours writing her eulogy in my head. Somehow, I don't think she'll understand.

"Look at all these people crowding up the city. I want to tell them all to go home and let me shop in peace," she says, and links her arm with mine so that we don't get separated by the acquisitive hordes. I take a deep breath and try to memorize everything about her. The warmth of her wool jacket next to mine, the smell of her Shalimar, which, it turns out, is slightly different from the way it smelled on my grandmother, the sound of her voice. As soon as we are inside, I am immediately overwhelmed by all the stimuli and annoyed that they are interfering with my total absorption of Ruth. Today is the day I will hold on tight, commit her to memory, so that whenever she is gone I am not left hollow.

But I can't focus, with the flashing lights, the perfumed

air, the elbows, the umbrellas, the fucking "Rudolph the Red-Nosed Reindeer," the mothers and daughters. Particularly the mothers and daughters, a holiday advertisement for everything I don't have and can't buy. A walking billboard of all the details I have forgotten. Or never thought to remember.

I look at Ruth and link my arm a little tighter. She feels like insulation. She leads me through the crowds and across the store and then does a loop, bringing us back to the spot where we started.

"What do you say we skip shopping and go eat instead?" Ruth asks, and even before I answer she begins leading me downstairs to the café.

"Yes, please." I can't walk through here today. I realize that now. It is suffocating, standing under the weight of a thousand shoppers, each hungrily consuming and checking off people from their endless lists. I picture men shopping for their mistresses and for their wives. Daughters shopping for parents and stepparents, brothers and sisters. Half brothers and half sisters. Cousins. Lovers.

My own list is so small that I don't even have to write it down.

"You look terrible," Ruth says to me, once we are seated across from each other in the crowded café. Here the atmosphere is still rowdy but contained. Here it doesn't feel like the collective tension is about to burst.

"Thanks." I like that Ruth feels comfortable enough with me to say it like it is. "I feel pretty terrible too."

"Yeah?" she says, asking without pushing.

"Yeah. I've been missing Andrew. He said he doesn't want me to contact him ever again."

"That must have hurt."

"Yup. But I asked for it, didn't I?"

"Yes, I guess you did. That doesn't make it any easier, though, does it?"

"No. And the holidays are hard for me, you know?"

"Me too," she says. "I always miss Irving most this time of year."

"What was he like? Irving."

"It's strange, but I hate describing him to people, because I can't do him justice. It diminishes him somehow to turn him into a list of details. The truth is, he was a mensch. You know that word?"

I nod yes.

"Well, that's who he was. He was just good, and smart, and kind. But shy, shy. I used to do the talking for both of us. His parents got out of Germany just before the war, and they moved to Brooklyn. If you could believe it, they moved right next door to my parents, and we were neighbors growing up. We went to the prom together. We went through everything together. He knew every incarnation of me—when I was a skinny schoolgirl, when I was an angry prosecutor, when I sat on the bench. It's hard now, because he didn't get to meet this version of me—Senior Citizen Ruth."

"You mean Kick Ass and Take No Prisoners at Poker Ruth?"

"That one too. He'd have been impressed. You know what? I think the holidays are hard for everyone. We are all putting on a big show. The holidays are an elaborate way of saying to the world 'I am okay.' If you have gifts to give and parties to go to, then your life must be all right, right?"

"I guess."

"Have you ever seen someone laugh at a funeral?" Ruth asks me out of nowhere, and I wonder if somehow she knows about my friends and me after my mother's wake. When we laughed in a corner—hysterical, shrill laughter—because it was the only thing we knew how to do.

"Yup." Because it is Ruth, I give more. "After my mother's funeral, that's what I did. And the funny thing was, it actually felt funny. Hilarious, even. It was so ridiculous, it couldn't be anything else but funny."

"Exactly. I think that's what people do with the holidays. They wrap it up all neatly with a turkey and clever gifts and lots of eggnog and laugh and laugh, but at the end of the day there are always people missing from the table. And you have to either sit with those empty chairs and laugh, or you can choose not to come to the table at all. I would rather come to the table," she says definitively, like she is delivering her verdict. Guilty or not guilty.

"You're saying I need to start coming to the table, right?"

"I'm saying you've got to go to the table, yes. But I'm also saying that eventually that laughter becomes real laughter, if you let it. You can't be afraid of that. You have to fight for it. And there are always going to be empty chairs, and that's okay too. Emily, I have to tell you something," she says, and I think, *Here it is, she is going to tell me she is dying.*

"Okay," I say, and take a deep breath to calm myself. *It will be okay. You can do this. You have done this before.*

"Jack is getting worse. I think we're losing him." I am confused. I know that we are losing Grandpa Jack; I was there when he disappeared. But I want to make sure I get what she is saying, since the first time she tried to have this talk with me all those months ago, I couldn't hear her.

"What do you mean, exactly? You can spell it out."

"He's dying, Emily. From something else. He's not eating very much. They think it may be colon cancer. But they don't know."

"I've been calling every day, and he didn't say anything. He said he felt fine."

I look down and play with my napkin. I rip it into long white shreds.

"You spoke with the doctor?" I stick with the technical details first. Always the easy ones first.

"Yeah. She stopped by a couple of days ago when I was sitting with Jack. Apparently your grandfather refuses to get a colonoscopy, so they don't know for sure that's what it is. But that's what everything points to." My napkin is now no longer a napkin. It is a pile of a hundred pieces of a former napkin.

"Okay," I say. "Okay."

"Do they know how long?" I ask because it seems like what I am supposed to want to know. Though I am not sure it matters. Grandpa Jack and I are past formal good-byes and counting time. I have stored a lifetime of him, and that will have to be enough. *It is enough*.

"They think soon. Probably not tomorrow, but soon." Her eyes rest on mine; they are warm and maternal. She wants to take care of me, and she wants to make it hurt less. But it is her look that hurts more than anything else, because it is the one I will keep, the one I will return to like an old photograph. I memorize her face, the lines that crisscross at random, her beautiful wrinkles, the kind that are disappearing as a whole generation is introduced to Botox. I want to copy them with tracing paper. I want to run my finger through their grooves. I want to feel that look forever.

I will not shovel dirt, I realize now. If or when, I will think of this look. This look will be her eulogy. No more, no less.

"Thank you for telling me. Like this. In a way that I can't run away from." I dump my pile of shredded napkin onto the table, making a baby mountain of useless paper.

"Of course."

"Do you think I should call my dad and tell him?"

"He knows." She aims her eyes downward so they don't have to catch mine.

"He knows?"

"He has been by every night this week. He must know." Ruth looks through the pile of lifeless napkins.

"But why didn't he call me? Why didn't he tell me?" I ask, though she is not the one I should be asking.

"I don't know. When I didn't hear from you this week, I figured your dad just couldn't do it," she says. "I hope I didn't overstep my boundaries here. I just thought you should be told."

"Thanks. Seriously, I can't tell you how much I appreciate this." I get up and walk around the table to give her a hug. She feels tiny in my arms, a stack of bones under her thick wool suit.

"This is for the best, you know. Grandpa Jack going this way. It's what he wanted. He said so." It feels wrong to say it like that before it is true. Like I am already counting Grandpa Jack among the dead.

"I know. This is better." Ruth rests her hand on top of mine, and it feels heavier than I would have imagined. Solid.

"Yeah," I say, "I know."

I take a deep breath and exhale in a rush. The napkin pile scatters to the floor, like kamikaze butterflies, but neither of us bends down to pick up the pieces.

* * *

Eventually, Ruth and I feel revived enough to face the rest of the store. We link arms again and walk through the crowds of people, barely noticing as they nudge us with overstuffed shopping bags. "Silent Night" plays just above the din, and a few of the shoppers subconsciously mouth the words. We get accosted by a few perfume-pushers, but other than that, we are left alone to wander about. We circle the cashmere scarves and indulge our fingers with the soft fabric. I buy gloves for Kate and Jess. Ruth buys a hat for her son and a Burberry shawl for herself.

As we continue walking together, I wonder if people assume that Ruth and I are grandmother and grand-daughter. I hope so. I would like for people to think that I have someone that special to link elbows with in Bloomingdale's. Today I am not envious of the rest of the department-store pairings. Having Ruth at my table is more than enough.

# Thirty-two

To: Emily M. Haxby, emilymhaxby@yahoo.com
From: Doug F. Barton, APT
Subject: Work

Hello, Emily. Happy holidays from the APT family. I didn't know you knew Ruth Wasserstein! What a small world. I clerked for her straight out of law school, and she has been my mentor for the last twenty years. Anyhow, she mentioned that you had decided to start looking for a new job and that you couldn't be convinced to come back to APT. So, long story short, I sit on the board at the ACLU, and they are looking for a new staff attorney. Unfortunately, the pay cut will be significant, but Ruth thought you would be interested. If you are, please get in touch ASAP, and I will arrange an interview for you.

Best,
Doug Barton

To: Emily M. Haxby, emilymhaxby@yahoo.com
From: Miranda A. Washington, APT

Hey, Emily! I didn't know you knew Ruth Wasserstein! She's my hero. I clerked for her out of law school, a million years ago. Smartest woman I have ever met. Anyhow, she got in touch and said that you were looking for public-interest work. I sit on the board at Legal Aid. Any interest in working there? I know the pay is shite, but you would get to do great work. It seems right up your alley. They can interview you on December 27, so let me know if you are available. They are desperate for help.

Happy holidays,
Miranda


To: Ruth Wasserstein, yourhonor24@yahoo.com
From: Emily M. Haxby, emilymhaxby@yahoo.com
Subject: Thank you!

THANK YOU, RUTH! THANK YOU!!!

You are my fairy godmother!

Now, do you happen to know of any cheap apartments available in Brooklyn? If I take a public-interest job, I can't afford to stay in my place without selling my organs on the black market.

To: Emily M. Haxby, <u>emilymhaxby@yahoo.com</u>
From: Ruth Wasserstein, <u>yourhonor24@yahoo.com</u>
Subject: Re: Thank you!

That's what Craigslist is for, my dear! Sell your organs! Much better option than selling your soul.

# Thirty-three

Maybe this is one of those times in life where you just go for it. Put your heart on the line. Let it hemorrhage. I have nothing to lose. Worse comes to worst, I find myself trapped back in a couch vortex. Unlike Meatloaf, I am hitting three out of three here—want, need, love—and there is no running from that. Enough is enough. Dr. Lerner would tell me to just do it: *This, Emily, is living your life.* And so I e-mail Andrew and finally say what I want to say.

To: Andrew T. Warner, warnerand@yahoo.com
From: Emily M. Haxby, emilymhaxby@yahoo.com
Subject: Couldn't help myself
  Hi, A. Know you don't want to hear from me, but couldn't help myself. I want to say a few things:
  I love you.
  I miss you.
  Let's try again.

To: Emily M. Haxby, <u>emilymhaxby@yahoo.com</u>
From: Andrew T. Warner, <u>warnerand@yahoo.com</u>
Subject: Re: Couldn't help myself

You have got to be kidding me. An e-mail? Grow up, Emily.

Please just leave me alone.

# Thirty-four

W hy do you think things turned out the way they did with Andrew?" Dr. Lerner asks at our next session. We have been through this routine before, and though we have "breakthroughs"—which is just another way of saying the good doctor made me cry—I don't know if I am getting any better. She can't stop Grandpa Jack from dying; she can't make Andrew love me again. She can, however, make me go bankrupt.

For the umpteenth time, we play the game: Dr. Lerner asks why things are the way they are, and I say I don't know.

"I don't know."

I look down at the Persian rug. I concentrate on the design, but I can't make out a pattern. There are circles within circles, and teardrops within teardrops. It is mostly burgundy, the color of dried blood.

"You don't know?" Dr. Lerner asks. She does this, too,

from time to time, repeats what I say, to keep me talking, to highlight that I am avoiding answering her questions.

"I screwed things up. I tried to fix them. That obviously didn't work. Game over."

"Game over?"

"Yeah, game over. I tried. I broke my own fucking heart, what, like three times now? It's time to get over it. Andrew doesn't want anything to do with me. It couldn't be clearer."

"Okay. 'It couldn't be clearer.' Right. Tell me, why do you think your father hasn't told you that your favorite person in the whole world is dying?"

"That's not a very nice way to put it. I thought you were supposed to be empathetic."

"No, I am supposed to be honest. So why hasn't he told you?"

"I guess we don't do that in my family. Clearly, communication is not my dad's strong point." I notice some gold in the carpet in the shape of small diamonds.

"How about you? Is it your strong point?" I can't quite read her tone. Today Dr. Lerner wears a robe and a white turban, with her hair twisted up into a knot. The turban gives off a sense of moral or religious authority, an unambiguity, so I assume she is not being sarcastic.

"Not really, but I'm working on it."

"With your father?"

Julie Buxbaum

"What am I supposed to do? Call him up and tell him to please start informing me from now on when one of my grandparents is going to die? It doesn't matter, anyway, because there are none left. Call him up and tell him that, though I completely sympathize with the impulse, canceling Christmas makes me feel even more alone than I already am? Call him up and tell him that I quit my job and broke up with Andrew? That Andrew hates me now? That I feel like a fucking orphan?" Who is Dr. Lerner to pass judgment? With her fake turban and unpatterned carpet. What does she know?

Dr. Lerner lets my questions hang there for a few moments and uses the dead air to convey her message. *Yup, that's exactly what you are supposed to do.*

"It takes two people to have a conversation." I know I sound like a spoiled kid, but I'm exhausted. Dr. Lerner just shakes her head at me and rests her wrists on her knees. She looks like she is meditating. I am tempted to remind her that I am paying her to help me, not to reach spiritual nirvana.

"He doesn't hear me. It's like talking to a brick wall."

"Who says that he has to hear you? This is not about him, Emily. This is about you. You can't change other people. Only yourself. *You need to learn how to communicate,*" she says, all in italics, like she is delivering the punch line to a New Yorker cartoon.

"Uh-huh," I say, intentionally inarticulate, intentionally

depriving her of the satisfaction of a real word. A private joke with myself.

"Uh-huh," she parrots back, and smirks. Her look says it all. *You're not smarter than me.*

I wish I could talk with my eyes the way Dr. Lerner can. Then I wouldn't have a *communication* problem.

"Okay, I get it. I need to communicate more. It's just easier said than done." She is right, of course. She is smarter than I am. That's why I keep coming back. "I tried with Andrew. I really did. I laid out all of my cards in that e-mail. And he shot me down. It was like getting run over by a tractor."

"Yup, sure sounds like you tried hard. With that *e-mail*. You tried."

"What's that supposed to mean?"

"You know what it means. So tell me what happens. What keeps you from saying what you want to say?" Dr. Lerner asks, reverting back to doctor–patient speak. I stare at the carpet again, but it still looks like a bunch of different rugs stitched together. "Please look at me, not the ground. I want to know what happens to you, what causes you to shut down."

"Sometimes, when I want to say something, the words just don't come out for me. It's like there is a space and I know I am supposed to fill it in. But I can't."

Dr. Lerner merely nods, sensing that I am not quite finished with the thought.

"But I guess part of the problem is I don't know what to say. Sometimes I can't even put a label on it. Like with Andrew. I couldn't tell him what I wanted, because I didn't really know. I get that I should dig deeper or whatever. But I have always felt like there is nothing there to pull from. There was nothing there," I say. I lean back into the couch and close my eyes. The room is completely silent. *This is where I start from*, I realize in the pause. *You start from quiet and you build the noise. You build yourself up from empty. You create that something to pull from. It's like eating.*

"Exactly," Dr. Lerner says, as if she can hear my thoughts. "Exactly."

We sit in silence some more, but now it's not really silence. My head is buzzing with words and with sentences, and I fill myself with them. It's not quite energy, but it's something. It's a start.

I walk home from Dr. Lerner's office, even though the temperature has dropped into the single digits. The streets are empty. Manhattan has unloaded its contents again, squeezed it through bridges and tunnels or packed it up into planes and cars, leaving behind a skyline in a rearview mirror, a handful of tourists wearing fanny packs, and a couple of bartenders to serve them. This is what happens every year on the eve of Christmas Eve. Most people leave Manhattan to go "home," whatever that may mean, or maybe to be anywhere else but here. The effect is a muffling of sound, as if all of the distinct noises of New York, its sirens, its taxi horns, its footsteps, are being smothered by a large blanket. It's not quite peaceful, more damped down.

Since my father decided to skip Christmas this year, I never considered the possibility of heading to the house I grew up in for the holiday. I don't really think of it as home anymore, anyway, since I associate the place with a rush of disorientation. It's not the same house once the insides have been taken down and rebuilt, the contents dispersed around the neighborhood via garage sale. I am pretty sure it's no longer mine.

When I feel like I do tonight—weightless and afraid that I may scatter into nothingness—I make a mental list of all the people in this world who love me. Today that includes: Jess, Kate, Ruth, maybe Mason (in his own way), and my father (also in his own way). Grandpa Jack is on there too, of course, but when he time-travels back a generation, I think it's cheating to count him. He can't feel left behind, he can't miss me, he can't *love* me, if he doesn't realize I exist. It's like that picture of my mom on the beach I often think about, a picture of a woman whose biggest concern is getting an even suntan. It is not a picture of a mother at all because it was taken pre-me; there is nothing pinning her in place. She, too, looks like she could float away.

Now I know sometime soon Grandpa Jack will be switching columns over to the tally marked *Dead People*

*Who Loved Me.* That's a separate list, for self-explanatory reasons.

Andrew, you might have noted, is also not on the list. Again, self-explanatory.

I do this frequently, this counting. I take comfort in the statistic, the ability to use some form of measurement. Does everyone do this? Count their love—their weight—in human units? I hold on tightly to my small single-digit figure, my five or my six, depending on how I count, repeating their names in my head as I walk down the city blocks. A mantra forcing me to take in breaths with each word and to lock a part of it in my abdomen. Each makes me heavier, more whole. A starting place.

*Twelfth, Jess, Jess, Jess. Eleventh, Kate, Kate, Kate. Tenth, Ruth, Ruth, Ruth. Ninth, Mason, Mason, Mason. Eighth, Dad, Dad, Dad. Seventh, Grandpa Jack counts. Grandpa Jack, Grandpa Jack, Grandpa Jack still counts.*

When I reach my building, I don't recognize the man standing guard at the door.

"Where's Robert?" There is a new person here, wearing Robert's uniform, wearing Robert's cap.

"With his family in Staten Island for Christmas. I'm covering for the next couple of days," the man says, and holds the door open for me. He looks about fifty, with a boxer's face of lumps and broken blood vessels, a face that says *You should've seen the other guy.* "Good night, ma'am."

We don't know each other's name, but his voice is the last voice I will hear tonight.

I miss Robert.

"Good night," I say, just after the elevator doors close. It doesn't matter if he hears me.

# Thirty-five

I know I didn't *have* to be alone today. Right now I could be in Providence, Rhode Island, or Short Hills, New Jersey, with Jess's or Kate's family, drinking eggnog and opening last-minute presents picked out by their mothers when they found out I had no other place to go. Ruth invited me to join her in D.C. with her kids and grandkids for a day of movies and Chinese food, and Mason suggested I fly down to Texas to experience my first deep-fried turkey. Though I was tempted by everyone's offer, I think it would have been lonelier to be the family mooch, to pretend to be a part of something I am not. I would have felt like a foreign exchange student.

Instead, I have my own plan. I wake up early, when the white glare of the sun edges through my windows, and eat a bowl of cereal standing up next to the sink.

*I will not wallow. I will not look in the direction of my couch and television.*

I shower, get dressed, put on my winter coat and gloves and hat and scarf; I bundle myself tight and heavy.

*This is easy. There are children being shot in Darfur. We are a nation at war. This is nothing.*

And then I go out the door, say Merry Christmas to the man who isn't Robert, and start walking uptown. The cold air sneaks under my sleeves and burns my wrists.

*One small thing you have to do. And that will give you strength for the rest. Get on with it.*

I walk faster, follow the path of the 6 train, but above-ground, as it snakes its way up the East Side. Past Union Square. Madison Square Park. The Met Life building towers over me, measures my progress.

I make it to Grand Central, which smells like body odor and coffee and feels like a refugee camp in Miami. The heat is on full blast, and the air is heavy and humid. Families gather in corners, trying unsuccessfully to corral wandering children, wiping sweat off their faces with discarded scarves. There are shopping bags everywhere, tucked under arms, cradled between feet, red-and-green wrapping paper peeking out of the tops. Every once in a while an announcement is made, and groups disappear behind grand doors marked with numbers onto trains toward home. The black flickering billboard propels the day forward, pushing us nearer to our destinations.

I wait for the shifting letters to announce my train. I don't think about what I am doing, certainly not where I am going. I just sit here, on the floor, eyes fixed to the board. If you happened to be in Grand Central right now, you would never notice me. I am one of a thousand people waiting for a train, blending into the walls. It feels like disappearing.

The train ride is uneventful. The voice in my head dissolves into the roar of the car as it moves along the tracks. I rest my head against the cold window, look out, but don't see anything. Only bland landscape. I could be any-where in the world.

When I get off at my stop, a taxi driver waits out front in an idling cab. It seems like he is waiting for me. I hop in the back, and though I don't have an exact address, he knows the place. The driver has pictures of his children pasted to the clear plastic divider, and I examine and memorize them, like they are on the back of a milk carton. Identical twin girls, both with two braids skimming their skulls, the girl on the right showing off a lost tooth.

The driver drops me off outside a stone-wall entrance, and I realize I am just a couple of blocks away from my dad's country club. I wonder if he is there, slapping people on their backs and shaking hands. Or maybe he is visiting Anne's family, though for the life of me I can't remember where she is from. Maine, maybe? She wears jeans like she's from Maine. I give the driver a big tip, twice my fare.

"Thank you, ma'am. Do you need me to wait?"

"No thanks. Go on home to your family," I say. "Merry Christmas."

"Merry Christmas?" he says back, but he sounds like he's not so sure. I nod at him again, and he drives off, leaving behind only the smell of exhaust.

I stand in front of the Putnam Cemetery and will myself to walk through the open metal gate and into the canopy of trees. There is not a single sound, not even the rustling of leaves. For now, I am alone.

I wander down the front drive and into the smattering of stones. The green grass is carefully delineated and contained by sculpted shrubs and a white fence. I have only been here once before, that first time when we buried my mother, and I'm not sure where her grave is. I realize that it sounds pretty horrible, that I've never bothered to get on the train before, to come here, to bring some flowers. But I haven't, and I won't make excuses like there just wasn't time, or the years escaped me, or any of that crap. Since I don't believe in an afterlife and have no other coherent theory that would make the piece of ground in which my mother is buried anything other than a piece of ground, it seemed silly to get on the train. Coming would have only been an exercise. Another reminder that a stupid stone slab is all that there is left. Which is nothing at all.

Today, though, I realize, coming here is all about me. This has little to do with honoring my mother.

I walk through the cemetery, hoping for clues to send me in the right direction. I read all of the stone inscriptions. I do lots of math while I walk, subtracting dates. I like passing by the graves of those who died old, especially the husbands and wives buried next to each other. I picture their bodies, deep in the ground, holding hands, extra support for the weight of the earth above them.

Babies are buried here.

I walk passed a grave marked *MacKinnon*, and I wonder if it is someone in Carl's family. There is a seventeen-year-old. A four-year-old. Lots of beloveds. A seventy-six-year-old. There is no pattern here. The stones are different shapes and sizes, some with elaborate etchings on them. Some matte, some shiny. A couple look like benches, and though I am tempted to sit down, I am not sure that's what they're for. There is no set distance between graves. No lines. Just a smattering here and there among the trees.

There are no rules.

There are Mothers, and Daughters, and Sons, and Husbands, and Wives, and Friends. I don't see a single grave marked Lawyer or Banker or Pharmacist. I recognize some famous names. Some Bushes that, based on the American flags, I assume are The Bushes. I see at least one grave without a first name. Just Baby Girl Davenport.

I want to lie down on a patch of icy grass and close my eyes. I want to stay here forever. Today I don't mind the quiet. For a while I forget that I am looking for one spot in particular and just wander around. Maybe this is my home. Among the stones, and the trees, and the dead. Maybe I could start a business right here, a little stand that sells flowers to people like me who forget to bring some. I would tell my customers not to feel bad, that it happens all the time. And at night I could sleep in a sleeping bag next to little Jenny Davis, who died at age fourteen in 1991. I wonder if she liked Madonna. If she wore braces, and if she did, if they took them off before they buried her. How do you die at fourteen? It seems a particularly cruel age to die. Old enough to know that it matters that you've never been kissed.

I find my mother among a bunch of graves from the late 1800s. She is set a bit apart from them, but I wonder how she got mixed up in this lot. It seems wrong somehow. There was a perfectly good spot next to Jenny Davis. I am glad, though, that my dad picked a simple stone for her. There are no elaborate etchings. Nothing that can go out of style. Just a vertical rectangle, with a big lawn around it, room for Grandpa Jack, for my father, and I guess, one day, for me.

## Charlotte Haxby
### 1950–1992

I like that it doesn't say *Beloved*, or *Mother* or *Daughter* or *Wife*. Nothing to pigeonhole her. I walk around it a few times, in a circle. I read the letters and do the math, though it contains information that I already know. I am not sure what to do now. Do I stand up and look at it? It feels condescending, this looking downward. Do I sit in front of the stone on the ground over which my mother is buried? Can I lie down here? That's what I want to do.

I want to lie in the shadow of the stone.

I sit but don't lie down, just in case someone comes. I rest a few feet in front of the stone, cross-legged, and wonder if I am being disrespectful or sacrilegious by choosing this spot, by adding weight to the casket. I figure it doesn't matter, and if it does, my mom would understand.

*Hi, Mom,* I say in my head. Not out loud. If she can hear me somehow, I imagine it doesn't matter if I say it out loud. In my head, at least, it doesn't sound like I am talking to a rectangular rock.

*Hi, Mom,* I try again. *Long time no see. You don't call. You don't write.*

*Okay, let me start over. I shouldn't be making jokes.*

*Hi, Mom, it's me, Emily. But you probably know that already.*

*Stop it. Do this right. You came this far.*

*Okay, okay, okay.*

I get up off the ground and circle the stone one more time to clear my head. I take deep yoga breaths. *I can do this.* I take my seat again, careful to sit in exactly the same spot. For some reason, I now think of that small piece of ground as mine.

*Hi, Mom. I don't know if you can hear me, or if it really matters if you can hear me, and I am sorry I didn't bring flowers, and that it took me fifteen years, and that I spent time with*

*Jenny Davis instead of coming right over to you. And I don't know how this all works, but if you get a chance to meet Jenny, tell her I say hi, and I'll be thinking about her. She won't know me, though.*

*I am not sure what to say. Is it wrong to tell you all about me? I could tell you about how much I miss you, which is more than you can ever imagine. I could tell you about how I think about you every day. Not always about you you, which I am sorry about, but I don't remember you you as well as I should. What I do remember, though, I hold on to tightly, maybe too tightly. And then there is the idea of you, and how you were everything, and how you were my mother, and that you are not here anymore. That I think about every day.*

*If you can hear me, I wouldn't mind sometime if you could give me your voice back. I would love to hear it in my head for a little while. Just some of your noise. I lost it a few weeks after you died, and I can't seem to get it back. No matter how hard I try to hear it. I hear you stopping breathing. That horrible space between sound. That's what I hear, and I would prefer not to hear that anymore. If you could do that—send me some of your noise— that would be great. If you can't, I understand.*

*I'm also sorry that I didn't remember you when I had the chance. I should have done a lot of things that I never did, and I wish I could do all of it all over again. Just press restart. I think now that it's better to say things that you can't unsay than not to say anything at all. I should have learned to ride a bicycle. I should have told Dad not to cancel Christmas, that we have to try to be a family, that it's no good to keep pretending. I should some-times say out loud,* Enough is enough.

*I will. I am now.*

*I guess I wish I had known to remember everything, because I think that would have made letting go of you a bit easier. Then you wouldn't really have been* gone gone, *right? You would have been inside me somewhere, and I wouldn't feel so empty now. Sometimes I try at night to picture your face, but all I see are photographs. It's not the same thing. You should know, though, that you look beautiful in the one right before you got sick, the one where you're all dressed up for my birthday party. My thirteenth. I remember you made a big deal about my becoming an official teenager, complained that I was growing up too fast, that you were losing me too soon.*

*In the picture, you look like someone I wish I could be.*

*It would be great if I could tell you Dad and I are just fine. I mean, we are, of course. Of course we are. But you can probably tell we are both a bit broken and haven't done such a good job of picking up the pieces. We're trying, though. I think we are both trying, and hopefully we'll get better at being a family. A two-person family is still a family. And I think it's time I fought for us.*

*Grandpa Jack is dying, which, if you can hear me, I imagine you know already. I am going to go see him later today and spend some time with him. I want to make sure I am there when he goes. You'll take care of him, if I am wrong and it's true that he actually goes somewhere, right? I like to think of you, and*

*Grandma Martha, and your parents too, though I didn't get to know them so well, all of you together laughing and eating turkey around the old oak table. I'm sorry that I don't really believe you are all somewhere together, though; I think these things just to comfort myself. Much like how I think you can hear me right now.*

*Does it matter? I can hear me, which is something. It's time I started hearing me.*

*I'm doing all right. Sometimes I feel tired, even when I haven't done anything at all. I have screwed some important stuff up lately, but I am getting myself sorted out, I think. I came here, which is more than a start. I made friends with a woman named Ruth, whom you never got to meet. She is a friend of Grandpa Jack's, and you would have loved her. She's smart and funny and looks after me. Is it okay that I still want looking after even though I am almost thirty years old?*

*When do you become who you are supposed to be? Or am I who I am, who I am?*

*I know I sound like a little kid. In real life, outside the walls of this place, I'm not. Well, only sometimes. Or maybe you are always a child around your parents? God knows I am still a child around Dad, and Dad is one around Grandpa Jack. I lied to Dad recently about a bunch of things, and he has been lying to me too. It is all very stupid and not worth rehashing now. Put it this way: We need to work on communicating.*

*Sometimes I think when you died, someone pushed a mute button inside me too and trapped the real me somewhere in here.*

*I quit my job, which I think was a good thing. And I broke up with Andrew, whom you never met but would have loved. He's pretty fucking special. I know now that you have to hold on to the people you would give your kidneys to. You don't just let them go because you are too fucked up to understand what you've got. Or too scared. Because the truth is, I was scared. If we kept going, I knew he could have chopped my heart up into a hundred little pieces. He could have eaten me alive.*

*Or maybe you do lose them, because when you are as fucked up as I was, giving away your kidneys doesn't mean all that much. But now it does, now that I understand what I lost, now that I understand I was running away. Now that I've started regenerating my lost parts. Now that I have kidneys to give, it means a hell of a lot. And if you have any pull with that one, I could use all the help I can get, since he has made it clear that he doesn't want anything to do with me. I am going to fight for him, anyway. For real, this time. Even if it means I'm too late. Even if it means I get fucking pulverized in the process.*

*Sorry about the cursing. I do that a lot now and should probably stop. I am a lawyer and a grown-up, for fuck's sake.*

*I wish I knew if you could see me or hear me, and when you could see me or hear me, because I am not sure I want you to see everything. But I guess if I could choose, I would pick everything over nothing, as embarrassing as that may be. But obviously it's not up to me. If it were up to me, you would be standing next to me right now, and we would be visiting some other person's grave, someone we liked but weren't going to miss all that much.*

*If it were up to me, I would rewind, at the very least to this morning, and come back with some flowers.*

*This is just a long way of saying that I love you. And I miss you. And I am going to try to do things better. I owe it to you— and to me, to me also—to at least try. And I love you, even though you are dead, and my love for you has no place to go now. And I love you even though I can't hear you anymore. And I love you, without any "even though"s. I want you to know that I'm going to be okay. Everything is going to be okay. Right? Right. It will, because it has to be. Enough is enough. I am going to fight for me.*

I stand up, for emphasis maybe, and to tell myself that I am done. *Good-bye, Mom.* I circle the rectangular stone one more time. Put my fingers along the grooves of the letters and memorize the feel of them. I close my eyes to isolate the sensation. Then I touch my fingers to my lips. Kiss them. Touch the stone again. Not quite flowers, but it's something.

I take my time leaving the cemetery. I walk by Jenny Davis one more time, kiss my fingers again, and touch her stone. *I'll try harder, Jenny. For both of us.*

On the way out, I notice there are a couple of other people here. But no one looks at me, and I don't look at them. This is a place to be invisible. This is a place where, for just a little while, the lack of noise is soothing, expected. I walk under the canopy of trees again and out through the front drive. I pass the stone wall. I tap it lightly with my fingertips. And then I walk out of the Putnam Cemetery and leave the silent and the lost behind, once and for all.

# Thirty-six

"M erry Christmas, Dad," I say, when my father's home number comes up on my cell phone. I am about a block from the country club, and from this distance I see a parade of Mercedes leaving the driveway. I pull my hat down further over my ears, partially to keep warm but mostly to keep from being recognized.

"Merry Christmas, sweetheart," my dad says, and then there is an awkward pause, neither of us sure where to go from here. He still hasn't told me about Grandpa Jack.

"Hey, Dad? What are you doing?"

"Nothing much." I wonder what that means: "nothing much" like solving Connecticut's budget crisis, or "nothing much" like fighting off an addictive love of his couch. Since I am talking to my father, who rarely sits down—not even to eat breakfast—I imagine it means the former. "Just listening to some music. The oldies station."

"Are you alone?"

"Yeah. Anne went to visit her family in Maine." So it's confirmed that he is dating her. *I knew it. I knew she was from Maine.*

"Listen, I'm near the club. Why don't you come pick me up there and we can go spend the rest of Christmas with Grandpa Jack?"

My dad doesn't say anything for a moment, and I hear Frankie Valli telling me to "Walk Like a Man" in the background.

"Okay," he says, and coughs. "I guess. Yeah, I guess I can do that."

When my dad picks me up, I don't comment on the fact that he is unshaven and wearing sweatpants, and he doesn't ask why I am in Greenwich or how I spent my morning. Neither of us volunteers any information. You can't change years of habit overnight.

"Listen, I need to tell you something," he says, after we haven't said anything for a while, and I wonder if he has been practicing in his head. He elaborately clears his throat.

"I already know, Dad. About Grandpa Jack." I save him the effort of having to say it out loud. I want to make this easier. For both of us.

"Oh."

"Dad?"

"Yeah?"

"Why didn't you tell me sooner?"

"I don't know. I guess I didn't want to hurt you. You and my dad have always been so close." He pauses. "I know he has been more like a father to you, and you've already lost one parent. It didn't seem fair."

"Yeah," I say, realizing that we both suffer from some perverse form of politeness. It seems futile to keep trying to protect each other from the truth.

"I didn't want it to be real." He rubs his face with his fingers. He looks down at his hand afterward, as if he is unused to the sensation, as if the stubble comes as a surprise. "It's enough already."

"I guess." We sit without talking for a little bit and let the car radio fill up the silence, our mouths moving to the words from habit. There is only empty highway in front of us, a corridor between the barren trees. We are the only two people left on the road.

"But still," I say.

"I know," he says. "I'm sorry."

"Dad?"

"Yeah?"

"It's okay, though. It's time, this time. He's ready."

"You think?"

"Yeah, I do. I'm ready too," I say.

"You are?"

"I think so. I'm trying to be."

"It isn't easy, though, is it? You know, your mom would

be very proud of you. She'd be pissed as hell at me for not being around the way I should. I know that. But she would be very proud of you."

"Really? You think?"

"Of course. Though it was kind of dumb of you to break up with Andrew. And some other time we need to talk about what you are doing about that career of yours." My dad keeps looking straight ahead, but the right side of his mouth lifts, just a little. "I have my sources."

"I was meaning to tell you. I just didn't, I don't know."

He waves me away, as if to say don't worry about it. But his voice grows serious again.

"Em, I don't know how to do this, to be a family, without Jack. I'll try, I promise. But I don't know how. I need your help. It— this—us—doesn't come naturally to me."

"Me neither."

"But we can try, right?"

"Of course we can try, Dad. I'm not sure we have a choice."

My father reaches across the seat and squeezes my hand. His gesture is both tender and awkward.

When we get to Riverdale, Grandpa Jack is sitting in bed and watching an old episode of *The Young and the Restless* that someone must have taped for him. It's a wedding scene, and the minister asks the crowd of beautiful people if there are any objections to the union.

"Hey, Pop," my dad says, and gives my grandfather a hug. My dad never hugs. He shakes hands. This is progress.

"Merry Christmas, Grandpa," I say, and give him a peck on the cheek. My grandfather reaches for the remote control and presses pause. The screen freezes on a goateed man standing up, a finger raised in objection.

"It's about time you two showed up," Grandpa Jack says, but he's smiling.

"How are you feeling, Pop?" my dad asks, though the answer is obvious. My grandfather is a miniature figurine of his old self. His eyes, only his yellow eyes, look huge and heavy, out of proportion to his shrunken face. Where did he go? I wonder. He can't weigh more than ninety pounds. Where did it all go? Is he in the air? Am I breathing him in right now?

"All right," Grandpa Jack says, and confirms that we Haxbys can't help but lie to one another. But would it be better if he told the truth, if he said, *My guts are rotting and this dying thing hurts like hell?*

"I'm glad," my dad says, and nods, like he is going to jot the answer down on a medical chart. Grandpa Jack looks small enough to pick up. Maybe I could stuff him in my purse and smuggle him home with me. Carry him around like a teacup Yorkie, safely tucked under my armpit.

Although I know how the game is played, I am not sure if I can keep this up. I feel like I may implode from this smile on my face. Grandpa Jack is going to die. I know it.

He knows it. My dad knows it. We don't need to pretend.

"Grandpa Jack?"

"Yes, Emily." I wonder if that is the last time I will hear him say my name. *Remember this*, I tell myself. *Remember how it sounds. This is important.*

"I'm going to miss you like hell," I say. Water gathers on my lids and the tears fall one at a time, one and then the next. My father looks away, out the window at the parking lot. He wants no part of this moment.

"I'm going to miss you too, kid," Grandpa Jack says, his voice like charred paper. "Come sit with me. I want you right here."

I take his hand and sit down next to him. My dad crosses the room and faces away from us. But then he changes his mind, turns around, and joins us on the bed. I am on the right side, my father the left, and we both stretch our legs out. There is plenty of room, because Grandpa Jack does not take up any of the space between us.

Someone presses play on the remote control, and we end up spending the rest of Christmas like this. Three generations of Haxbys—Grandpa Jack, my father, and me—lying in one bed.

The three of us watching old episodes of *The Young and the Restless*.

The television volume turned up as high as it will go.

# Thirty-seven

My first thought when I show up at Andrew's apartment door at six a.m. the next day is maybe I should have called first. Showing up unannounced at the crack of dawn the day after Christmas is not the best way to prove my sanity or my love. I don't know if he is home and, if he is, if he's alone. Maybe he's inside with another woman, just ten feet away, blissfully humping away to a Christmas song, a gross one, like "Santa Baby." Or worse, maybe they are fast asleep, his mouth resting on her shoulder, his body snaked around her limbs.

I bet she's blonde and has recently paid a Russian woman to give her a Brazilian wax.

Maybe I should turn around and go home. Send an e-mail or a card or pick up the phone. Maybe I should turn around and go home and give him up for good. Accept that I had my shot, that I blew it, and move on. But I can't. I won't. I am fighting for us. Building up from empty.

Still, I am paralyzed in this spot, standing on his *Welcome!* doormat, unable to press the button and unable to walk away.

I am not sure how long I have been standing here, but it's long enough that my legs are tired and that I now know that the paint on his door frame is cracking in exactly one hundred thirty-two places. I have done the "on the count of three" thing fifteen times. I have read the front page of his *New York Times* twice. I have tried yoga breathing.

I have gotten nowhere.

I spend some time thinking about what I might say, if I am ever able to ring the doorbell, and if he is home, two gigantic ifs that give me a clinical distance from the reality of what I am trying to do. If X and Y, then Z. I am not over-come with the love mania you see on television, where you have to tell the person immediately how you feel. Instead, I feel nothing but terror, knowing that at some point in the near future I will have to speak directly to Andrew. That I will have to talk. That I will have to explain my behavior over the last few months. That I will have to apologize.

That I will have to say stuff that can't be unsaid and undo stuff that seems like it can't be undone.

I will ask for a restart. A game over, try again. The odds are against me. I will much more likely lose than win.

I feel nauseated and consider the possibility that if I stand here for much longer, I may throw up on his doorstep. My organs feel like they are pressing up against one another, like there isn't enough room in my body for all the pieces that go inside. Like I am the game Operation, and the tweezers keep touching my edges, sending electric currents straight through my core. When the sensation becomes too much to take, I take my finger and press the doorbell. I put my whole body into it, so it sings loudly and for a long time.

And then I wait. I don't hear anything at all on the other side of the door. I ring again; it's easier the second time. And then I wait some more.

Eventually, I hear shuffling inside.

"Who is it?" Andrew asks.

"It's me," I say, and then realize that I am no longer in the "it's me" inner circle. "It's Emily."

"What the fuck?" I hear him say, and then a loud banging noise, followed by another "Fuck." And then, "Damn it. Motherfucker."

"It's Emily," I say again, though I'm sure he heard me the first time. "You have one hundred and thirty-two cracks in your paint."

"What?" he says, and then the door opens and Andrew is standing in front of me. He wears the green polka-dot boxers I bought for him on sale at the Gap and no shirt. His eyes are half closed, squinting at the assault of morning. His right hand is massaging his left elbow. His funny bone. But he is not laughing. He looks at me but doesn't say anything. He doesn't welcome me inside and doesn't tell me to leave. He just stands there squinting and rubbing his elbow.

"Hi," I say.

"Emily?" he says, like he is just noticing me. It feels good to hear him say my name, even though his tone is not friendly.

"Hi," I say again. "Merry Christmas." Andrew tilts his head to the side and stares at me.

"Can I come in?" He opens the door wider and I follow him inside. I am not sure if I should sit down or keep standing. Andrew doesn't sit, so I don't either. I can do this standing up. I had pictured us having this conversation on his couch, but I can improvise. *I can do this.*

"I know it's early, and I'm sorry for waking you up. I wanted to talk to you, even though I know you don't want to talk to me." I take a breath and look around his apartment. I haven't been in here since before Labor Day. It looks exactly the same, still just like an Ikea showroom—beige pullout couch, loopy brown carpet, pre-framed black-and-white photographs on the walls. This gives me encouragement, somehow. Like his furniture has been staying in place, waiting for me to return.

"Is this a bad time?"

"It's a little late for that question, don't you think?"

"Yeah." I look down at the floor. I notice a stray potato chip, and I'm tempted to pick it up and put it in his garbage can. I don't, though, because it feels presumptuous. "Are you here alone? I mean, I need to talk to you, but I need to talk to you alone."

I can tell I have said the wrong thing, because Andrew looks angry, like he is about to start yelling at me.

"No, it's just me. No one else." He is screaming without screaming. "It's the crack of dawn. What do you want?"

"Just to talk. Can we sit down?" My legs are wobbling. I sit without waiting for an answer. He follows me and perches on the end of his couch, as far away from me as he can go.

"You know I am not very good at this." I pause, hoping he will rescue me, but Andrew looks down and waits me out. He would get nowhere in therapy; he has no fear of awkward silence. "I have a lot of stuff I need to say to you, and I hope you'll listen. I don't deserve it, really, but I hope you will anyway.

"I know I should have called as opposed to just showing up. I know it looks weird, and not in a charming way. So, sorry about that. Sorry about everything. I clearly don't know how to do this right."

"Em, it is not a crime to break up with someone. I am over it," Andrew says, and shrugs like it was no big deal. He no longer looks angry, just apathetic. Which now, I realize, is much, much worse.

"I screwed up," I say. "I mean, I don't regret breaking up with you."

"Okay." He shakes his head, as if to say *Then what the fuck are you doing here?*

"I had to."

"Okay."

"Because I wasn't ready for you. I mean, I was a mess, and I didn't know it. You see?"

"No."

"I was pretending that everything was all right, but it wasn't. I was wearing a life preserver around my heart. You get it?"

"No."

"I was running on empty, you know what I mean?"

"No."

*Must stop asking rhetorical questions.*

"But now I'm different. It's like I woke up. I have a kidney to give." I'm not making any sense.

"But I don't need a kidney."

"But if you did, I would give you one of mine," I say. "In a heartbeat."

"Thanks."

"Anytime. Seriously."

"Okay." Andrew stands up, a signal that the conversation is over. "Well, thanks for the potential kidney."

"Andrew." I look him in the eye for the first time this morning.

"Andrew," I say again. "Please, just wait."

I take another deep breath to calm myself, but it has the opposite effect, and I start to cry. Big, ugly, gulping tears, hysterical tears, the kind that signal he should run away, or possibly rubberneck, but under no circumstances get involved. To his credit, Andrew sits back down on the couch and doesn't watch me. He stays perfectly still.

After a few minutes, Andrew gets up and comes back with a glass of water and a box of tissues. He puts them both on the coffee table in front of me.

"I'll stop soon, I promise," I say. "It'll pass."

"I know. I'll wait."

There is something about hearing Andrew's voice that breaks through, and my pulse slows, my tears stop. I blot my eyes with the tissue and blow my nose. I walk to the bathroom and throw cold water on my face. When I look in the mirror, a swollen, distorted version of me stares back. *What are you doing, Emily? Make this right. Enough is enough.*

I come back to the couch, sit down, and turn to face Andrew. *I can do this. I am ready.*

"Okay. Sorry about that. I'm back now."

Andrew nods, but he looks exhausted. And tired of me.

"I know I screwed everything up. But I love you, Andrew. And I did that time in the movies when I didn't say it back, when you said it first. And I loved you when I broke up with you on Labor Day. I wish I could explain it all to you, tell you why I ran away from the best thing that ever happened to me, and I'll try. But it's complicated. I needed to learn about me first. I wasn't ready to give anything to you back then. I wasn't ready for an Andrew.

"But now? Now I am. I am no longer numb, you know? And I wish it were all simpler, and I could explain it like

'Well, Andrew, I broke up with you because I was afraid of loving you and losing you and having to go through all that,' which would be true, but that's not the whole story. It's not that simple." Andrew shifts his body to face mine. The move is subtle, but enough that I take it as a sign to keep talking. He is listening.

"I guess what I am trying to say is, I screwed everything up, but I think I did it for a reason. You wouldn't have wanted to be with the person I was a few months ago. I was unhappy and empty and didn't know it. And now, well, now I am better, I think. At least I am working on it."

"Okay, I'm glad things are better for you. Really, I am," he says. "But, Emily, I don't know what you want from me. You left me, remember?" He looks down now and starts drawing circles on the couch with his fingers. Around and around and around.

"I know I can't undo the past couple of months. I think of it as breaking us. I broke us, and I take full responsibility for that. But I would love, love, love if we could try again. If I could have a do-over. If I could try to put us back together again. Unbreak us. Or reglue us, or something."

I take a breath and wait. *This is it.* Neither of us moves or breathes, and I wonder if we could float away on this nothingness. This absence of sound. It doesn't hurt, really. It's like the cessation of feeling. I almost don't want the moment to end, because then I will know. Maybe that's why I have stayed mute for so long. Maybe, after all, it's easier not to know. Then, at least, you have hope.

"Emily," Andrew says, and then stops. "Emily."

"Yeah," I say, and look down. He has not taken me into his arms. He has not kissed me. It's over. *Game over.*

"It's okay, you don't have to say anything. I get it." I wonder if you can see a broken heart. Can Andrew see it, right now, on the floor, smashed into a hundred little pieces, scattered among the potato chip crumbs?

"No, no, you don't get it," he says, and his voice is low. Barely noise. I hold my breath.

"I love you, and I don't know what the fuck to do about it. I didn't stop feeling that way on Labor Day, when you ruined everything, though God knows I wanted to. Wanting to be with you, worrying about you, caring about you doesn't feel good, though, or at least it hasn't these last few months. You're like a fucking curse. Why do you think I asked you to leave me alone?" Andrew stands up and starts pacing in front of the couch, and with each word, each step, his voice gets louder.

"A fucking disease," he says. "You're like the fucking flesh-eating virus.

"But now you're here, and I don't know. There is so much we haven't said to each other, and that's not all your fault. I know that." He points at me, like it's an accusation. "Don't think I don't know that. I should have pushed you or not let you get away with just not dealing. But I did. I thought . . . I don't know, that you would eventually just get what we had. Wake up already. But then you didn't and then you broke us. That's the right expression. Funny that you found exactly the right words for it.

"You broke us," he says, and points at me again with his index finger.

"I broke us," I say.

"And now you are trying to fix us? Fuck, I don't know. I just don't know." He stops in front of me and bends down, so he is on both knees and we are at eye level. There is nothing left to say, except for everything, and I realize it's time to go for it. I can't hold it back anymore. It's not fair to either of us.

"I love you, Andrew," I say. "I love how you laugh in your sleep. Who laughs in their fucking sleep? It is the most beautiful sound I've ever heard. And it's you. There are six billion people in this world, and granted, a lot of them are babies and women and men who don't speak English and people I haven't met, but that's not the point, is it? It's you. That's the point. That's not complicated. We can pretend like it is, but it's not. At the end of the day, I can't walk away from that. I am not afraid anymore. Okay, that's a lie. I'm still scared shitless, but I won't let the fear hold me back. I can't and I won't." I say it like it's final, like I have made a decision for both of us, though I know that's not true. This doesn't work without him.

"I laugh in my sleep?" he asks, and puts his hands on both sides of my face.

"Yeah," I say. "You didn't know that?"

"Nope, I didn't." He moves his face in closer, as if he is trying to get a better look at me.

"You do. A lot. It's not normal."

"There are six billion people in the world?"

"Maybe closer to seven."

"You cry in your sleep," he says. "That's not normal either."

"I do?"

"Yeah, you do. It's the saddest sound I've ever heard." He leans in an inch more. His hands still rest lightly on my cheeks, and he kisses me on the forehead. I close my eyes and memorize the kiss.

"But I'm not going to lie. It's not beautiful when you do it. Not at all. It's heartbreaking. Please, please stop doing that," he says, and then kisses my cheek. I don't want to look at him. I don't want to see if this is his way of saying *Let's be friends*.

He doesn't stop, though. He kisses the tip of my nose. My eyelids. My forehead again. He moves in slow motion, deliberately, as if each kiss is a conscious decision. A word that he wants to articulate just right.

Andrew takes my hands in his and kisses my fingertips, lightly dusting them with tingles. *Kiss me for real*, I want to scream, but I don't. I can wait for as long as it takes.

Instead, I take back my hands, kiss my fingertips again, and touch them to the grooves at the corners of his eyes. I trace them slowly, noticing where the lines crisscross, trying to decide if the pattern was different the last time I was this close to them. They feel deeper somehow, as if they have recently set.

"Look at me," Andrew says, and I look him directly in the eyes. The world goes quiet again. "Are you sure?"

"I'm sure.

"I'm sure," I say again, loudly, to make him hear me, to make me hear me. A tear sneaks out of the corner of my eye, and Andrew catches it with a kiss. "Are you sure?"

Andrew doesn't answer me, though. Instead, he brushes his lips against mine, a whisper of a kiss. He kisses me again, this time harder, and I kiss him back hungrily. The kiss is a promise. A vow. A declaratory sentence.

Later, when we are naked in his bed, we lie facing each other. Our limbs are tangled, stitched together, like a zipper. It is here, within the safe confines of the gray duvet cover, where it is warm and soft, that Andrew and I begin to talk.

"I don't want to go back to the way things were," he says, and tucks a stray hair behind my ear.

"Me neither." I trace my fingers up and down his arms. I draw balloons, and hearts, and circles.

"I'm serious. We can't just pick up where we left off. I'm not going to do it."

"I know. That's not what I want. I want a do-over. Can we

still get do-overs as adults? Is it possible, you think?" I ask.

"I don't know."

"I don't either." I shrug. Andrew kisses my bare shoulder. "But I want to try."

"Me too."

"Really?" I ask, even though we are already naked, and it seems like that decision has been made. But I want to hear him say it again.

"Really," he says, and I savor the word. I feel like I can pluck it out of the air. *Really*.

"I need to know your thoughts on Brooklyn."

"Brooklyn?"

"Yeah, Brooklyn. Or maybe Queens."

"Cheaper rent."

"More space."

"Might be nice."

"Really?"

"We could get a dog."

"Really?"

"Yeah, I have always wanted a dog."

"Why?"

"Unconditional love," he says.

A little while later, we have moved our heads under the covers. Andrew's bed is now like a tent, and we whisper with the reverence of ten-year-old campers.

"Grandpa Jack told me to wait for you," he says.

"Huh?"

"When I went to visit him. I didn't think he recognized me, but while we were playing poker, he stopped the game out of nowhere. He told me to wait for you. That's all he said. 'Wait for her.' And then he went right back to playing."

"He said that? What did you say?"

"I didn't say anything. I just went back to playing. It didn't really matter, though. Even though I didn't want to or would never admit it, I was already waiting."

"I have to say something to you right now, but please don't say anything back. Not yet, okay?" I say.

"Okay."

"I love you."

Andrew doesn't say anything, and I am glad the words aren't reduced to an echo. I don't want them to bounce off the walls and back at me. Instead, I want to wait until we are heavier, more rooted. It's my turn to wait.

I cuddle up next to Andrew and press my body even closer to his, to erase any seam. This is as near as I can get to what I really want. I wish I could eat him, maybe start with his fingertips, so that he can share my skin and become part of my insides. I want to mix our blood, to fill myself up with the double helixes of his DNA, to make us one whole. One being.

I want us to have three spare kidneys. I want us to have a spare heart.

# Thirty-eight

Today I am a superhero, dressed as a lawyer, dressed as a superhero. Ready to save the world. I am put back together again. Better than Humpty Dumpty. Reassembled. Sleeker.

Better to play it down, though, not kick open the door with a dramatic *Help has arrived!* No, sir. I will walk in, shake the interviewer's hand, and woo him and all of Legal Aid with my sharp legal skills and analytical mind. I will mention Yale Law School. I will exaggerate my experience. I will. *Get. The. Job.*

I have psyched myself up. Drank multiple cups of coffee from my Wonder Woman mug. Used expensive exfoliating body wash. Shaved my legs. Did not miss my ankles. Did not skip my knees. I have pored over the Legal Aid Web site and memorized its mission statement. That mission has become mine. Andrew practice-interviewed me for hours, made me wear my "SuuuperLawyer" suit for the boost of confidence. I am ready as I will ever be. Here is my shot.

"Ms. Haxby, Barry is ready for you," the receptionist says, and leads me down a narrow corridor of gray industrial carpet, set off from a maze of half-walled cubicles. This place is the opposite of APT. No shiny nameplates, no frosted glass, no marble. Definitely no window washers. Instead, there is Formica, and cheap metal filing cabinets (hand labeled), and makeshift doors. It is perfect.

"Barry Stein, nicetomeetcha," says a woman with a frizz of black hair and thick appendages.

"Emily Haxby," I say, and try to hide my shock that Barry Stein is a woman, which means if I work here, my boss would be a woman, which means my boss would not stare at my cleavage and would *in no way* resemble Carl. This place rocks.

"So, tell me about your public-interest experience."

"Well, I don't have much. I spent the last five years at a large law firm, so . . ."

"How about *pro bono* cases?"

"Not really. No. There were these billable-hour targets, and never enough time . . ." *Emily, get it together. Don't blow this.*

"But you have litigation experience, right?"

"Yes, absolutely. I am very experienced. I am a very experienced litigator."

"Have you ever been to trial?"

"Yes." *No.*

"Made an opening statement?"

"Yes." *No.*

"Cross-examined a witness?"

"Yes." *No.*

"Sat first chair?"

"Yes." *No.*

"What kinds of cases?"

"Uh, usually for smaller matters. The partners like to sit first chair on the larger stuff. A few insurance cases, some real estate. I don't want to bore you with the details."

"You won't bore me."

"No, seriously, it's very dry stuff. Insurance, reinsurance, subordination of claims, nonmutual offensive collateral estoppel, *carpe diem*, anti-enterprise immunity doctrine, ERISA, perfected security interests."

"*Carpe diem?*"

"Excuse me?"

"You just said *carpe diem*. What did you mean?"

"I didn't say *carpe diem*."

"Oh, I thought you said *carpe diem*."

"Haha. No, you must have misheard me. *Carpe diem!* That's very funny."

"I guess."

"Seize the day, and here I am seizing the day." *Emily, shut up. Just shut up.*

"Are you a little nervous?"

"Yeah, sorry. It's just this is a really great opportunity—"

"So you're not on drugs, then?"

"Drugs? No."

"Good. It seemed like you may be."

"No. Absolutely not. I am way too uptight for drugs. Think I went overboard with the coffee this morning, though."

"That explains the leg."

"Huh?"

"Your leg. It keeps jiggling up and down."

"Too much coffee."

"Right."

"Right."

"So here's the thing. You come with great references, Yale Law School, you worked at one of the most reputable law firms in the country, yada, yada, yada. You are a bit weird, but lucky for you, I like weird."

"You do? I mean, thank you."

"So let me tell you about the job."

"Okay."

"Basically, we are looking for a staff attorney for our family-law unit. So you would be doing intake, working on adoption issues, custody, divorce, that sort of stuff. We do a lot of work on behalf of battered women, temporary restraining orders and the like, which is actually why I am here over the holidays. Our caseload always skyrockets during Christmastime. For some reason, husbands like to beat the crap out of their wives during the holidays. Seconded only by the Super Bowl."

"Really?"

"Yeah. Sick, right? We need people who are aggressive, who can give a voice to the voiceless, a platform for the disempowered. We need people who are not afraid to speak up."

"That's totally me. You just described me. I always speak up."

"Okay, I have one final question for you. Why? Why are you here? Not in an existential way. Why do you want the job?"

"Because if I am going to spend at least seventy-five percent of my waking hours doing something, I want that something to have meaning. I am tired of wasting my time. I am starting to realize that I want my life to matter in every way that it can."

"Finally, a perfect answer. When can you start?"

"You are offering me the job?"

"Yeah, I think I am. Truth is, we are desperate for help. So, do you want it? The job?"

"Yes. Yes, I do."

I want to kiss Barry Stein flat on her strawberry-colored mouth or throw my arms around her fleshy neck. I want to say thank-you, you-won't-regret-this, I-will-be-the-best-lawyer-that-you-have-ever-hired, you-won't-regret-this, did-I-say-that-already? But instead, I shake her hand in a firm and professional manner, arrange to start the week after next, and walk back down the carpeted hallway. A confident swagger. I wait until I am four blocks away to put my hands together in front of my head. To run quickly down the street. To simulate flying. To sing the words "SuuuperLawyer."

# Thirty-nine

This is where it ends. Right here, on the constant-care floor of the Riverdale Retirement Home. We are ready. Or prepared, because you can never really be ready, can you? You can have the doctors spell it out, say "It's time," like these words mean something. You can be nervous, and braced, and have practiced in your head. But you can't be ready. If you think you can, you're kidding yourself. Because later, when you go to the movies, you'll think, *Grandpa Jack would have liked this film.* And when you have a problem you don't know how to solve, you'll think, *Grandpa Jack would have known what to do.* And when you stand at the altar in a white dress and pledge your life to someone else, you'll think, *Grandpa Jack should be here to see this.* For a long, long time, maybe even forever, it's going to hurt like hell.

When this day is done, after someone takes a shovel to my insides, I will have no choice but to attempt to regenerate my lost parts. And because he is old, and because he is ready, and because this is the natural order of things, I am okay with that.

Grandpa Jack lies in the middle of the bed. My dad and I each sit on one side of him, taking our usual places. We have been here almost every day since Christmas and have our routine down by now; I sit on the right, my dad sits on the left. Andrew stops by when he can, hops on a train in between his shifts, and explains all of the gadgetry. What is dripping into the tubes attached to my grandfather's forearms, why the doctors keep drawing blood when there seems like there can't be any more left, who are all these specialists in white coats with clipboards. When we feel like we could be comforted by more cold, hard facts, we turn to Andrew, and he dutifully gives us our fix.

Grandpa Jack keeps on shrinking in the space between my father and me, and I wonder if this is the way he will go. Maybe his molecules will disintegrate right before our eyes until he is just a small pile of matter on the soiled hospital sheets. Or maybe he will implode, spiraling toward an invisible vortex. Maybe he will blow away, like a pile of paper in the wind.

For the past couple of hours, since Andrew left to go back to work, Grandpa Jack has slipped in and out of consciousness. He hasn't spoken much. When he does, it looks like talking hurts.

"I brought you a present, Grandpa Jack," I say, when the

nurses stop coming in to check on him, like he has died before he has died. I reach into my bag and take out my tiara. My grandfather smiles at me and motions for me to put it on his head. I balance the tiara on his white tufts of hair, and he transforms into an infant prince. Shriveled, regal, and unafraid.

"Thanks. Kid. Love. It." Each word feels like a victory.

Without asking, I take his newsboy cap that has been sitting on the window ledge and put it on my head. It is mine now. I don't need something tangible like this to hold on to Grandpa Jack, but I allow myself the additional comfort nonetheless. I pull the cap down low on my forehead.

My dad looks at his father in bed in a tiara and hospital gown and lets out a noise, halfway between a laugh and a sob. It sounds like the click of a camera, and I imagine both of us mentally taking pictures of Grandpa Jack as fast as we can. *We will remember you. In a tiara and a gown, maybe, but we will remember.*

It is our turn now to wait for Grandpa Jack. We talk to him while he is awake, tell stories from the small trove of family recyclables that gets pulled out from time to time. We try to include my grandmother and my mother in the recounting, so that Grandpa Jack can think about going to them as opposed to away from us. I still don't believe that's how it works, but at times like these, it doesn't really matter what you believe.

We stroke Grandpa Jack's hand, which looks exactly like

Julie Buxbaum

ours, except shot through with blue and brown spots. Every once in a while we squeeze to remind him that we are here. That he is not alone.

"Remember, Grandpa, when I broke my arm that time in fifth grade and you took me to the hospital? Remember?" I ask, though my question is rhetorical. It's not important now whether he remembers. I just want him to hear my voice.

My dad nods at the story, as if he remembers too even though he wasn't there. Tears spill from his eyes, they march one by one down his face, and he wipes them with his sleeve.

"I should have listened to you more, Pop. I should have come here more." My dad rests his forehead against Grandpa Jack's hands.

His body is bent in the shape of an apology.

My father and I are talking in that way young children do, without the back and forth of dialogue, off on our own parallel tracks.

"Remember when you visited me in Rome during my semester abroad? You said you came because my voice sounded lonely—"

"Don't worry, I found that will you asked me to look for. Right where you said it was. Under the kitchen sink on the left—"

"We went to that restaurant that's supposed to have the best pasta in the whole world. And we ate so much we felt a little sick afterward. Remember—"

"And the arrangements will be exactly the way you asked. Promise—"

"Remember when you chaperoned that school trip to the Museum of Natural History, and my teacher got mad at you for not using 'child friendly' language? We laughed so hard afterward, almost peed in our pants, picturing you writing on the blackboard *I will not say damn in front of children* a hundred times. And that became our inside joke. *I will not say damn in front of children*—"

"I know we didn't always see eye to eye, Pop, but—"

"You whispered it to me just before my mom's funeral. 'I will not say damn in front of children.' You always just got exactly what I needed. Oh, God, it still makes me giggle. Even now, sitting here with you like this—"

"I'm sorry. You don't know how sorry I am—"

From time to time, I whisper in Grandpa Jack's ear, so only he can hear me say the things I haven't had a chance to let him know.

"Thank you for telling Andrew to wait, Grandpa," I say, and adjust the tiara so that it sits straight on his head.

"Thank you for waiting for me to be ready. I'm going to be okay now," I say, and fix the blanket so that he is warm and tucked in tight. To keep his molecules in place.

"I'm ready if you are," I say, my voice cheery, like we are about to do something fun, like jump off a diving board.

I move the uneaten tray of food into the hallway.

"I miss you already," I say, when Grandpa Jack doesn't respond and his eyes no longer focus.

"I love you," I say, again and again.

Later, when my grandfather slips back into sleep, we somehow know it's for the last time. The air feels different. Heavier and expectant. We listen and wordlessly count his breaths. *One two. One two. One two. Am I ready for him to stop? He's ready. He's ready. One two. One two. I'm ready.*

When Grandpa Jack stops breathing, when that two does not come, the room is still. A suspension of time and sound, as if the universe takes a moment to adjust to the loss of another soul. It is the end of a symphony all over again.

And though my father and I want to do anything else, anything but wait here—run from the room, scream, yell, maybe even clap—we don't; instead, we force ourselves to sit and absorb the silence.

# Forty

It's about six-thirty in the morning, and although it's the dead of winter, the sun still shines through the windows, the light sharp and cutting. It slices the floor into long strands of pointed triangles. If I were to walk across the room, I would go from shade to light, light to shade. I am tempted to get up and wander back and forth to warm and cool the bottoms of my feet. To stand up next to the bed and watch Andrew breathe.

"Hey there," Andrew says, when he wakes up and notices that my eyes are also open. I am curled up against him, with my back to his stomach, and Andrew rests his head on his elbow so that he can see my face. He takes his other arm and tucks me in closer.

"Hey," I say in a whisper, and smile up at him. "It's early. We should go back to sleep."

"You okay?" he asks, and kisses me lightly on the bit of my neck that rests just below his jaw.

"Yeah." I close my eyes and open them again. "I am."

"I wish I was there with you the other day." He pulls the covers over my shoulder. A protective gesture, one that says *I would have tried to make it hurt less.*

"I know, and thanks. But it was probably better that it was just my dad and me. Just us saying good-bye." I still whisper out of respect for the early hour, the word "good-bye" too harsh to say with force.

"I understand." Andrew puts his nose to the spot where he kissed just a few moments ago. The movement makes me wonder if he remembers by smell. *Is this his way of memorizing me?*

"Are you ready for today?"

"As ready as I'll ever be."

"At least your suit fits this time. Hopefully no wedgies."

"No, no wedgies. And this time you'll be there with me. That'll make it easier." I lean up to give him a kiss on his shadow of a beard.

And then I close my eyes and go back to sleep, for just a little while longer.

I don't listen for Andrew's breath, though. I know it's there.

The funeral, unlike every other funeral I've ever been to—and I've been to quite a few in my day—has a distinctly upbeat vibe. Yes, we are in a church in Connecticut and we wear black suits and we hear talk of Resurrection and the like, but the tone isn't particularly sad. Instead, all of us are abiding by an unspoken agreement that today should be a rockin' celebration of Grandpa Jack's life.

My father arranges to have music playing throughout the ceremony. Music from the 1940s, the kind that makes you want to slap your knee in time to the beat. The church fills with trumpet and trombone and piano. With wistfulness and energy and optimism. It plays softly in the background, loud enough to hear, but not loud enough to distract. It's music unafraid of silence or of sentimentality or of mourning.

The place is crowded, so much so that a group of people is forced to stand behind the pews, cooling the back of their heads against the church walls. I recognize some of them, but not all. From the predominance of white hair, I can tell they are mostly friends of Grandpa Jack from Riverdale. When the minister finishes his eulogy, he invites up anyone who would like to say a few words about my grandfather. A line immediately forms up the aisle to the pulpit.

The first to speak is an older gentleman with a bush of nose hair. He recites the stand-up routine that Grandpa Jack performed at the talent show in Riverdale, recounting it word for word. The jokes are childish and simple—*an Indian had a cup of tea before he went to bed, and in the morning he drowned in his teepee!*—but he hits every punch line. *Teepee!* The laughter and the clapping make the air lighter in here. Afterward, he walks slowly back down the aisle to Maryann, who greets him with a kiss on the lips.

When it's my turn behind the pulpit, it becomes clear that all that eulogy practice in my head did little to prepare me for the real thing. I say a few things about Grandpa Jack, about how much he was loved and how much he will be missed, though my words are neither poetic nor original. I don't say anything that hasn't been said before about someone loved and lost. I tell the crowd that he was loved more, though—more, more, more—but it sounds unfairly flimsy. There are things I want to say but don't: that Grandpa Jack was both my father and my mother during the times when I felt like I had neither. That even as an adult, I believed that Grandpa Jack was my own personal superhero. That I will not say damn in front of children.

It doesn't matter, though, that I don't speak these words out loud. They are still mine to keep.

"I met Jack when I was an old woman, after my husband died, when I thought a huge part of me had died too," Ruth says, when it's her turn at the pulpit. "But Jack changed that for me. He taught me that there is humor in loss and even in death. That those we love stay with us long after they are gone, in a form beyond memory and in a form beyond consciousness. Thank you for teaching me that and for making me laugh every day."

When Ruth says "Good-bye, Jack, we know you are now here within us," the entire congregation bends its head forward and repeats it with her again. It becomes a collective wish, a prayer, a farewell.

A man with a combed mustache and a green polyester suit steps up to the pulpit after Ruth. He looks nervous to be in front of the crowd, and he takes out a handkerchief to wipe sweat away from his temples.

"I work in the diner in Riverdale," he says in heavily accented English. "Jack was the most generous person I have ever met. He was always friendly and always left a twenty-five percent tip. Always. Except when he just came in for coffee. Then he would leave double the price of the cup. A one hundred percent tip. Even when he stopped recognizing me, he still remembered to give twenty-five percent. Let me tell you, there are few people in this world who always leave a twenty-five percent tip, even when it's raining. Did you know people tip less on rainy days? They do. Once he left me thirty dollars on a two-dollar bill. It was snowing. I thought it had to be a mistake, so I ran after him to give it back. He said that there was no mistake. That he had won it in a poker game and that he knew I was putting my Irena through college. He said, 'Here, take the thirty bucks. I like to pass things along.' I am proud to have known someone who likes to pass things along. I will miss him. Thank you for your time."

There it is. The perfect eulogy. Better than anything I have ever scripted in my own head. The invisible hand behind all those pickles and cups of coffee and strawberry milk shakes, someone I have met over a hundred times and never met at all—it is he who captures for the congregation who Grandpa Jack was. *Someone who likes to pass things along. Someone whom we are all proud to have known.*

When it is my dad's turn to speak, he doesn't go up to the pulpit. Instead, he relies on the music to speak for him and turns the volume up as high as it will go. He plays a medley of my grandfather's favorites—Benny Goodman, Tommy Dorsey, the Ink Spots, a little Duke Ellington. We all close our eyes to listen, and for a moment it feels like the entire place is huddled around an old radio. Together, we are all young and scared and hopeful. Already nostalgic for today.

After the funeral, my dad offers to take Ruth, Andrew, and me into the city for dinner. There will be no post-service gathering back at the house. The funeral was our good-bye. It was perfect, and now it's over. When my dad says that he's craving barbecue, Andrew leads him to that fated restaurant on Third Avenue, the one with crayons on the table and peanut shells on the floor. The one where I broke us.

We sit at a table far too large for four people but close to the jukebox, which we feed constantly with quarters. I am not sure if it plays any of the songs we request, but we hear some more Ellington, and some Radiohead, the Beatles, Lynyrd Skynyrd. I compose an iTunes shopping list in my head so that I can recreate the soundtrack should I need to rely on it one day.

"That was a fun funeral," Ruth says. "Am I allowed to say that? I hope you don't think I am being disrespectful."

"Of course you're allowed to say that. You are allowed to say anything you want in this family. It's the new rule," my dad says. *We are a family*, I think. *He knows that we are a family.*

"You are absolutely right. It was a beautiful funeral. Exactly what Grandpa Jack would have wanted," I say.

"Definitely," Andrew says, and lifts his beer for a toast. "To Grandpa Jack."

"To Grandpa Jack," we repeat, and clink our glasses.

"And to a Happy New Year, because he would have wanted that too," my dad says.

"To a Happy New Year," we repeat, and clink our glasses again.

The waiter brings over a platter of hot wings. We dig in, ring our mouths with sauce, burn our lips until they swell, wear bibs like babies, tied around our necks. We feel pride as they get finger-painted red. We feel no fear when the waiter brings over a second batch with extra hot sauce. Though we don't compete to see who can eat the most, we don't surrender to the meal either. We conquer it.

After we have stuffed our stomachs and run out of quarters, after we leave nothing behind but a thirty-dollar tip and a pile of chicken bones, after I feel full for the first time in as long as I can remember, we walk out into the swill of Third Avenue.

We line up, shoulder to shoulder: my father with tousled hair, condolence kiss marks still on his cheeks, Ruth, her wrinkles capturing years of expressions on a single face, Andrew, his fingertips circling my hip, and me too, watching and waiting.

There is no camera, so there will be no picture. But for once I am not worried about forgetting. This I will remember, this overlapping of moments, the four of us standing together, the four of us caught somewhere between holding on and letting go.

THE END

# Acknowledgments

Thank you, thank you, thank you to my agent extraordinaire, Elaine Koster, who guides me with honesty, patience, and kindness. I am eternally grateful. And, of course, many thanks to my editor, Susan Kamil, who consistently astounds me with her insight, wisdom, and sense of humor, and who has managed to make every step of this process pure pleasure. I feel blessed, reassured, and incredibly lucky to have landed in Elaine's and Susan's capable hands.

Francesca Liversidge and the whole Transworld team, I am so grateful for all of your support.

Special thanks to Chandler Crawford, David Grossman, and Helen Heller.

I am grateful to my first readers who were willing to wade through a very rough first draft: Pamela Garas, Lena

Acknowledgments

Greenberg, and Mark Haskell Smith. MHS, thanks also for being such a fantastic mentor.

Special thanks to Laurie Puhn for her extreme generosity with time, advice, and direction.

And though the list is endless, many more thanks to: Megan Dempsey, Melissa Fien, Meredith Galto, Marion Goldstein, Seth Greenland, Halee Hochman, Scott Korb, Liz McCuskey, Jenna Myers, Jonathan Pecarsky, John Schowengerdt (who coined the term "funemployment"), and to Walt and David Zifkin.

Thanks to the Flore family, and Sunny, of course, who gets a special shout out—don't ever say I don't keep my promises . . .

Endless love and thanks to my father, Fred, and my brother, Josh, for not telling me I was insane when I decided to quit my job to write. Your support is everything. And though anyone who knows my dad already knows this, let it be said, once and for all, that he in no way resembles the fictional father in this book.

And finally, there aren't enough words to express my gratitude to my husband, best friend, and partner in crime. Indy, I love every last one of your molecules.